"I'M A SUCCESS, FLETCHER. I'M RICH."

Char stepped forward, trailing the black silk behind her. She was grinning now, holding out her arms, still in her gown of blue and green beads.

"I know."

Char didn't hear the note of sadness buried deep in that acknowledgment. Fletcher wasn't even aware he had spoken with such melancholy. The adventure was so great and he remembered it so well. He also remembered the moment he had to let it go.

Char was very close, her face tipped up just a bit, her lips invitingly near, her skin . . . ah, her skin.

Carefully he plucked a rose petal, rubbing it gently between his fingers as though to gauge its softness. Without hesitation, he drew it over Char's throat, slowly, cautiously, past her collarbone, down her chest to the point where her breasts rose with tempting fullness above the beads of her gown.

Char held out her silken cape as her body trembled with ecstasy under the touch of the petal. She threw her head back, her eyes fluttered closed, a gentle moan bubbled from her throat.

In a moment she had wrapped Fletcher in a mantle of black silk. Her mouth was on his, probing, insisting that they now finish what he had begun. His arms were around her, his lips on her flesh, following the trail that a single rose petal had blazed, following it with exquisite accuracy.

REBECCA FORSTER
Golden Threads

ZEBRA BOOKS
KENSINGTON PUBLISHING CORP.

For Jenny

ZEBRA BOOKS

are published by

Kensington Publishing Corp.
475 Park Avenue South
New York, NY 10016

First printing: December, 1992

Printed in the United States of America

Chapter One

"I thought we might take some time off now that it looks like I'm going to own Montreal Foods by the end of the month. That will be quite a feather in my cap, that little takeover. Four and a half bucks on every share of common stock is going to be the turning point. I can feel it. So what would tickle your fancy? A cruise in the Aegean? Maybe climbing the Pyramids? Or just lazing around on the beach . . . in Monte Carlo. . . . Maybe now's the time . . . Now that Montreal Foods . . ."

Ross fell silent, his eye caught by a flash of bare skin, the curve of a slightly raised leg. Appreciatively he watched long-fingered hands ease a taupe stocking over a slender foot, sliding it up a shapely calf, unrolling it gingerly past an endearingly bony knee until it slipped — well, up seemed appropriately descriptive.

Raising his glass Ross smiled just as the bourbon and water slid past his lips. The fact that what he had just witnessed was only a reflection in a dressing table mirror made the moment all the more exciting. Ross shook his head, never taking his eyes off the mirror. Reflected in it now was the corner of a bedpost hung with something green and gold, a mattress covered in peach satin and a glimpse of the well-tended blond wood floor.

Reluctantly Ross pushed himself off the faille-covered sofa and headed to the armoire that served as a bar in this minuscule palace. Pouring himself a splash more of bourbon, he tried to figure out what it was that drew him to this place again and again.

It was a box of an apartment the likes of which he hadn't seen since college. He, and most of his friends, lived in lavish homes—ocean-front condominiums at the least, mansions at best. But he loved it here. She was the only one who didn't have the financial security to live in either and the only one he knew who didn't seem to care. An unusual acquaintance for him, but he loved it here with her. He felt somehow comforted and excited all at the same time, as though something unique and wonderful was only a heartbeat away in this small home. How odd that a bedroom door that didn't quite shut could provide him with one of the most erotic experiences he had ever had. Strange that the woman in the next room was the most singularly remarkable woman he had met in his entire life and that he was content to simply be with her, listen to her, watch her without insisting they take that last intimate step toward commitment.

Ross always felt as though he was staking out new territory, making sure he knew the lay of the land before moving in to take what he wanted when he was with her. Nothing was ever the same with her, and he hated the thought he might take a wrong step. This was one takeover he didn't want to be hostile. When he, and the lady in question, decided the time was right for a more serious commitment, Ross Parnell was sure the payoff would be spectacular. A few more scenes like the one just played out in front of him, and he would have to make this relationship exclusive, if not permanent.

A step or two and he was back at the sofa. Through the door, reflected in the mirror he saw a streak of teal and a starburst of something gold then, in the blink of an eye, the bedpost and the floor again as the object of his attention drifted away once more.

"Char, are you listening to me or am I just impressing myself with all this?" he called, knowing this kind of provoking behavior was no way to start an evening. Hours lay ahead of them before he could do anything about this incredible desire that was building with each reflection in that mirror.

"Don't be silly," came the reply, as the warped but lovingly painted bedroom door was flung open. Char Brody stepped into the living room speaking as she turned to a brass lamp and, leaning close, adjusted her earring. "I heard every word you said. Four and half bucks on each share above, well beyond its worth on the current market. Boy, I wish I wasn't such a good girl. Do you know what I could do with the information you spew out? If I bought in on just one of your deals, I'd be a millionaire, and I could be manufacturing CB Designs as ready-to-wear instead of one-of-a-kind creations. As to how I'd like to celebrate your business acumen, how about a nice dinner? I'd feel awfully naughty if I let you lead me astray in Monte Carlo. What do you think?"

Satisfied with her earrings and her dutiful recitation of Ross's soliloquy, Char straightened as she threw out her long bare arms, twirling for Ross's scrutiny. He accepted her invitation without hesitation. There was nothing he liked more than looking at Char Brody. From the moment he first saw her at the Anderson's fund-raiser, he'd been enthralled.

The fact that she was gorgeous was only one reason she caught his eye. Actually, gorgeous was the wrong word to describe a woman like Char. She was exotically stunning. Though not overly tall, she seemed to stand head and shoulders above the other women at that gala event. She held her body like a dancer, her short hair curled around her square face naturally, in sharp contrast to the studied informal do's atop other heads.

Though she spoke to people, laughed with them, put her hands intimately on their arms as she leaned toward them to whisper something, Ross could tell she was not exactly part of the group of men and women who could get Anderson elected senator. Rich-looking, she wasn't wealthy, he knew. Familiar and friendly, she didn't seem to be an intimate of the powerful and wealthy crowd. She wore chartreuse that day. An unusual choice of color, he thought, for a staid political event. He remembered her skirt had been short, pleated. "Saucy" was the insipid word that popped into his mind as he admired the dimples behind her knees, the slender stretch of her legs and her taste in shoes. High, high heels had always been one of his favorite female accessories.

So he had circled, letting her come into full view slowly. In profile he saw that she was reed-thin without looking sickly. Rather, she wore her slightness with a wily strength, not a daintiness. And under her little cropped top with gold buttons he could see the swell of her well defined breasts and the nip of a waist that defied description because of its smallness.

A passing waiter hesitated for only an instant when Ross reached out and took two champagne flutes from his tray. It was time to make his move. Carrying them toward the woman in chartreuse, he was delighted when her companions drifted away just before he reached her.

"You've been left alone."

She turned toward him and, with that first look, Ross Parnell was impressed beyond words. Her forehead was broad and smooth. The short wispy curls that danced over it had touches of gold in the brown, streaks he hadn't seen from faraway. Her eyes were wide — doe eyes of gray — shadowed with the colors of smoke and dawn that made them look innocent and sexy all at the same time. Her nose was short and straight and her lips so full that, had it not been for the slight parting of them, he would have thought them too dramatic for her face. Her skin was golden, too, but not tan; her scent that of the Orient.

She smiled and those full, full lips widened into one of the most gloriously open smiles he had ever seen. There wasn't a wrinkle on her face. She hadn't a worry in the world.

"I don't think anyone is ever alone at a party like this, do you?" She took the champagne from his hand. Not exactly a forward gesture but one of such natural grace that he wasn't peeved she hadn't waited for him to be gallant. She dipped her head, sipped, raised her eyes above the glass and looked about. When she finished drinking, she lifted her face again and her gray eyes were looking right into his brown ones as though they had been looking at them forever. "Loyal Republican or curious Democrat?"

"Both and neither," Ross laughed, raising his glass in a silent toast to the happy couple. "The candidate is my favorite banker. His wife, a Democrat, used to own Gentry Products before I raided the company and bought it out from under her."

"And you're still friends?"

"It was only business. I'm very fond of her. I also respect her business acumen. She gave me a run for my money. She wasn't married then. Now she'll turn her talents elsewhere. This time she'll have David's money to play with. I think she'll find success a lot more entertaining when she doesn't have to struggle for it. From the looks of it, David won't have to either."

"I don't know. Struggling has its own rewards. You just have to struggle with style." She held out her hand, flashing her toothy grin. "Char Brody."

"Ross Parnell." He took her hand and shook it.

That had been a year ago. It seemed like yesterday. But it wasn't until four months after that first meeting he had run into her again, this time at a charity fashion show where her designs were featured along with Perry Ellis, Donna Karan, and Armani. The second time around, Ross was as impressed with her work as he was with her. Since then they had seen one another regularly, scheduling their dinner dates, their lunches, their theater engagements around his hectic travel schedule and her seasonal rushes.

Now, standing in front of him, draped in a waterfall of teal chiffon, her breasts encased in some sort of gilt fabric, she was asking Ross what he thought of her. Well, his opinion hadn't changed

11

in all these months. Char Brody was . . .

"Incredible, as always, Char," Ross murmured, tipping his glass her way.

"Thank God you aren't a buyer. 'Incredible as always' does not indicate that you think I might be able to set fire to the fashion world with this particular number."

Char plucked at the sheer fabric, holding it between her fingers as she contemplated it before letting it flutter down around her marvelous knees. Her rose tinted lips pouted and her smoky eyes rolled toward the window as Ross set down his drink before moving close and sliding his arm around her waist, pulling her into him.

"You creative types amaze me. So touchy. Always needing so much praise. If it's good, you know it's good. Now admit it. You know you look like a hundred million dollars."

Char laughed and turned her sparkling eyes up to him. "Coming from you that's high praise indeed."

"I mean it," he whispered, suddenly serious.

Char's lips closed slightly before parting once again in anticipation. Face to face, Char and Ross felt the spark that might ignite a flame between them. It was this way so often — the closeness, the intimacy, the anticipation. Then he kissed her. His handsome patrician face coming close until his lips covered hers and she felt his arms tighten about her. Instinctively Char's arms wound themselves around his neck. She kissed him back.

Gently at first then with more intensity until she realized this was not to be the day. Passion wouldn't blaze between them. Someday they would find what was missing in the equation.

Embarrassed, not wanting to look deeper into herself than she already had, Char let the kiss end, then leaned back in his arms and brushed at his lips.

"We're going to be late," she murmured, rubbing her lipstick from his skin. Hesitantly, affectionately, she ran her fingers through his almost blond hair and stepped out of his arms. "You look perfectly turned-out as always."

"Nice to meet with a fashion maven's approval." Ross reached out and took her hand just as she turned to fetch her purse. Quizzically she looked back at him. "Are you really going tomorrow?" he asked.

"Of course I am. What a silly question," Char laughed. "I haven't been working overtime with Maggie just to ship the clothes off by themselves, you know. Pilar is counting on me. Besides, it's been ages since I've been in Paris. I'm dying to go." She picked up her purse, snapped it open, and checked the contents before snapping it shut. "The invitation is still open if you want to come."

Ross shook his head, "No, thanks. I just realized I'm going to miss you, though."

"Ross Parnell, are you getting sentimental in your old age? No self-respecting corporate raider would admit something like that. Haven't you al-

13

ways told me sentiment is the kiss of death in your business?"

"But this isn't business, Char," Ross reminded her as he picked up his jacket. "This is personal. Not that I haven't tried to get you interested in a loan and give our relationship that extra dimension. Put business and pleasure together and I think the fireworks might really begin. You could actually make a go of CB Designs with the right capital."

She picked up the length of chiffon she would use as a wrap and wound it about her shoulders while she spoke.

"We've talked about that, Ross. Much as I'd like to have my own ready-to-wear line, I'm not going to take your money. I'm doing well with the one-of-a-kind, and I'll get the capital from that business when the time is right."

"Don't be absurd, Char." Ross ushered her through the door. "The minute you start making a decent profit, you throw it all back into exotic fabric or Venetian beading or some other cost-ineffective item. You'll never get to the big time that way. Everyone who's ever made it big in fashion has had backers and the good sense to know style has to be tempered with cost control. Why not let me be your backer?"

"I can't," Char answered quietly. How could she explain that his money would mean the end of her freedom. Idealism was still something she felt. She wouldn't let it go so easily. "I will make it on

14

my own. Things are happening. Once Pilar's boutique opens, I might be able to pick up a few international clients. That should help the bottom line."

Ross threw up his hands. "Don't be ridiculous. You're trying to run before you can walk. Take my advice and my money. Start a mass market line of clothing and establish yourself in the United States before you count on any business overseas. It's a headache you don't need." Opening the door of his racing green Jaguar, he touched her lightly before she slid in. "I'm only looking out for your best interests, you know."

Char raised a hand and cupped his close shaven cheek. "I know you are. And that's sweet. But I think it would be terribly exciting to have a small international clientele. It would do me a world of good with all the ladies I design for here. They adore that sort of thing."

"Adore it or not, this kind of haphazard marketing is never going to make you rich. I can't even believe you promised Pilar you'd let her have that much merchandise without billing her in full. Sometimes I wonder about your business sense."

Char laughed, her gray eyes dancing, "I have none. I create, I don't legislate. And I know you're absolutely right. I shouldn't even be thinking about clients in Europe when I have a hard enough time clothing the wealthy ladies from San Diego to Del Mar. I know there will be problems with licensing, customs, fittings, and fabrics if Pilar comes through. I know I'm crazy to bring twenty thousand dollars' worth of my finest work to Pilar without so much as a letter of agreement. But you know what, Ross?"

"What, Char?"

"The thing you always forget is that sometimes you've just got to go with your gut, and this is one of those times. Sometimes you gotta rely on love and luck and the fun of it all."

With a quick kiss on his cheek, Char settled herself in the Jaguar. Ross might want to worry about business, but Char was ready to party. The evening was beautiful, she was headed out with one of the most eligible bachelors in the country, her designs were going to be on half the bodies at this extraordinary bash, her own dress was fabulous, and life was full of promise. Only the way Ross's hand covered hers for a moment made her feel less than perfect. She glanced his way, smiling sweetly, knowing she should be feeling more for him and wondering why, after all these months, she wasn't. With a sigh she leaned back in her seat, closed her eyes, and banished that worry as they drove toward Del Mar. After all, feelings like this weren't new.

The men in her life had been wonderful, interesting to look at and listen to, so attentive. What they hadn't been able to do was share her visions—her creative sense—and so they remained in her life until they drifted away almost without notice, replaced by her desire to create. None had been forceful enough — in personality or temperament — to capture her interest, arouse the desire buried deep within her, and pique her curiosity. Someday, she knew, she would marry and have children with a man she loved dearly. But Char had long ago given up hope of reveling in a hungering passion. Because for her, the passion was grounded in a second sight of how the world should be created. No man had ever been able to look at the world through her eyes. More than likely there was no man who could.

She swiveled her head on the leather covered rest behind her and smiled at Ross. He was the best of them and she adored him for all the things he was. She wasn't going to fault him for being unable to do what all the others couldn't. When he returned her smile, Char slid her hand behind his neck. She was too happy to worry about perfection now. There was a marvelous party ahead of her and tomorrow — Paris and Pilar. Life couldn't be better.

"Didn't she just look stunning, Ross? Char is such a talent she could make anyone look just fabulous." The woman waved a hand Char's way but kept her hungry eyes on Ross as she grinned widely and, she hoped, alluringly. With mock coquetishness she put that same hand to her lips and batted her lashes. "Oh, that didn't come out right at all, did it?"

"That's all right, Evelyn," Ross reassured her as he wound his arm around Char's slim waist and pulled her close. He could feel her muscles tensing as she fought to keep her chuckle quiet. Ross continued to speak as though the woman were the soul of discretion. "I'm sure we both know what you mean. And I agree. Jennifer is a lovely bride . . ."

"Again," Evelyn reminded him emphatically.

With great patience and a killer smile Ross agreed. "Again, Evelyn."

"At this rate," the woman muttered, casting a hateful glance toward the bride, "she's going to marry all of our ex's twice. Her portfolio must be twice the size of mine by now just because her settlements have been so wonderful. And now she's got her claws into the wealthiest man in Del Mar. Well, what can you do?"

"You can cheer yourself up with a new outfit," Char laughed, "it always works for Jennifer."

"Oh, Char, always thinking about us, aren't you?"

Evelyn giggled, perfectly charmed by the designer. Women who made their own way fascinated her. She couldn't imagine actually having to labor for a living. Just keeping herself looking like the wife of a wealthy man was enough to exhaust her, especially since she was desperately looking for a wealthy man to marry.

"Just reminding you of the age-old wisdom of women. A new dress does wonders for the soul,"

Char commented, shrugging prettily.

Evelyn Masterson was one of the most influential women in the social set that populated the most southern reaches of California: Del Mar and Coronado and San Diego. But Evelyn had slipped out of Char's fingers a dozen times, stopping at Char's studio on Coronado Island to try on but never buy. Now, though, with the bride looking so splendid in one of Char's exquisitely beaded dresses, Evelyn Masterson was obviously having second thoughts.

"You might be right. I'd much rather have a new gown than a face-lift. Besides, with your prices, I don't have to wear it until it sags before I can have another one. I'll stop by soon, dear. Oh, there's Franklin." She leaned close and whispered. "I think you may be designing another wedding dress before long. Must go now. Ta."

She was off in the blink of an eye. A woman of impeccable figure and face dressed in a Saint-Laurent suit of the palest lavender, Evelyn Masterson was as far from perfectly happy as you could get. Yet, as Char looked around her, her eyes lingering on all the beautiful people who hadn't a financial care in the world, she felt that awful twinge of envy once again. So much wealth with so little purpose. How she would love to have a tenth of it.

"Char? Earth to Char?"

"What?" Smiling, she turned to Ross, letting her long, strong fingers slide beneath the yellow silk of his tie as she pulled him close in apology for letting her attention drift.

"I have to go," Ross whispered, tightening his arms around her. She began to sway in their confines.

"You can't go," she said with a pout. "The sun is set and all the lights have come on and the orchestra is just starting to play down at the pavilion. Oh, Ross, I want to dance under the stars and listen to the ocean and look at this incredible hotel Jennifer and her new husband call a home. I want to pretend I'm dancing on gold and every woman here is wearing a CB Design. Ross, please."

He laughed and twirled her about. They were alone now atop the marble stairs that led to the formal gardens below. Beyond that the acres of grass were so well tended they looked as though they had been shaved by a master barber rather than cut. And the acres reached beyond that, with the grass skirting a seawall until it trailed into the beach beyond.

This was careless wealth in every sense of the word and those who walked into this world were enfolded by its magic, its promise, its rarity, and above all, its safety. They left behind all the worries of their lives to become as beautiful and privileged as everyone else. It was so easy to give into wealth's seduction, but Ross knew better than to simply enjoy the moment. It took a great deal of cunning to pay for the carefree hours, the fancy dresses, the mansions, and cars. He, for one, enjoyed the getting of the money more than the actual reward.

"I think I'd like nothing more than to dance with you," Ross murmured, enthralled with the way her eyes darkened along with the sky, "but you'll have to wait."

"I don't want to wait. I want to dance now, with you," Char laughed, as she slipped out of his arms and held his hand while she skipped down a step or two. "I'm going to teach you that business isn't everything if it's the last thing I do. We work far too hard. It's time to pretend work doesn't exist."

Ross stood his ground, stopping her so that she had to turn and look back up at him, "I never pretend, Char. That's what makes us such a lovely couple, don't you think? I'm the dreamer and you're the dream."

Char grinned, her eyes sparkling. "That's beautiful. See? Given half a chance, I could teach you to be more like me."

"Given the other half of that chance, I could teach you to be like me. But that's going to have to wait. Fielding is hesitating on the limited partnership we were talking about regarding the Golden State Banks deal. He promised to meet me in the library when the dancing started. His latest girlfriend drives him to the brink of a heart attack on the dance floor, so he thought he'd use me as an excuse to beg off."

"All right. Go." Char pouted without sincerity and released his hand. "But not too long."

She did so like Ross. He looked amazing standing above her, the alabaster façade of the mansion his frame. With the lights behind him, his hair looked like fresh straw, and his face was shadowed so perfectly he could have been carved out of a perfect piece of golden oak. Not quite tall, his athlete's build made him look powerful.

"I won't be," he said, "I wouldn't want to lose you to one of these guys whose bank account triples mine."

"Never. This lady prefers to make her own millions, thank you."

Ross laughed, shook his head, threw her a kiss, then disappeared through the bank of leaded glass doors on his way to make deals and change the face of the business world. Char watched him, frowning without realizing it. His laugh was insulting, though she knew it wasn't meant to be. It only showed her that Ross didn't really have faith in her talent as a designer, even though half of Southern California's wealthiest women wore her one-of-a-kind clothes. According to Ross, her business was respectable, boutiqueish, too creative for the mainstream. He admired it. He just didn't think it would ever grow. And as far as he was concerned, if it didn't exist to make her rich, it was simply a hobby.

Turning, Char peevishly clicked down the steps in her silk mules. She wasn't exactly angry at

Ross. After all, he had offered her a great deal of money to start her own ready-to-wear line because he knew with the right marketing her clothes could be a success. But she wanted victory based on her creativity, not her marketing strategy.

Striding through the lovely gardens, her crossness vanishing, Char was ashamed she'd even felt angry. How on earth could she even think of supplying major chains when she couldn't control her own creative urges? She grossed over three hundred thousand dollars a year and still lived like a pauper because every cent she made went right back into materials, new machinery, and hiring specialty artists when necessary. Char could never resist the unusual. That's why Jennifer's wedding gown was stitched with insets and gussets from antique kimonos. Jennifer had paid five thousand dollars for it. But by the time Char secured the kimonos, cut them properly, and paid her seamstress to hand-bead three thousand reflectors and bugle beads onto the gown, it had only paid for itself. There was never enough left over to rent larger space or hire more help or purchase a computerized pattern cutter. Yet no one seemed to mind. Not Carol, her assistant who had joined Char without even asking about her salary, not Theresa or Ilsa, not Maggie. None of the women she considered family seemed to mind that Char Brody wasn't the next Chanel.

Hesitating a moment before stepping out of the gardens, Char looked toward the raised dance floor, gaily lit under the striped tent, and resolved not to think about her handful of employees anymore that evening. Looking at the bride, she could see, even from a distance, the perfect fit of her gown, the extraordinary detail, and Char knew she could never compromise her artistic bent for anything.

Char had almost reached the tables when she changed her direction. A strange ennui had seized her. The thought of socializing with the ladies of means, even though they treated her as one of them, was just a bit much now. She was only human, after all. Char knew she might look like she belonged, but she was well aware of the delicate line drawn between those she draped and those who did the draping. If she were Saint-Laurent or Givenchy or Ellis or any number of other designers, she would be a peer. But she wasn't.

Unique, talented, she was a close-mouthed woman with no interest in any of their husbands. These were the qualifications that endeared her to these women. Char was their change of pace, like using a new florist at a party.

Altering her course, Char headed away from the music and the revelry, away from the waiters and maids, and walked down the grassy slope, stopping only at the retaining wall that kept the sea from claiming what Jennifer and her new husband called theirs.

Immediately Char felt the poetry of the moment. Behind her the rarefied world of privilege whirled and laughed. Illicit assignations were made under the noses of spouses and business partners. Too much was drunk and too much was eaten. A world of excess was behind her but, ah, in front of her . . . now that was something.

The sky was black as velvet, the stars abundant and glittering like crown jewels. In the center of the sky, hanging low and heavy above the inky horizon, was a moon blazing with golden light. It shone a sparkling path across the indigo ocean, tripping over the froth of waves before brightening the white sandy beach.

Though there was a slight chill in the breeze, Char faced it gladly, enjoying the way it pricked her skin, picking up the chiffon of her short dress, making it dance around her knees. When she breathed deeply, she felt her breasts strain against the corded gold braid that covered them. Closing her eyes, preferring the feel of natural perfection to the lavishness she had left, Char let the music filter into her brain, entertaining her without thinking much about it. The sound of voices was nothing more than an indefinable chorus. This was where she needed to be; this was where she felt happy. An outsider who could walk back through the door anytime she chose.

Then her eyes were open. No sound had alerted her to his presence, she only knew he was there. Slowly she turned her head and peered into the darkness until she found him. He moved slowly, like a shadow, up the beach. His head down, his shoulders hunched, he looked like so many people she saw on the beach who had nowhere to go and nothing to do. She stood rigid, her breathing shallow, as she willed herself into nothingness.

Char considered fleeing, but it seemed impossible to move. The sight of this lone vagrant on the beach was somehow enthralling. She could see he was tall even though it would be another twenty yards before he walked into the path of the moon's light. Perhaps, she thought, she had second sight because she could see so many things about him in the darkness. A man lost in his life, a man who had lost interest in trying to play by the rules. She could see all this, but she preferred to pretend he was something else. Until he passed by her, she would imagine him an explorer, alone on the beach of a deserted island. He was a poet, anxious for inspiration. He was a shadow and only she could fashion his face and determine his reason for being.

Closer he came and, with a pang of sorrow, Char realized he was a young man. Only a young man would have such a slim build and hair that gleamed even under starlight. How sad that he had nothing. How sad that he sought refuge on land that belonged to people who threw away more than he ever owned.

He was almost upon her now. A few more yards and he would pass by without noticing Char keeping watch in the darkness. She tensed, waiting to see him in full, waiting for the moon to spotlight him while she remained invisible. But nature chose to put them on an even footing. A cloud passed in front of the moon, plunging them into total darkness. When it peeked out again, only a sliver of it now, the man was in front of Char, so close she could see that he stood, not with an air of defeat, but with confidence. He raised his face to the moon as though drawn to it. And, with this gesture, Char felt herself drawn to him, so moved by the moment, she knew she would never forget it. The sight of the lone man raising his face in absolute appreciation of nature's beauty was a picture she recognized for its uniqueness. She felt somehow ashamed to be witnessing so private a moment.

Slowly now, the man turned and looked directly at her. It was as though he had always known she was there. There was no sense of surprise at his discovery. Char breathed in, feeling her lungs fill with cool, salty air. She had made no sound, she had hardly moved. Her arms remained at her sides. The breeze suddenly became a gust, blowing the chiffon of her dress behind her so that in the front it lay against her body, outlining every curve of her figure.

They stared at one another, shadowed eyes locked in an embrace. Now she could see parts of him: black, black hair, a hint of darkly lashed eyes, skin that glowed red as though burned from weeks in the sun. She saw the hint of a high slash of cheekbone, the stubble of a beard, and the hard line of lip that would speak only true words even if they hurt the one who heard them.

Neither of them moved. Neither spoke. It was the man who interfered with the magic. Slowly he lifted something in his hand. It was something metal, dark and foreboding. In the night he pointed it at Char with a purpose that both excited and fascinated her. Fear, she thought. She should be feeling fear. She should be threatened. Instead she was frozen, unable—not unwilling— to feel these things. She was a prisoner of this man's gaze and at the mercy of whatever he held, whatever he wished to do to her.

It was only when she heard a click, a whir, that she realized he had taken her picture. In his hand was a camera, its zoom lens now looking hideously arrogant. Slowly he lowered his camera and walked toward her. He didn't stop until he stood at her feet, looking up at her with the blackest of eyes.

He was the stuff of adventures. He the hero lost in a dark continent. A dark man, hardened in body, his soul held closely and revealed only to those he felt should know it. She a sacrificial virgin waiting for his rescue, or a queen holding his fate in her hands.

Char looked down at him, her face revealing none of what she was feeling. It was a moment of intrigue, as exciting as if this stranger had just made love to her without a word spoken between them.

For the longest while they stood that way. Slowly the man pulled the strap of the camera over his shoulder. He looked down while he adjusted it, then raised his eyes to Char once more. His voice broke the silence between them.

"You are the most beautiful woman I have ever seen."

Chapter Two

"Then again it could be a trick of the light. I won't really know until I get this film developed. That dress might have something to do with it, too. Teal really is your color. The gold?" He shrugged, his eyes narrowing without embarrassment as he considered her breasts. "Too Egyptian—Roman—something. It wasn't necessary. But that blue. Did you know there's a bird in the jungles of South America whose wings are tipped with just that color?"

The sound of his measured, overly-familiar voice released her. Blood flowed again in her veins, and her breath, held so long, eased out from between her parted lips in a thin vapor of disbelief. The wind, so at odds with her dress, decided to ebb, allowing the layers of fabric to once more drape around her. Fascinated, yet wary, Char eyed him.

"And did you know this is private property? I don't know how you got past the guards, not to mention the fence, but if I were you I'd be on my way. You're no fashion critic, and I doubt you've been within a thousand miles of South America."

"My goodness. Here I had you pegged for a party girl, all dressed up and taking a breather from the festivities." He nodded toward the celebration, letting Char know in no uncertain terms he wasn't as impressed as she thought he should be. "But I guess I was mistaken. You don't sound as if you'd know a good time if you tripped over it."

With a laugh, he put his hands on the retaining wall. Char stepped quickly back and folded her arms like a sentinel, though she wasn't sure if she was protecting the party or herself from this disarming man.

"What are you doing?"

Grinning, he cocked an eyebrow and pushed himself up on strong arms until he was sitting on the low wall. In an instant he was standing, dusting off his khaki slacks, adjusting the oversized cotton shirt he wore with sleeves rolled up.

Tensed for action but curious nonetheless, Char watched him check his camera. It was a fine piece of equipment. No doubt he had "borrowed" it from one of the estates on his little trek over this stretch of beach.

Her concern for her safety, or anyone else's for that matter, was fleeting, pushed aside by the realization that this man was indecently attractive. Older than she had first imagined, he appeared to be in his late thirties. His body, though, was that of a man ten years younger. Lean and sinewy, its appeal was evident even under the billowing shirt of raw cotton. His skin was the most beautiful color. Somewhere in his ancient history Char knew there had been a slave girl or a sultan who could lay claim to his family tree. His face, as she had first seen, was well defined. Long, an inverted triangle, lovely from his broad forehead to the rounded point of his strong chin. Those eyes, hidden before, were now seen for what they were: black on black, lashes and orbs. Deep set, unafraid, perhaps all-knowing. Char wanted to turn away from them, but didn't. His brows were as dark as his hair and his hair, worn long, was sliced neatly mid-ear so that it fell in a curtain about his face in a multitude of shades: ebony and coal and jet and raven. Yet it was his lips, sculpted under a straight broad nose, that intrigued her. Just long enough, just wide enough, they wore an expression of sensitivity that almost disguised the . . . what?

The adjective escaped her and the fact that this perturbed her made Char angry. He shouldn't be standing next to her, so close, above the beach where he didn't belong in the first place.

"Look. I don't know who you think you are, but I'm giving you fair warning. Get off this property or I'll have to call security. I don't think you know what you've stumbled into, but this is no place for a beachcomber. You're going to force me to do something I'd rather not if you don't leave under your own steam."

The man lowered his eyes and kicked at the grass. His brow furrowed as though he was displeased. As he turned away, turned into the breeze, Char was struck by the scent of him. It was as though he was part of the greater essence of the outdoors. But she refused to be drawn in by him again. Just as she was about to repeat her threat, he spoke, so softly Char had to take a step forward to hear him.

"Do you really think the Great Spirit," he looked over his shoulder and raised an eyebrow, "God or whatever you'd like to call it, really meant for man to fence off portions of this world? Do you really think he meant for mere mortals to hire guards to make sure other mere mortals don't walk on a stretch of beach?"

Seeming to tire of looking at Char, he swiveled his head seaward once more. She marveled at how thick his hair was, how straight it fell, almost touching the collar of his shirt. Inexplicably she, too, looked toward the horizon, almost moving closer to him. It was at that instant the orchestra struck up a waltz, a delightful Strauss waltz, and she wrenched herself away from the spell he was weaving. She felt somehow disloyal standing in the dark with a fascinating stranger, a man who worked magic . . .

"This is absurd. Completely absurd," she snapped, blushing at her thoughts and the knowledge that she could, indeed, enjoy sitting down with this man to discuss anything in the world. "Who knows what God wants us to do with the beach. And if you tell me you can ask him and find out, then you're a loony. Loony, trespasser, or just plain obnoxious, I don't care. I'm not going to stand here and discuss philosophy with you. This property is private and it's legal, and that means that you've got to go. Now. If you're not going to, then I have to do something about it. I'm going to get security and I would suggest you make tracks while you can."

Char turned to leave, but one heel of her mules caught in the soft grass. Angrily she yanked it out, glaring at the dark-haired man while he laughed gently. She hated clumsiness, especially her own long-legged brand.

"You'll ruin the heel," he clucked.

Once more she started out, the lesson of the soft grass forgotten in her pique. Frustrated, furious at herself and him, Char reached down and took her shoes off, almost losing her balance as she did so. She wasn't sure when he moved, but he was beside her in an instant, his long, strong fingers cupping her elbow as he steadied her.

"There's no reason to be that mad. Your shoes haven't done anything."

"I'm not mad at the shoes," Char muttered through clenched teeth, "and if you don't get your hands off me, you're going to have more than a trespassing charge to answer to."

34

He backed away, holding his hands in the air, that horribly delightful smile still on his face. Char was several steps away before he decided it was time to set her straight.

"I think there's something I should tell you before you run for the gendarmes," he called to her retreating figure.

Char stopped, throwing her shoulders back. She didn't bother to look at him. His lazy voice drifted her way, irritating her all the more for its shiftlessness

"I'm a guest at this soiree. Now you may still want to have me thrown out, but I think you're going to have to come up with a better excuse than trespassing."

Char's shoulders trembled a bit before drooping in defeat. He imagined the look of utter humiliation and disappointment on her face. How he wished he could have seen it, photographed it. Hers was a marvelous face, too exquisite for words. Only film could capture the essence of her beauty — of her.

Head held high, Char stalked on with dignity. He might have put her in her place but she had her pride. He liked that. He liked that very much.

Loping behind her, he raised his camera and snapped. Hearing the sound, Char glared at him over her shoulder, then huffed on. He snapped again. Now they were in the circle of lights from the dance floor, Char weaving her way between the tables and still she could feel the eye of the camera on her. Cheeks blazing, she slipped into her shoes. But before a step could be taken, she was captured.

The man from the beach, his camera discarded somewhere, took her in his arms. He lifted her up, sweeping her expertly between the couples on the dance floor until he had twirled them to the center of the raised platform. Her feet had simply followed his lead, her arm finding its place on his shoulder as he raised her other hand in his. All this in the blink of an eye. Then they were waltzing as though this were Vienna and she a favored lady at the queen's ball.

"You're not Scarlett O'Hara and I'm no Rhett Butler," he whispered, "so let's not pretend. Life's too short for these pretenses. You're curious about me. I know you are. And I'm dying to know about you. Who wouldn't want to know a woman who stands against the wind happily alone? Admit it. You want to know more, just as I do. Admit it, then tell me your name," he held his cheek against her soft, short hair and twirled her confidently once more. "Tell me."

"Char Brody," she whispered.

It seemed she hadn't said it. Rather she had thought her name, and his mind had heard it. But she felt him smile, his jaw moving against her hair.

"Fletcher Hawkins," he murmured back.

Char leaned away from him, looked deep into his eyes, and smiled. It was then he slowed their dance and pulled her hand close to his chest. While the rest of the party waltzed around them, Char and Fletcher swayed slowly back and forth, their eyes locked onto one another's. Only their hearts were very aware of what their bodies were doing.

"Isn't that better?" he asked.

"I'm not sure. I haven't heard anything to ease my curiosity. You don't look like any of the other guests."

"I'm not. That just confirms my suspicion about you. You're smart and appreciative of things that are different. Actually, I could almost say the same about you. I don't think you really belong here either."

"You first," Char insisted. "You told me I was curious. Why not tell me what I'm curious about, and save me the effort of asking?"

"Lazy wench," Fletcher laughed, his fingers tightening over her hand. "All right. I'll humor you just this once since it will only take a minute. Let's see. Start with the vitals, I suppose. Name: Fletcher Hawkins. Age: thirty-eight. Marital status: none." He looked at Char with those black eyes waiting for a reaction. She humored him with only the slightest tilt of her full, wide lips. The bold flash in her eyes suggested she had little interest in the last piece of information. He shrugged, adroitly turned her into the next step and continued. "Citizen, without residence, of the United States. There, is that enough?"

"Hardly. If I'm dancing with an exile, I want to know why said partner has felt the need to flee — or be thrown out of — his home. I don't condone political terrorism anymore than I do a man running off with the gardener's wife to a villa on the French Riviera."

Fletcher threw back his head and laughed, showing strong white teeth as he pulled her just a bit closer. He hesitated with a beat of the music, letting her long leg rest against his muscular one. Both felt the instant flash of desire. Neither allowed a physical expression of it. Fletcher liked that challenge, Char was empowered by it. They began to dance again. "Hardly anything as exciting as either of those options," he said. "I'm afraid it was self-imposed exile." Char raised a well shaped brow in silent query.

Suddenly he melted into her, as if the closeness of her was necessary to his explanation. They danced on in silence, his mood serious for the moment while he carefully considered his answer.

In his arms Char felt his thoughtfulness and was amazed at how his mind seemed to control every fiber of his body. For a crazy instant she thought she might wrap both arms around him, gathering him into her or, at the very least, run her long fingers through his hair, all the while murmuring that it didn't matter what had driven him away. Then he changed. He remembered the music and the dance floor and that the woman in his arms was almost a stranger. He stood back only enough to let the breeze squeeze between them for an instant as he looked down on her up-turned face.

"Sorry," he apologized in a low voice, "it's actually been a long time since I put into words why I felt the need to travel, to be away from my home. I suppose it's quite simple. The American dream didn't do it for me."

"I beg your pardon?"

"The American dream. Pulling yourself up by the bootstraps, making a fortune, having it all. You know that one. Well, I did it. Twenty-three years old and I was being hailed as the next Edison, and I knew I didn't deserve that kind of praise." He chuckled, gently now, a self-deprecating laugh. Char leaned her head closer to his until his cheek rested on hers. For both, it was as natural as eating when they were hungry, sleeping when they were tired. His voice lowered to a gentle tone. "I thought that was the funniest thing I'd ever heard. Edison! I'd discovered that computers could be fun and happy things and these 'people' that ran the world decided that I'd hit upon something quite revolutionary.

"How that mess in a rented garage became a multimillion-dollar enterprise was almost beyond me. I had cars, homes, and all the money I could ever spend. I was surrounded by people I thought were friends, but best of all I had purpose. Unfortunately the purpose became just business at some point. Suddenly I had to worry about markets and price structures and not about creativity. I was processing information, no longer creating it. My sole objective had always been to find things that had been hidden. I'd found a way to do one thing right and it gave me too much. This talent limited me at the same time it liberated me. I didn't want to be limited by anything, certainly not by money, so I left it all."

"Everything?" Char asked, her eyes wide with disbelief. No one walked away from millions of dollars unless they were crazy.

In answer he grinned that marvelous, mysterious straight-lipped grin and danced her toward a corner of the floor.

"All right. I'm not a saint. I didn't leave the money. I sold the company for a lot of cash, stocks. There was a good deal of creative financing. There's so much it just sort of manages itself."

"So you just walk around the world pointing your little camera at women on the beach?"

Fletcher let his eyes flit to Char's face. He hadn't heard it in her voice—that overwhelming excitement that gripped most women when they found out he had more money than he could count. All he heard from the woman in his arms was polite curiosity. He was dancing with a miracle.

"I like to think what I do is a bit more serious than that. The urge to create doesn't go away just because you have a lot of money. No, I found I had a real talent for taking pictures, for capturing things on film that no one is really supposed to see. You know, the hidden agenda behind a politician's eye, the ugliness in a piece of land made beautiful by developers. I've been a photojournalist for the last seven years.

"Luckily, because of my financial independence, I can pick and choose my projects. I don't have to compromise my artistry. I can become blissfully passionate about my subject. I accepted assignments in the most exotic foreign countries and I lived like a king because I had my own money. For that I will be forever grateful to big business and big buyouts. Seven years after that marvelous success, I set out in search of knowledge and happiness and never looked back."

"How nice for you. I assume then you've found them? Knowledge and happiness, I mean." Char found her hand tightening over his shoulder as she awaited the answer.

"I think so. Yes, I do believe I have. Knowledge, of course, is something one never masters, but I certainly am content."

"That's not what I asked," she said, surprised that her voice was almost a whisper. "I asked whether you'd found happiness."

Fletcher's feet stopped moving just as the music faded away and the waltz was done. Yet he didn't release Char, nor did she step out of his embrace. Rather they simply looked at one another, each admiring the strength and openness they saw in the other.

He sighed and smiled gently. "Yes, I believe I've found happiness. I'm a student of the world and a citizen of it and I am happy."

"How lucky for you. That's unusual. I don't understand how you could have given it up, how the security and the chance to work in a business you loved could have been confining. I would kill to have what you had. But I'm sure you know that." Char sighed and smiled a pretty little smile. "Like Alice's rabbit you become curiouser and curiouser with each explanation, Mr. Hawkins. It's been so interesting."

As Char spoke, she took a half step toward the tables on the lawn. Intent on finding Ross, needing to be away from this unusual man who touched her in so many different ways, she was slipping out of his hold. But Fletcher caught her hand just as the orchestra struck up a fox-trot. Twirling her into him, he led them in no particular step, preferring to hear a waltz in his head rather than follow the quick pace of the dancers around them.

"I couldn't possibly let you go. Not until you satisfy me."

Char lifted an eyebrow. "I have a feeling it would take a good deal of work to do that, Mr. Hawkins."

"You do me an injustice. I only want to know something about you. I've bared my soul, now it's your turn."

42

"I'm afraid I've nothing quite as exciting to share with you. I'm a designer. I drape wealthy women in silks and satins, tailor their day suits in the finest linen and give them play clothes in Egyptian cotton. I'm probably one of the people you had so little use for when you scurried out of the mainstream. I would venture to guess you buy your clothing off the rack."

Though she hadn't meant to, Char realized she sounded defensive and immediately chastised herself. She was proud of her work. And if this man laughed she would . . .

"How wonderful," he enthused. "Let me guess which of our sinfully rich party-goers are in your originals."

Char couldn't help grinning at his obvious delight. This was not something she had expected. She relaxed in his arms, turning so she could survey the crowd with him as he forged ahead with his guessing game.

"Let's see. The bride definitely." He cocked an eyebrow for confirmation. Char nodded. "A most lovely creation. And, if I may say so, you did wonders with her hips. Try as she might, the lovely lady could never be as slim hipped as . . . you for instance."

"I thought the drape of lace was a nice touch," Char offered warily, his compliment putting her on guard.

"I would assume Ashley is in one of your gowns also. It truly is stunning. Poor Ashley. So much money and so little to do with it." He sighed and narrowed his eyes, looking through the dim light, then brightening as he found his mark. "And I think Barbara Long is wearing one of yours. Barbara who is never satisfied with anything her husband does. Not his immense compensation, not her home, not even her sex life."

That was it. Char pulled out of his arms, standing away from him but not running away.

"You seem to find this quite amusing. Are you telling me that you find my designs to be predictable? Or that only a disgruntled, grubbing, imperfect woman would consider wearing them so they are easily identifiable? Whichever it is I take exception to it, Mr. Hawkins. These are not only my clients, many of them I count as friends. Which is more than I can say for you. For someone so true to himself, so concerned with finding wisdom and knowledge, don't you find it just a bit contradictory that you accept the hospitality of people you can't stand?"

"Char," Fletcher cooed, reaching for her. She pulled her hand away but he grasped it again, brought it to his lips, and wouldn't let go. The warmth of his touch melted Char's urge to flee. She felt her resolve weakening but kept her eyes angry as best she could, her mouth set.

"I didn't insult your talent or these people. The reason I was able to pick out your designs is because they are distinctively yours. The angled cuts at the neckline, the body consciousness of them, the otherworldly way the fabrics fall as though they had been poured, rather than stitched, to shape. I think you've a marvelous talent. Too much talent to restrict it to this small segment of the universe.

"As to my comments about these people, well, I've been friends with most of them for years. Some of these men sold me parts for my computers. One or two worked with me on financing and seed money. Others owned stock. I know their wives and their children. And when I'm not snapping pictures of the rain forest being destroyed in South America, I come and take a few Polaroids of the kids and dogs and horses that hang around out here. I stay in their houses and eat at their tables. I like these people individually. They like me because I was once one of them and I'm fascinating because I'm not anymore. But I don't think I said anything out of turn. Ask them and they'll give you the same analysis of themselves. I don't find the truth distasteful or disdainful. And I don't think you do either. If you didn't see the truth of these women, you wouldn't design the way you do."

"I beg your pardon?"

"Think about it. Why would you have draped that wedding gown the way you did if it wasn't to create the illusion of physical perfection. If you weren't aware, or couldn't acknowledge, the bride's flaws, then you wouldn't have chosen to do what you did. See? Underneath it all we are as

45

alike as two peas in a pod."

Fletcher grinned, enjoying more than he thought possible, not only the conversation but the feel of this woman in his arms. She seemed light as air yet substantial, too, as though she had pared herself down to muscle and bone in anticipation of taking a strong leap at life. And oh, that face. Had his camera ever focused on such an unusual and divine face? If it had, the memory of her rival was gone.

She glowed golden skinned. Her eyes were a mystery, all smoky and wide set. But it was her lips that enthralled him. They parted minutely, then closed again; he could hear a whisper of breath and then think he imagined it. Those lips gleamed not only with the coral lipstick but with a softness that was inborn. She was so lovely and he wanted this night to go on forever. His lonely trek on the beach seemed eons ago. Fletcher no longer thought of this place as a facade for living. Here he was holding a most alive woman, a most interesting woman. Fletcher almost didn't realize she was speaking he was so lost in the joy of discovering her.

"I'm not sure I'd go that far," she murmured, her voice as warm as the ocean breeze.

"As far as what?" he asked, snapping out of his reverie.

"To say that we are as alike as two peas in a pod. I think you just have a way of twisting things around to make it seem that way," she teased, forgiving him his candid transgressions.

"You might be right," he acknowledged, "but my gut tells me differently."

"Well, mine tells me that you're a wizard with words and with your camera. I simply design dresses. I don't look for the mystery behind my clients or my clothes. I stitch up what I think is pretty and leave it at that."

"I won't argue with you. Not on this lovely night, not with the sound of the music and the smell of the sea making this a much more perfect encounter than I ever imagined. Oh," he sighed and threw his head back, his thick dark hair dangling in a perfect line above his shoulders for only an instant. "I'm so glad they held this party outside. I couldn't bear to have to spend the whole evening in that."

Fletcher jerked his head toward the mansion that sprawled over the lush grounds. Instinctively Char's eyes followed. She eyed the structure with the discrimination of a designer.

"It's a beautiful home," she noted, "exquisitely put together. The detail is marvelous. Have you seen the library? They had an artist paint the walls to look like mahogany. Truly a work of art."

"Yes, yes and yes. I've seen the library and the work of art and I've rattled around in there until I couldn't figure out if I had to head north or south to find a bathroom. I'm sorry. I can appreciate the structure, it's the utilization of the space I can't abide. Two people in a place like that. It's absurd."

Char giggled, "I'm afraid we must agree on that point. I tend to like something a bit more intimate myself. But then I don't have fifty thousand a year to spend on upkeep, so I suppose it's all relative. Maybe if I had the money I wouldn't be so quick to condemn living in a place like that."

Fletcher shook his head, "You're wrong. You'd never condone such waste even if you had unlimited funds. I can tell. You're much more practical than that. Besides, it's not a love house."

"A what?"

"A house for loving," Fletcher explained. "It's perfect for the couple who could care less about each other. It's so big you'd never have to see your partner. But if you loved the one you were with, it would be an impossible house. You'd never find them. Or by the time you did, exhaustion would win out over lust every time."

"No exceptions to that rule, Mr. Hawkins?" Char said, baiting him playfully.

"Perhaps. If that mausoleum belonged to me, for instance, and I happened to be trying to find a woman dressed in teal chiffon, I imagine passion might win out."

"Really?" She murmured, charmed by his playful words and his black gaze and the feel of muscle rippling just under the thin cotton of his shirt. Coyly she raised her eyes to his, her lips parting to test the truth of what he said. But he wouldn't let her speak. Now the hand that had lain protectively on her back tightened, his fingers splaying as he drew her closer, closer and closer still until his lips touched the tip of her ear and his whisper was only a gentle breath.

"I think the chiffon is a smoke screen, Char Brody. I think we are kindred spirits and we should try to discover exactly what that means."

Char closed her eyes as the timbre of his low voice reverberated in her mind. In her self-imposed darkness Char imagined the two of them dancing. Already she had memorized every nuance of his expression, every purposeful movement of his body. Aware that she held him close without clinging to him, without committing any part of herself, she also was clearly wanting to continue this assignation. Opening her eyes, she pulled away slightly. But before she could speak, Char saw Ross striding purposefully toward them, oblivious to the crowd of stunningly turned-out guests surrounding the dance floor.

Without thinking, she distanced herself from Fletcher Hawkins. He let her go easily, sensing she needed this from him. He watched her, his expression never changing as he considered the transformation in her. She seemed embarrassed, skittish, yet still she smiled at him.

"I'm afraid your charm isn't quite potent enough, Mr. Hawkins. I'm traveling in the morning and even if I weren't . . ."

She let the words hang, unable to say Ross's

name. But Ross was upon them and his arm was sliding around Char's waist protectively — or was it possessively? Turning into him, she smiled and let her fingertips touch the side of his face reassuringly before curving back to the dance floor, the first syllables of an introduction on her lips. Char's heart fell when she realized that Fletcher Hawkins was gone. He hadn't waited. He had flirted with her and they had both enjoyed it immensely. Now it was over.

Char smiled sadly. Why should he be any different than the rest of this strange community of people who tended to think first of themselves and then of others?

"I was going to introduce you," she said quietly.

"I know who that was," Ross said, his eyes darting over the crowd. He disliked the fact that the man had disappeared. Ross felt as though he had been made to look foolish. "That was Fletcher Hawkins. He's a fool. Walked out on a company that was ready to skyrocket."

"I think he decided it was time for him to leave. He didn't walk out," Char sighed, linking her arm through Ross's and stepping off the dance floor. He pulled her back.

"Leave, walk out, it's all the same. He couldn't hack it. I hear he's kind of wandering around now. Actually working freelance as a photographer. Strange what power and money can do to some people." Ross looked back to Char and smiled, his musings forgotten. "But he's gone and you're looking lovely."

Ross tugged on her hand as he moved back onto the dance floor, waiting for the orchestra to start once again. Char pulled back, shaking her head, suddenly tired. Laughing he drew her up and toward him.

"Don't tell me Hawkins wore you out?" he murmured as the music began. Without waiting for an answer he led them through the steps.

Char smiled just before she laid her head against his shoulder. She was tired and not at all interested in dancing. Not now anyway. It was too soon, too easy to compare Ross's soft, well manicured hands with those hardened ones of Fletcher Hawkins. It was too easy to compare the expensive scent Ross wore to the unique and manly smell of Fletcher Hawkins. Dancing with Ross, it was far too simple to realize that Ross's muscular frame was choreographed by a trainer and Fletcher Hawkins's body was made perfect by nature. She tipped back her head, her eyes hooded just as they turned under a lantern.

"I'm so tired, Ross. Not from the dancing. You were just gone so long and I have an early flight tomorrow. You don't mind leaving, do you?"

Ross shook his head. "If you really want to."

"I do," she said apologetically. The glitter of the event had dimmed, the warmth of the night had cooled.

"Your wish is my command. I'll have you home in no time."

51

Ross kissed the top of her head and Char could feel his lips linger in her hair. She raised her face. He looked closely at her, as though trying to figure out what had changed. At a loss, he lowered his lips to hers and kissed her properly. Char ran a hand up his back, leaning into him as she waited for the fireworks to begin. When they didn't, she kissed him again because of her guilt. The chemistry should be so much better. She knew that in her head, too bad her heart hadn't quite figured it out yet.

"Let's go," she murmured.

Hand around her waist, Ross guided her through the thinning crowd. They weren't the only ones to feel the night closing in. Char smiled and shook hands, made arrangements for fittings, small talked until she thought she would scream. Why couldn't they just *leave* one of these parties! Why did it have to be business *and* pleasure — ending with so little pleasure, at that?

Finally, their car brought along by a uniformed attendant, Char stepped up to the open door. As she turned to smile a thanks to the young man who opened her door, she couldn't help but feel *his* eyes were on her.

Fletcher Hawkins watched her from somewhere and wondered about her. His thoughts pulled at her like the song of the siren, and Char wanted just once more to see him, to look at him, to find some fault with him so her dreams wouldn't make him more than he was.

But all she saw was the white mansion illuminated by the blazing lights from within. Slowly Char got into the car. And, as she leaned out to thank the attendant once more, she was unaware that Fletcher Hawkins had taken another perfect picture of her.

Chapter Three

"*Naturellement!* But you are a genius, *ma petite amie!*"

"I am not your 'petite' anything, Pilar. You make me feel like a munchkin when you call me that. I've been trying to break you of that habit since design school. You know, if you'd stuck with designing, you wouldn't talk so much because it's impossible to keep up a conversation with a mouthful of pins. But no, you had to become the toast of the Paris runway. Now enough of this 'petite' business. At home I am considered rather tall, you know."

"But to me that is what you look like. Can I help it if God has made me stand head and shoulders above you?" Pilar clucked, giving in to that famous pout of hers. Char had seen it on the cover of countless magazines, but in person it was even more charming.

"Above me and most men and women on this planet, you monster."

Char laughed up at her gorgeous friend. In the five years since they had actually seen one another, Pilar had become even more beautiful. Her cocoa skin was without blemish, her eyes, once limpid with innocence, now were softened with understanding of how life was lived. Her generous mouth still tipped naturally in a Madonna-like smile, belying her wonderful sense of fun. Her black, black hair cascaded down her back in a fall of natural waves and kinks and frizzes mortal women spent small fortunes to achieve. Her tall, slender body now looked downright angular as Char looked up from her position on the floor. But Char knew from fitting Pilar that she was all woman, curves in exactly the right places. Over the years, Pilar's French with its exotic Martinique accent had given way to the purr of the Parisian. Design school had been so long ago and both had neglected transatlantic visits. How amazing that so much, and so little, could change.

"Hush now," Pilar scolded, waving a jeweled hand toward Char. "I want to look at this magnificent piece you have brought me, and not speak any longer of monsters. This boutique is to open tonight and all must be perfect."

Pilar stood back eyeing the pearl white gown Char was draping on a white-haired mannequin. The plaster mannequin, a cross between Madonna and Marie Antoinette, did justice to Char's creation. Pilar stepped to the left, leaned forward and plucked at the bodice, then bent back and eyed it again while Char became impatient.

"Pilar, I am tired of lying on my back under this thing. Can you tell me if you like the sweep of this skirt or should I tent it more?"

"Mais non! C'est magnifique, Char. Just perfect. I was lost in the beauty of it. Come now. Come look at your handiwork."

Pilar reached out and, with a tug, Char was up and standing by her friend's side grinning like a fool.

"Not bad, if I do say so myself," Char mumbled, unable to keep the pride from her voice. Pilar hugged her, then wrapped her arm around the shorter woman's shoulders while they continued to consider the gown.

"Exquisite. I think I should sell many of these if you made them for me."

"I can't make them, Pilar, lovely as they are. I haven't the capital to expand and make this an off-the-rack item, much as I'd like too." Char sighed.

Pilar shrugged, chagrined. "And I have taken this on consignment when you could have sold it to your ladies at home. *Je suis désolée, ma chère."*

"Don't be ridiculous. You're not sorry in the least to have this in the shop, and I wouldn't want this dress shown anywhere else but here. I do think the beading came out well, don't you?"

Char moved forward and ran her hand over the cape of silver-tipped white bugle beads. She tugged at the intricate braiding of the belt until it lay just so on the mannequin's unnaturally flat stomach.

"But of course, the beading makes the gown," Pilar agreed.

"What a pity I haven't a million dollars," Char answered dreamily. "I would manufacture these for every upscale store in the United States and then some. I would put gowns on the ready-to-wear market the likes of which no one has seen since Edith Head. Oh, Pilar, wouldn't it be wonderful if I could do that?"

"Mais non," Pilar said instantly and offhandedly as she bent to open a box of evening purses.

"No?" Char turned startled eyes toward her friend, who was arranging a Judith Lieber bag on a low glass table.

"Non!" Pilar shook her head emphatically, flicking a speck of dust off the jeweled bag. "If you were to put such a gown out for everyone to purchase, you would find the gown no longer held the allure it once did. Imagine, Char, such a work of art on a less than perfect body? The beading must fall just so over the breasts, the fabric just close enough over the hips." Pilar straightened, motioning with her long-fingered hands to the appropriate body parts before tiring of her explanation. "Oh, you see, don't you?

57

This gown is not for everyone."

Pilar tsked and Char laughed outright as she tackled a box of much needed accessories that had arrived only that morning.

"You're right. I can just imagine Gertrude Palley in this. She's that lady I told you about whose father was responsible for developing the marina area in San Diego. This dress would never work on her. But if I had her money, if I even had Ross's money, I could create clothes that would look right on everyone and still design my one-of-a-kind wearable art. Wouldn't that be marvelous?"

Char pulled out a silver belt, its buckle set with onyx. She ran her fingers over the stonework and wondered how the artist managed to balance the weight so well. It was a moment before she realized that Pilar continued to unpack her box in silence.

"Pilar? Is there something wrong?"

The model shook her head, *"Non, ma chère.* It's only that you've talked so much of other people's money since you've been here. Ross's money, I think?"

"Have I?" Char sat back on her heels. "I'm sorry. I didn't realize."

"Oui, you have. I am wondering now if, maybe, you have something to tell me. Is this Ross making you feel ashamed that you haven't money of your own?"

"Oh, of course not!" Char laughed. The no-tion was ludicrous. "Ross is absolutely wonderful. He has so much faith in my talent. He's always drawing up plans for my expansion — if and when it ever happens."

"And he wants to give you money to do this?" Pilar asked.

Char shrugged as she unfolded the last of the belts, "Yes. But I wouldn't take his money. I want it to be my own money. I want to do it on my own when I expand."

"And what if you were to marry Ross? Then his money would belong to you both," Pilar suggested.

Char pulled another box toward her and spoke almost sadly, "I'm not sure we're headed in that direction. He hasn't asked me. Hell, we don't even sleep together and we've been seeing each other for ages. Marriage is a big step, Pilar. I'd have to be absolutely sure we have what it takes to be married before I commit. We like each other. A lot, in fact. But it's so easy for us to leave each other sometimes that I worry. Does that make sense?"

"Naturellement!" Pilar arranged the fine silver chain of a lizard shoulder bag that it lay snakelike over the beveled glass tabletop as she thought out loud. "If you had the same money, would that make you feel better about Ross? If you brought the same dollars to this relationship that Ross does, then you would feel good about him? Maybe it wouldn't be so easy

59

to think of leaving."

"Pilar!" In frustration Char wrapped a coil of skinny little purple leather belt around her neck and tugged dramatically. "I'm not thinking of leaving. We don't have that kind of relationship. It isn't one you stay in or leave. At least I don't think it is. The only thing I do know is that we mean something to each other. Someday I think we will be very important to one another."

Char wrinkled her nose considering exactly what type of relationship she and Ross did have. It was comfortable. One of mutual respect. Interesting — God, it was interesting. Ross knew everyone who was anyone and then some. He was handsome and easy to be with. She sighed.

"I don't know. I haven't dissected our relationship or how I feel about the wealth I'm surrounded by. Oh, sometimes I'm jealous a little bit, but not of Ross and not of his money. I'm just envious of the freedom it brings. Look at him. He's master of his fate. If Ross wanted to, he could open a chain of restaurants tomorrow and not blink an eye. If he wanted to retire and travel the world, he'd never run out of money. And these women I design for! Hah! They spend as much on one dress I make them as I spend all year on food. It's amazing to watch. They have no idea what a wonderful resource they have at their fingertips. To them money is just a toy. It's not a means to an end. It is the end. Oh, Pilar, I wouldn't be normal if I wasn't just a wee bit resentful—of those ladies and Ross and everyone else who has money to burn. But at least Ross earned what he has. I admire that. I don't think it would make our relationship any deeper if I had as much money as Ross or any of them. It would only make my relationship with all of them," Char put a finger to her lips, "well balanced."

Pilar rolled her eyes heavenward. "I think that was a joke about money, Char. Balanced like a money scale?" Char giggled at Pilar's perception of what a joke was, then removed the belt that was still wound around her neck. Pilar pulled the last bag from the box, then packed up all the papers.

"I think it is time we stopped this nonsense. We've only the scarves to finish up after you display the belts. That we can do tonight, just before the party. Let's go and play like we used to. We shall find a bottle of wine and a loaf of bread. We will sit and whistle at the handsome men strolling about. You and Ross are not so serious we cannot whistle at the handsome men?"

Char laughed. "We are not that serious. Maybe someday. You know he comes closest to what I've been looking for in a man. Ross is the most undemanding man I've ever known." Char wrapped herself in a capelike scarf of sorrel cashmere, draping it like a cowl over her short hair.

"*Mon Dieu,* Char, you are so American. Love, it is no fun unless the man demands a bit now and again. You can pretend you only want to say no, then say yes only when he is mad with desire. You must learn to play a game or two. What you American women think is perfection is only settling for the boring. Come, I'll teach you over our wine how you must look for the excitement in a man first, then you won't worry about what it is he demands. When you find the right one, everything he wants from you will be heaven, like a request from an angel's lips. You will see."

With that Pilar pulled a red fedora over her cascade of hair, dragged on thigh-high canary yellow boots over black leggings, donned a swing coat of kelly green and kissed Char on each cheek.

"Your idea of heaven sounds like too much work, Pilar," Char sniffed.

Pilar shook her head sadly, ushered Char out the door, then turned to lock it.

"I suppose you're right. You live only for the fashion, Char. That is the only thing you wish to work hard at. Pity the man who loves you well. He will work himself to death to please you and you will see nothing but the next design, you will long for nothing but the caress of silk running through your fingers, not his hands running through your hair."

Door locked, Pilar buried her hands in the

deep pockets of her coat and turned a smiling face toward Char, her philosophical meandering forgotten. Behind her Char was stunned almost to speechlessness. She put her hand on Pilar's arm, stopping her before she started down the street.

"That's not true, Pilar," Char whispered.

"What, *chérie?*"

"That I don't want to love someone. That I can't love someone." Char moved a step closer to her friend, looking for some confirmation that she hadn't believed what she said. But Pilar's eyes were hooded and the January sun shone weakly on her beautiful dark face.

"I did not say you couldn't, my friend," Pilar answered evenly. "I said it was the fashion you loved and were willing to work for. I only say you haven't chosen to love deeply. There is a difference. When the fashion is number two, that is when I'll believe you love deeply. Now, come, Marcel will have a table for us and I will treat you to the marvelous *crêpes au sucre* before we must get ready for tonight."

Winding her arm through Char's, Pilar chattered about the boutique opening. The winter wind whipped around them as they crossed the Seine on a bridge that had played host to history's most beautiful women.

By the time they sat with a bottle of wine between them, Char was laughing at Pilar's account of her final altercation with the eminent designer Vachel. The same great designer who, at one time, couldn't create a line without Pilar standing by his side, who couldn't show unless it was Pilar floating down the runway in the final bridal gown, and who was now not only content to design without Pilar's inspiration, but chose to ignore her.

"Just as well," Pilar sighed. "I get more of the publicity without his blessing. Thank the Lord my contract is so tight. He must pay me through the summer. By then, Pilar's, that magnificent fashion house, will be making me more money than I know what to do with."

"To success," Char chimed in, holding her glass aloft, catching Pilar's optimism.

"To happiness," Pilar responded, her glass meeting Char's just as Pilar's eyes met those of her friend. "To success," she whispered.

"I'm not sure you can have both," Char said, lowering her glass.

Pilar laughed gently at the silliness of her friend.

"Most of the time they are one and the same thing."

"Char! Char! *Chérie,* I haven't my other earring. *Que faire?* Ten minutes and they will all be here. Char! Where are you?"

"Right here."

Char peered out of the back room where she

was overseeing the caterer's work. The bar had already been set up, Jean-Luc presiding over enough wine, liquor, and liqueurs to satisfy anyone's taste. The ladies who were to serve stood about, chatting quietly. Their starched pinafores and black dresses were exquisitely turned out. The most marvelous treats lay ready on trays of silver: new potatoes topped with sour cream and caviar — black and red — *prosciutto e melone,* smoked oysters, and an oddly puffed concoction that reminded Char of bite-size Moroccan *bastilla.*

Now, in the quiet of the elegant boutique, as everyone reverently awaited the arrival of the press and the fashion elite, Pilar was shrieking like a banshee and looking like a vision.

"Pilar," Char sighed affectionately, moving slowly into the main room so that she could enjoy this moment of utter panic by one of the coolest women she had ever known. "You're wearing one of my designs. You look lovely, but the gesture was unnecessary. To choose my work over Saint-Laurent and Givenchy? That's true friendship."

Pilar tossed her head back peevishly. Carefully she picked up the purse she had taken such care displaying only that morning and looked underneath.

"It isn't here," she grumbled returning the bag with little thought while continuing her search for the errant earring. Nervous, feeling she must talk, Pilar berated Char. "What gesture? I do not make a gesture. I've chosen the best to wear because I want to look so . . . what do you say? Unforgettable."

"Well, you do, even if I say so myself," Char laughed as she walked toward the small gilt secretary where Pilar would discreetly conduct her business after the boutique opened. Now it was the place Pilar had left her enormous jade earring. Scooping it up, Char glided to her friend, tapped her on the shoulder, and held the gold encased green jewel under her nose.

"Ah! Ah!" Pilar cried, snatching it from Char and clipping it to her ear. *"Merci."*

The jade earring was so large it almost covered her ear. Char laughed and shook her head. Pilar of the must-have school of shopping. She had made a fortune as Vachel's muse and she had spent every penny. Luckily her contract with Vachel had proven unbreakable and she would receive another six months of her salary to carry her through until the boutique turned a profit.

"Chérie, tell me true. How am I looking?"

"Incredible. You look like the proprietress of the soon-to-be-hottest boutique in Paris." Char took Pilar by the shoulders and shook her gently. "Now you must calm down. It's no good to look like a goddess in green silk only to sound like a fishwife the minute you open your mouth."

"D'accord! I am so stupid. Of course." Pilar

66

took a deep, calming breath, her countenance becoming serene. "A good trick you learn on the runway. Now, all is calm. Let me see you." She twirled a finger imperiously.

Char obliged her, feeling as special as the occasion demanded. There in the tastefully decorated boutique, surrounded by the glitter of haute couture, Char drew attention to herself through simplicity. For this most special occasion she had chosen a dress of indigo shantung. Fitted exquisitely to her body, the dress lay against it without a wrinkle or pull from the exaggerated neckline, which bared her décolletage as well as an inviting expanse of shoulder, to the scalloped hem that bared half her thigh. In typical CB fashion, Char added the sparkle of jeweled buttons in every possible shade of blue, securing them so they marched up the seam of her long slender sleeve and down the side seam of the dress, a glittering outline of her body. She wore no jewelry except for thinly hammered hoops of gold. Her short, short hair was moussed into witty little licks of curl and her makeup glistened with an underlying sheen of sparkled taupe.

"Char, but you are marvelous. We shall sell the dress off your back." Pilar clapped in delight, lightly plucking at a button or two to check *la qualité*. Char laughed. Pilar was so transparent.

"I hope not. I'd like to keep this one."

"But you shall let me take orders if there is

someone who would rather die than not to have it?" Pilar asked slyly, knowing Char would refuse her nothing. But before Char could answer, they felt a puff of icy air and the first of the press had arrived. Pilar was in her element, turning from Char with such grace that Char wondered if she were watching reality or dreaming a dream.

"Paulo!" Pilar cried, floating toward the dark-haired man in an oversized cashmere coat. "How good of you to be first. I was hoping the friendliest face was the one that would arrive before the others. Let me show you, darling, my small business. You must tell me what you think in your heart, Paulo . . ."

It had begun. Grinning, Char disappeared into the back room, leaving Pilar her moment in the sun. There she busied herself making sure the food and wine flowed without interruption.

Every once in a while Char would wend her way through the crowd. Introducing herself, charming the reporters with her all-American straightforwardness, catching Pilar's eye now and then before disappearing once more to make sure the details of the party were attended to.

Finally, Char pulled a delicate Louis XIV chair to the small wall that partitioned the main room from the tiny alcove in which Pilar had placed only the most exclusive eveningwear. Exhausted, she sat down and leaned her head on the carved back of the chair as she listened to the excited babble of the grand-opening party. All was going well.

Just as she smiled, Char's reverie was broken by the flash of a camera. Her eyes flew open only to see spots dancing in front of them. Anger flashed at the photographer's intrusion. But as she let her eyes clear, blinking away the spots, Char smiled most engagingly. Heaven help her if she alienated any of the press on this of all nights.

"I'm sorry," she stammered, "was I in the way? Were you shooting the gowns?"

Char blinked again, sitting stick straight. Finally, her vision clearing, she turned toward the photographer as though drawn to him. There was an aura in the little room that hadn't been there before. And there was a scent that reminded her of something. A hand took hers. His voice, when he spoke, was so close to her ear his lips might almost have touched her if she hadn't tipped her head as though trying to remember why this touch should be so familiar. Her eyes remained closed now, not because of the flash, but in an attempt to recapture a memory as she listened to his voice.

"How could I possibly think of focusing on anything else when you're here?"

There was no doubt now. Memories of amusement and that odd pull of desire, where there should be none, returned with full force. Unwanted, but inevitable, a sly smile claimed her lips. She knew who had taken her picture, who held her hand, and who spoke to her as though in one moment he would laugh and the next he would talk of love.

"Fletcher Hawkins," she said, opening her eyes to see Fletcher's smiling olive-skinned face filling her line of sight.

He hadn't changed in the few days since she'd seen him. His hair was still raven black, falling too long without care for convention, his eyes still burned, deeply set under thick lashes. His features still lacked categorization yet strangely came together with such an exotic and intense beauty it almost took Char's breath away. The only nod to the protocol of the evening was the Missoni sweater he wore, its shades of sienna and ocher a perfect complement to his coloring. Baring his chest just so, the V-neck allowed Char a glimpse of the blanket of dark curling hair. His jeans were pressed and a scarf of cashmere had been added, more for warmth, Char imagined, than for style. His style, it would seem, was his own and Paris was not about to change it.

"You remembered," he laughed. "I'm touched."

Fletcher, still holding Char's hand, drew her out of her chair, up and toward him. Surprisingly she didn't resist. The alcove was small, the dresses expensive. It would be a shame if the button of her dress caught on any of the garments, or if Fletcher should inadvertently move too quickly and a gown fall to the floor. It was natural, under the circumstances, to stand close to one another, holding hands to balance. It was so . . . natural.

"Don't be," Char sallied. "It's hard to forget someone with your particular brand of charm."

"You can't still be mad at me for the misunderstanding at the beach."

"I'm not mad at you about anything. If I were angry, that would indicate I had thought about you during the last few days, which, I can assure you, is about as far from the truth as you can imagine."

It was then Char slid her hand out of Fletcher's and turned her attention to a gown that didn't look quite right on its hanger. But Fletcher moved in, standing just to the side of her, casually inspecting his camera as he spoke.

"Isn't it interesting how a person can say one thing and their eyes say another? I suppose that's why the Indians think the eyes are the window to the soul. It's only by looking deeply into them that one can know the truth."

Char suppressed a grin, giving the heavy silk-satin skirt of the lace-topped gown one final tug. Slowly, cockily, she faced Fletcher, tipped her chin, and planted her hand on her hip.

"Okay, Mr. 'Traveled-the-World' Hawkins, why don't you tell me exactly what it is you think you see in my eyes."

Fletcher barely moved, yet Char felt him overwhelm her with his presence as she waited. It took all her willpower not to look away from his smoldering eyes that both disconcerted and delighted her. When his lips opened to speak, she knew she had to listen, otherwise she would be lost in assessing the intricate pattern of his bone structure.

"I see a woman so single-minded in the pursuit of her art that she has the ability to block out all other thoughts. Thoughts both pleasurable and not so pleasurable. But that doesn't mean those thoughts aren't real, it only means they aren't acknowledged. And that is why I know you've been thinking of me. Admit it. I've been there," he tapped the side of her head, the little hollow just to the side of her brow, "since the moment you saw me on the beach."

Fletcher grinned suddenly, flashing his white teeth like a badge of distinction. For an instant Char thought he was going to drag her off to a dance floor once again, only this time he wouldn't let her go, no matter who wanted to cut in.

Fighting every urge to return his dazzling smile and encourage his fantastic ego, Char let a tick of time pass. Her eyes traveled the length of him, her expression giving no indication that she admired what she saw. Slowly she lifted a hand, made a fist, extended her finger, and punched him lightly in the chest.

"If I had been thinking of you, you would have known it. As for your assessment of my single-mindedness, I can't argue with that. And I always acknowledge pleasurable memories; it's only those that aren't gratifying or aren't even important enough to fall into either category that I ignore. Now, if you're so anxious to take pictures, I suggest you take ones that count. Pilar is the star here tonight, not me. Or did you neglect to introduce yourself when you crashed this party?"

Char tried to sidestep around Fletcher but he blocked her way with a graceful slide. She feinted right, only to be blocked by the wall of clothing. She raised an eyebrow as though to say further-conversation-wasn't-worth-the-bother-and-please-excuse-her. While she waited for him to move, Char tried desperately not to think of how perfectly suited they were to one another in height. For an instant her body remembered the feel of his against it as they had danced on Jennifer's wedding night. But the physical memory evaporated and she found herself caught up in that amazing grin of his.

"But I'm not here to photograph the owner of this boutique, no matter how enticing an offer that is. I've come to find you."

"All the way to Paris to ask me for a date?"

Fletcher shrugged. "Paris or around the block. It's all the same to me. I work for myself."

"It must be lucrative if you can manage Paris

as easily as your neighborhood block," Char drawled, suddenly tired of his pretense and their bantering.

"You forget my fortune was made long before I took pictures," Fletcher said matter-of-factly.

"Of course. Boy billionaire. How could I forget?" Char looked askance as though to say he had better try harder if he wanted to impress her. Unfortunately, both of them knew he was doing a reasonable job of that. Fletcher grinned.

"You did remember. But that's neither here nor there. I didn't come all this way to ask you for a date but to chronicle your journey. Did it ever occur to you that I might have been in Del Mar for professional reasons the night we met?"

"I didn't think that much about it once I knew you were a guest," Char sniffed.

"That's fair, I suppose, though I'm not sure I believe you." Char opened her mouth to protest. But he spoke over her with ease. "So, I was there for a very specific reason. I'm working on a photographic editorial on the quiet wealthy. You know, those people with a zillion bucks that no one ever hears about. They may be written up in the *Wall Street Journal* on a regular basis, but they'll never be on the front of *People* magazine. Nor would they want to be."

"Actually," Char commented, "that is quite interesting. But I'm in Paris to help a friend open her business. You could have sent me a card if you thought I had some burning desire to know

74

why you were at Jennifer's wedding. In fact, I'm so uninterested I'm not even going to ask how you tracked me down. Now, if you'll excuse me."

"But I can't," Fletcher protested, putting his arm out to block another attempted escape. "I mean I can't let you go. I can tell you Jennifer told me where you were. And if you walk out on me now, you'll be missing out on one great business opportunity. You are an exquisite package, mind you, but even I wouldn't follow a woman across the ocean just to get to know her better. This is business—mostly." Her lips tightly shut as she tried to find something pithy to say, Char slipped back into the gilt chair realizing she had no choice but to listen to him. "I knew I'd get you with that. No good business person can walk out on a proposition until they've heard all the details."

"Actually, I'm just being practical. I don't feel like fighting my way out of this room."

"Smart and talented. I like that." Fletcher laughed, kneeling beside her, draping his strong arms over the dainty little ones of the chair. "Okay, here's the proposition. You design for half the wealthy women in San Diego, Del Mar, and Coronado. They represent the better halves of a good percentage of the *Forbes* list of wealthiest men in America. These are women who can afford any designer they want and they choose to trust you with their fashion image—to a certain extent. You're their one-of-a-kind, witty type of designer whose work is a must-have-one objective.

"Now I think that says something not only about these women, but about you. Obviously you not only are talented, you've been able to convince those monied ladies that you're worth their attention even though you don't have an international reputation."

"That's my business," Char reminded him. "If they wanted off-the-rack they could go to Neiman's. If they wanted haute couture, they would jet off to Paris or Milan. What they want is something easy, close, stylish. They realize I understand the Southern California lifestyle. Rich or not, the lifestyle transcends labels and trends. It's a meeting of the minds, an encounter with a special soul that lives in California . . ." Char stopped, sat straight up in her chair, her cheeks flushed. "What *are* you grinning at?"

"You are perfect. Just perfect."

With that he laughed, took her hand, and dragged her out of the alcove into the heart of the party.

Chapter Four

"Wait! Fletcher, what are you doing?" Char groused as he tugged her on. "Excuse me. Sorry." She apologized as Fletcher led her right into the arms of a gentleman in a burnoose, then bumped a lady who obviously was enjoying the wine. She smiled through clenched teeth and tugged back on his hand as discreetly as possible.

"What are you complaining about, woman?"

Fletcher stopped so quickly she ran right into him. Char bounced back slightly, jerked her hand from his, and smoothed her dress hoping they were not going to make a scene. The few people who had taken notice of them seemed amused, as only Parisians can seem, but it appeared a scandal was not in the brewing.

"I would like to know where it is you think we're going." Char smiled broadly and made her demand without even moving her lips.

"Out to see Paris as if neither one of us has

ever seen it before. I'm going to take you to the top of the Eiffel Tower and tell you exactly how you fit into the grand scheme of the story I'm doing. I'm going to convince you that I not only find you incredibly attractive, but that I have your best interests at heart, too. I'm going to . . ."

". . . Stop this right now is what you're going to do," Char finished for him. "I'm here to help my friend with the most important night of her life. And I am not going to run out on her so I can go sight-seeing in the middle of January with someone I hardly know."

Fletcher grinned, his dark features transformed by the sweetness of his smile. "I promise, you won't be deserting anyone. Your friend will understand. In fact, she probably won't even notice you're gone."

"Don't be absurd," Char scoffed, shaking her head in disbelief. As she did so, the crowd parted. There stood Pilar just like Moses contemplating a cooperative Red Sea. Fletcher followed Char's gaze, saw their hostess and took advantage of his opening. His hands cupped Char's shoulders, his fingers straying from the shantung onto the velvety smoothness of her skin as he propelled her forward, leaning down to whisper as they went.

"I'll prove her feelings won't be hurt in the slightest," he insisted.

Pilar looked quite delighted to see Char. She

held out her long arms. Char grinned. Now Fletcher Hawkins would see what was what around here. He couldn't keep pushing and pulling her about like this. Taking her away from places where she had obligations. But it was Char who was surprised, Char who was once again handed a pretty package only to find an explosion of confetti inside.

"Fletcher! *Beau* Fletcher!" Pilar cried exuberantly, as she came round to wrap her arm about his shoulders and kiss both his cheeks. "You have found her. I am so glad. But you cannot take her without her coat, she will freeze at the top of the tower. Unless you will take her in your arms to warm her, eh?"

Together they laughed. Fletcher, his hand still on Char's shoulder, wound his free arm around Pilar's slender waist and soon their laughter infected Char. What could she do but enjoy this moment with Fletcher? Wonderful Pilar obviously saw something special in Fletcher, too. She allowed him her friendship so easily and so openly.

"I can't fight it," Char admitted, leaning into Fletcher, who tightened his hold, releasing Pilar without a second thought.

"But you should, Char. Remember I told you to say *non* until he is mad with desire," Pilar warned, wagging her finger playfully. "Fletcher, he has come to find you. He says for business, but I say on this lucky night it is for some other reason. Yet I think his blood doesn't boil enough for you yet."

Char's laugh faded to a sigh and suddenly she felt almost shy in his embrace. She would have moved away, but he kept her still.

"He came because he is crazy, Pilar," Char answered without looking at Fletcher.

"Crazy can be good, my friend," Pilar answered. "And I have already decided he is a gentleman despite the fact he makes a living with his camera."

"But I shoot the truth, Pilar, not just the beauty," Fletcher reminded her.

"That is why I give you my blessing," she answered, then sighed as she raised her fingers to his black hair. "Such a pity you are not lighter. I like my men with the blond hair. If you were blond, I might take you away from Char."

"If he were purple, pink, or anything else, I would give him to you, so you could make sure he doesn't keep popping up at the most inopportune times, Pilar," Char joked, wanting to stay here with Pilar. Alone with Fletcher she would have no hope, she knew that now.

"I think she doesn't know her own heart," Pilar said with an exaggerated aside.

"I think I know my own mind," Char interrupted. "Now why do I get the feeling I'm in the middle of a conspiracy?"

"Because you are," Fletcher answered. "Pilar gave me permission to take you away an hour ago. I told her my intentions were strictly honorable. She said she hoped that wasn't true and that was that."

"You asked for her permission?" Teasingly Char raised a beautifully shaped brow.

"It was the only way to get you out of here. You've been working this whole night while I have been playing queen," Pilar reminded her.

"I've been having a marvelous time," Char objected, even as she longed to go.

"It would be better with him, *ma chère.*" Pilar winked. "Now go. I have seen Pierre and I must talk with him immediately, or I shall have to spend the time after this party alone. See how lovely and light his hair is. Oh, Fletcher, such a pity."

With that Pilar floated off in pursuit of her sometime lover and dear old friend, leaving Char and Fletcher alone in a roomful of people.

"Well, Ms. Brody. Now that we have your guardian's consent, may I have the honor of seeing Paris with you on this beautiful night?"

Slowly Char turned to Fletcher, wanting so much to stave off the moment she must be completely alone with him. Yet when she looked into his face, her lips parting ever so slightly in surprise, her heart softened, and her mind found the words it was searching for.

"I'd be delighted Mr. Hawkins," she said softly.

In his face she had seen such sincerity, such

81

honest and open hope that she would go with him that she was touched. The one Fletcher, the brash and unexpected one, was exciting. But this Fletcher was endearing. And for Char, that moment when she looked into his eyes, that instant when those black orbs didn't shine with the twinkle of sport, was the point she knew she was lost to anyone else. At least for a night. Just one night in Paris.

She clung to him because if she didn't, she was going to fly into the black, black night. Straight up, like a shooting star, she traveled like a projectile. But if Fletcher held her, perhaps together they could remain grounded. Char didn't want to become part of the universe. She was much too content to be a mere mortal at this heavenly moment.

"Scared?"

His lips were on her hair, he whispered against it so that the sound of his voice was muffled. Char shook her head against his chest and closed her eyes even tighter. She heard him chuckle, a deep sound that came from his heart. Char's fingers tightened around the fistful of sweater she had grasped as this third, and final, elevator shot them to the top of the Eiffel Tower.

With them in the cage was the man who seemed to run the contraption with an interest bordering on the negligent. He paid little heed to them. He had seen it all before.

In the silent night, with the bored conductor as their only witness, Char was wrapped, as Pilar had instructed, in both her cashmere throw and Fletcher's arms. She could hear so many things she had never been aware of before: the beautiful bass of a beating heart, the gentle drift of a breath, the sound lips make when they speak against a cloud of curls. It was as though, for the first time in her life, Char had stopped running, jumping, and looking for the ever more interesting things in life. For the first time, in repose, she listened and felt what was around her. For a fleeting instant Char wondered why she had never paused to listen to Ross—his heart, his mind—then the moment was gone and the door of the elevator was open. Char and Fletcher stepped out into the room on the top of the Eiffel Tower.

"Do you want to go outside?" Fletcher indicated the observation ramp outside the glass enclosed deck.

Char shook her head and left him, her arm sliding away from his body reluctantly as she went to the window and placed her hand against it. Then she heard what was now familiar. The click and whir of Fletcher's camera. Without looking over at him she spoke:

"Why do you do that so often?"

"Because you're beautiful. I told you that in Del Mar. I'm telling you again and I will continue to tell you until you insist I go away and leave you alone. Maybe you never will. Then I'll be content to point my camera at you and chronicle your life until you're ancient."

"Maybe you'll want to go away. When you find someone more beautiful."

"Maybe," Fletcher said without conviction.

"Tell me about this layout you're working on," Char said, afraid that here on top of the tower, alone with him, she would forget another life and crazily choose to make one with him if he asked. Fletcher had to speak of things other than beauty and desire and a lifetime entwined if she was to retain her reason. He moved next to her and leaned back, facing away from the window.

"The quiet wealthy. Greedy yet incredibly generous. They shy away from publicity because it tries to categorize them, yet there is a pecking order in their own societal hierarchy. They put on no airs. The silent rich, as opposed to the nouveau riche or celebrities, have no need to impress anyone. They have old money or money made from manufacturing the most boring necessities.

"They live in and for a rarified group. Without each other they feel naked and alone in a hostile world. And all around them there is an army that works to keep them rich, beautiful, and comfortable. They don't have to strive for money or position, they only have to maintain it.

"And you? You're a general in that army to emperors. They trust you with their vanity. My God, that's an incredible trust for people like this."

"They trust other people, too, and more often," Char countered. She turned toward him intrigued by the way he saw the world she moved in but was not a part of. "They fly to Paris, to Milan, to New York to visit this designer or that. They snap their fingers and the latest gown is in their closet. Mine just happen to hang alongside world famous designers. Why not include them in your story?"

"Far from original." Fletcher waved away the idea with disdain. "That story's been done a thousand times. I want the reader to find out about people who drive the world economy without so much as rippling the everyday waters of life. I want them to find out about people like you who create incredibly beautiful things for people most of us never see.

"I don't want to just show your designs, Char, but the soul behind the design, the care taken with each stitch and the final glorious conclusion of all that hard physical and mental labor. I realized how important a part of these people's lives you were at that wedding. The bride's dress was spectacular, but she took for granted it would be. You envisioned it, created it. Do you see what I mean? Do you understand that a month in your life translates to an evening of presumed glamour in theirs?"

Excited, Fletcher faced the expanse of window that kept them safe from the buffeting winds outside. As though at a loss for words, he raised his camera to chronicle the moment he shared his inspiration.

"You make me sound rather noble," Char said quietly. "Almost like an attendant to a court of kings and queens. It sounds as though I slave away by candlelight, embroidering kid gloves for a pittance."

"I like that analogy." Fletcher adjusted the focus on his lens and stepped back. "Move in a bit. I want to just get the shadow of your brow and cheek with the lights of Paris stretching out behind you." Strangely, without hesitation, Char did as he asked. "Perfect. Thank you."

"You're welcome," she acknowledged quietly, taken aback by his courtesy. The camera clicked. She knew the shot would be lovely.

Lowering the camera he looked at her. "Stitchers of the court weren't paid according to their talent. I'm sure that you're not proportionately wealthy to your clientele because yours is not a recognized name. There's a three hundred percent markup for that little bit of marketing wizardry."

"Well, I'm not rich, that's true," Char admitted.

"Even close?" Fletcher prodded. She shook her head. Fletcher chuckled. "How could you be?

From what I've seen at the wedding and in Pilar's boutique, you can't resist going the extra mile on each of your designs. I noticed you line in silk, not acetate or one of the new silklike substitutions . . ."

"I think it feels better against the skin . . ."

"And your beadwork. It's not machine done. All of it's handwork . . ."

"These are one of a kind. No plant would take on a onetime beading project . . ."

"And your seams are flat felled . . ."

"Okay," Char put an end to his cross-examination, "you're absolutely right. I don't charge enough. Even the rich have their limits for an unknown. I don't have the label recognition to go along with the talent, so I can't charge the way a couturier might. I can't license because only a handful of people know who I am. But happiness isn't dependent on money. I create beauty, I do it well and I control the end product. I'm very, very good at what I do. And you are welcome to come and photograph my workroom, my helpers, my beaders. You're invited any day you wish to come."

Without answering, Fletcher held out his hand and took Char's. Raising it to his shoulder, he cradled her other hand, holding it out ready to begin with the next beat of a song she couldn't hear. Her breath came sharply into her lungs and suspended there as she waited to see what he would do. He had pushed her to a point of defense, then reached out and caressed her as though to say, "We're not at war."

He smiled now and pulled her close. The tune had begun for him. Slowly he moved her back, to the side, forward, and back again. Their eyes never left one another's.

"I don't want to come for a day, Char Brody. I want to photograph your life. The entire fabric of it. I want to come for as long as it takes. Do you understand?"

Char nodded. "It's a lot to ask, Fletcher. Almost too much."

"But don't you think it might be worth a great deal, all this attention I'm willing to lavish on you?"

Char cocked her head. She felt her fingers entwine themselves in his hair without her knowing when they had moved. His hair was so soft and thick she wanted to put her cheek against it. She heard his question as from a great distance. Above her the stars illuminated France, below her the lights of Paris blinked and flickered. In the middle of all this heavenly light, she was an angel dancing with a very agreeable devil. If she had ever wondered what love felt like, she had her answer now. Luckily she also knew it was the dark, the starlight, the feel of thick straight hair beneath her fingertips, and a tall strong body moving with hers that made her feel this way. Tomorrow, when the sun came out, things would be different. Tonight, though, Char would forget about tomorrow. Tonight she would be whatever she wished to be, enjoy whatever it was she felt.

"How will all this attention be worth my while?" she asked dreamily.

"The notoriety, for one," Fletcher whispered, twirling her ever so slightly to pause at the door leading to the observation deck. "People will know your name, they will admire your talent. They will fall at your feet. It's what you want, isn't it? It's what everyone wants." With one swift motion he opened the door, dancing them out until they stood in the open sky above Paris. The cold made Char draw close, the force of the wind made her cling to him for support and reassurance. She lifted her face and Fletcher saw clear gray eyes that desired so much in that moment.

"I don't want the world to fall at my feet."

"Then there is the other benefit," Fletcher continued softly, coming close until his lips hovered just above hers.

"And what might that be?" Char breathed back, her lips parting in hope and anticipation.

"I might fall at your feet. Adoring you for the time we're here together or, perhaps, forever."

As the last word was picked up by the wind and driven away before it could become an actual promise, Fletcher Hawkins's lips covered Char Brody's. Their bodies melted into one another without question or reservation. Char and

Fletcher were alone, two more stars in the Parisian sky.

As their kiss deepened, as Char forgot Coronado and Ross and Pilar, she realized that given another time, another life, Fletcher and she could have been lovers of epic proportion. But there was no room in her real life for him. Not for a man who lived by his wits, who threw away a fortune in search of truth, who believed that life was simple and that security came from the mind, not from the pocketbook. No, there was no room in her life for him to stay, but she welcomed him that night when nothing was real.

"It is too soon for you to go!" wailed Pilar for the hundredth time just as the cab skidded to a halt in front of the international terminal of de Gaulle airport. The driver lacked even an ounce of grace as he slammed on the brakes. Fletcher held the two women back as they pitched forward, keeping them from being thrown into the terminal before they could get out and walk.

"Mon Dieu! Quoi? T'es aveugle? Ou complètement bourré?" Pilar screamed, leaving the poor driver not an ounce of dignity as he pulled toward the airport curb. The man shrugged sheepishly as he hopped out of the cab with Fletcher on his heels. Both men were happy to have reached their destination in one piece.

"Pilar, you're too hard on the poor man. I

have no idea what you told him but it sounded absolutely horrible." Char laughed, her long-ago-learned French completely forgotten save for the very basics.

"I tell him he is either blind or blind drunk to drive the way he does. He doesn't keep his eyes on the road," she huffed.

"Well how could you expect him to? He couldn't keep his eyes off you. Who could think about the road with the marvelous Pilar in the backseat of their cab?"

"Hmph! That is a silly excuse. If he wants to look at me, then he should wait until I get out of the cab, not when I am still in it."

"A man in love cannot bear for the woman of his desire to be out of his sight even for a moment," Char teased happily, as she turned to see how Fletcher was coming with the luggage.

"And the same is for the woman, no?" Pilar asked slyly.

"What?" Char mumbled, engrossed in the sight of Fletcher's hair dotted with diamonds of mist as the gray sky tried desperately to rain.

"I said I think that you and this Fletcher are crazy not to have made love while you are in Paris. A waste of the city."

Incredulous, Char slipped back onto the seat, giving Pilar her full attention.

"I beg your pardon?"

"I say it is a pity you came to my apartment every night alone while Fletcher, he went to the hotel." Pilar flipped the end of her huge silk scarf up and picked at a nonexistent piece of lint. Her lips were pushed into a knowing pout. Carefully she avoided Char's questioning gaze.

"I'm not in the habit of sleeping with photographers who want to do a story on me, Pilar," Char said evenly.

"Ah, he is not just a photographer, *ma chère.*" Throwing down the edge of the scarf, Pilar decided she would play no more games. Time was short. Char had done so much for her in the last few days that the least she, Pilar, could do would be to open her friend's eyes. "Fletcher is a good man. There are the sparks here between you. We are together in Paris for days, and it is as though I do not exist, he wants you so much." She wagged a magenta-tipped nail in front of Char's eyes. "He is a fine man, Char. Do not throw him away."

"He is with me because of business. I explained all this to you," Char answered, exasperated because she knew Pilar was telling the truth.

"Your words sound smart but your eyes, your body . . . oh, Char, they say so much that is different. And Fletcher too. He wants . . ."

"I don't care what he wants," Char snapped, disliking where this conversation was going.

She had commitments, after all. Ross was waiting for her. Better she put a little energy into that relationship. She had to figure out where

92

they stood rather than worry about a nonexistent love affair with a man who had no roots and no intention of putting any down as far as she could see. A wanderer, a free spirit, a man who could walk away from a successful business was not the kind of man who could take Char's dreams of expansion seriously. The only thing Fletcher Hawkins took seriously was whatever he trained his camera on at the moment.

Indignant, she reached for her carry-on. Pulling the zipper back, Char felt her anger dissipate as she looked at the beautiful antique laces she had spent far too much on at the *le marché* at Clingoncourt. Lovingly she fingered the delicate fabric, then zipped the bag once again. She was being unfair to Pilar. Pilar's big heart only wished Char well. And for her efforts she got a verbal slap on the wrist.

Char laid a hand softly on Pilar's arm. "I'm sorry. I didn't mean to be so short. I feel it too, Pilar. Fletcher is a very special man. But he's not for me. Ross understands what I need and what I want from life. Fletcher is exciting, but you must remember we are in Paris and Paris is magic. And, Pilar, magic isn't real. It's time to get back to reality."

Char glanced over her shoulder knowing this would be the last time she could really look at Fletcher. Once they were back at her small factory on Coronado Island, things would be different. Her handful of employees would see romance where there was none. Hadn't they all hinted more than once it was time Char got serious about a man? And there would be Ross and work, her clients, and so many other things to keep her from looking at Fletcher Hawkins the way she did now.

Pilar covered Char's hand and leaned close to whisper, "But, *chérie,* this is reality. To feel so much is a sign. They do not say people have electricity for nothing. Electricity must light something. It is inevitable—you and Fletcher."

Char laughed softly. "Nothing but death and taxes are inevitable."

"I like him, Char," Pilar said sincerely. "You must give him a chance."

"I like him too, Pilar. But I can't afford to give him a chance. Time is slipping away. I don't need Fletcher's love. I need to be part of his story. I need to make a success of my business now, and his kind of publicity will help me do that. I don't want to be fifty and still hanging in with the ladies in Del Mar and Coronado. How can I think of anything but my business now?"

"So who is talking of what you need? I see only what you want," Pilar sniffed.

"They are one and the same, Pilar. What I need and what I want are to validate my abilities as a designer." Char shrugged as though to apologize for her single-mindedness before she leaned over, bag between them, and hugged her friend. "You and I are both going to be perfectly marvelous successes, Pilar, and we're going to do it on our own. Then we're going to find true love and all will be well with our lives."

"As long as I don't need to sleep with success, I will take it. There are not enough francs in the world to take the place of a lover."

"But love must come from a place that makes you happy in all ways. For me, wanting someone, being attracted to them is not the same as loving."

"Not for me either."

"Then we agree on Fletcher?"

"Never." Pilar huffed with a smile that admitted defeat only due to the restrictions of time. "You are, both of you, from the soul. How do you say? Soul mates?"

Char laughed and released Pilar. "We are late is what I say. It's been wonderful. The shop is marvelous. I can't thank you enough for letting me be a part of it."

"It is I who should thank you," Pilar said sincerely. "I have already sold three of your gowns. You will not forget to send others to replace them?"

"Not on your life. Between your boutique and Fletcher's story, I'm going to be the toast of the fashion world yet," Char intoned brightly.

"You don't want to be that. Look at Vachel. He is a miserable little man, yet he is thought to be *extraordinaire!*

"Well, I'm me and I would never . . ."

"Char?"

A cool breeze blew into the cab as Fletcher held open the door and touched Char's shoulder. Her head swiveled, her heart turned round. Paris was, indeed, a magical place. Char only hoped that in the days and weeks to come, the magic would wear off and her life would be her own again.

"I'd almost forgotten about you," Char laughed. Pilar snorted her amazement and crossed her arms as she shook her head. Fletcher only grinned as Char turned to look at her friend.

"Isn't that always the way?" he said. "Out of sight, out of mind. Your incredible amount of luggage is now on the way to the plane and I think we should be headed that way too. Pilar?" Fletcher leaned over Char, his chest pressed to her shoulders as he reached for the dark-skinned woman. Pilar came to him, willingly offering her cheek and her hand. "It's been wonderful, Pilar. I can't thank you enough. I doubt if I'd ever have seen the nooks and crannies of Paris if it hadn't been for you. I think I got some great shots. I'll send them."

"*Au revoir,* Fletcher. I will see you again."

"I hope so."

"*C'est bien,* Fletcher," Pilar said speaking of friendship because she liked him, and because both of them loved the woman who sat between them.

"Again, *merci*. The hospitality was wonderful. Char?"

Fletcher and Char left Paris forty minutes later. Sitting side by side, they spoke quietly, touching now and again and excusing the breach because of the closeness of the quarters. Both had a feeling, though, that the seating arrangement had nothing to do with it. And when the plane finally landed, when Fletcher had to reluctantly wake Char, moving her from his shoulder where she had fallen asleep, he knew things were going to change in his life and in hers. When they walked off the plane to find Ross there to meet Char, Fletcher couldn't help speculating how long it would take her to reach the same conclusion.

Chapter Five

"I can't give you what I think you want from me, Ross."

It took all Char's courage to look Ross right in the eye and tell him she could no longer, in good conscience, continue seeing him on an exclusive basis. She had known it a week ago when, with Fletcher by her side, she had stepped off that plane and saw him waiting for her. She had been happy to see him — not thrilled, not ecstatic — just happy. That wasn't the way people serious about each other were supposed to feel. So after a week of soul-searching, they sat down to talk on neutral ground.

"I see. It's Hawkins, isn't it? He's caught your eye," Ross said, leaning back in the small wrought iron chair. No normal human being would consider it comfortable, but its rigidity didn't seem to bother Ross. Char, concerned and considerate, hoping she wasn't bringing him too much pain, narrowed her eyes trying to determine if she really did note a glint of amusement in her companion's eyes.

"Ross, it has nothing to do with Fletcher or the story he's working on," Char answered, fully believing it herself.

She noticed Fletcher, of course, as he worked around her studio. Sometimes felt the odd twinge of need, the fullness in her body that signaled he was near. Luckily she knew these things were nothing more than a normal, natural feminine reaction to the presence of a handsome man. Her decision regarding Ross, though, had nothing to do with Fletcher. Of that she was sure.

"Char, I can fully understand how a woman of your creative bent would be fascinated by a guy like that. It's the Indiana Jones complex. A cowboy riding across your range. Tarzan swinging in your jungle. And a ton of money in the coffers on top of all that sensitive, macho stuff."

"Ross, that is ludicrous." Char waved away his assessment, peeved because that he had the nerve to chuckle.

Much as she admired Ross, Char was now sure that her feelings began and ended with that emotion. His intelligence, his clear-sightedness, his head for business, his style were all to be respected, but weren't the things of a lifelong relationship. For an instant she almost regretted seeing all this so clearly. Many people, she knew, built wonderful lives together with just such criteria as a foundation. Then the moment was gone and the regret was gone. If there was one thing

Char knew it was that there had to be more . . .

Click. The now familiar sound of Fletcher's camera snapped her out of her daydream. Aware he was close, Char didn't look at him. It was disconcerting to find him studying her without a hint of a smile or a glint of admiration in his eye. When he worked, his intensity was incredible, his professionalism without question. Fletcher exuded an incredible power when he had camera in hand, as though he could orchestrate the universe with a word or a flip of his hand. That, above all, irked Char. In the same way she didn't want to be beholden to Ross, she didn't ever want to feel powerless in Fletcher's company. It was moments like this when she wished she and Ross were still an item. He, at least, was so predictable.

"Ms. Brody?"

"Yes?" Char shook her head slightly, clearing it of all memories of Ross, all consciousness of Fletcher, and gave her full attention to the design student who stood beside her.

"You're on next. Do you want the lectern?"

"I'll use the lectern, thank you." Char grinned through her nervousness, trying to put herself and this incredibly unstylish young woman at ease.

"Too bad. It's a shame to cover up that dress. Actually, we ought to put the microphone behind you so you can give your speech backward. That back is so cool. Did you design it?"

"Sure did. I'm glad you like it."

Char smoothed the glittering beaded silk over her hips with ill-disguised pride. From the deep scoop neck the dress fell in a column of blue and green beads in the pattern of a churning sea. At the front the hem skimmed the tip of her satin mules, but in the back she'd let the hem trail across the floor. With that one element of design, Char brought back an age when women's gowns were not only clothing but extensions of the sensuality a long, languid body exuded. As though defying gravity, the heavy beaded gown was held up by straps as thin as thread. But the real excitement, the wizardry of fabric manipulation, was behind her. Char had designed the cowl back so that it bared her skin from neck to waist, ending in a drape of beading that swung out over her tiny derriere. Cut on the bias, the fabric clung to the curve of her waist. She could have been a mermaid stranded in the Four Seasons Hotel in the heart of Beverly Hills.

But she wasn't a mermaid and she definitely had a purpose here. For two days Char had been at the hotel preparing for the next five minutes. She was the Design School's featured designer at tonight's annual award banquet. Her collection would be spotlighted on the runway. The fashion press would snap photos, jot comments, eye the garments critically before deciding whether her efforts deserved the giddiest praise or the pithiest contempt. She should be concentrating on what was ahead.

"Okay, Ms. Brody, you're up." Char shook her head, again caught off guard.

"Is everyone ready backstage?" she asked intent

on the task at hand.

"Everyone's set. Five seconds. When the light hits . . ."

Before the girl finished her instructions, she put a courteous, but pressured, hand on Char's back and pushed her into the spotlight. A dutiful, polite applause filtered up from the audience. Char hesitated, then walked toward the podium. The applause swelled as the audience took in the full effect of her gown. It swelled until finally, behind the lectern, Char had to raise her hands to quiet them.

Glowing, grinning into the blaze of light, Char experienced what other designers dreamed of. Tonight she was the glorified one. She had never realized how wonderful it could be, applauded by the many rather than the few. For one moment, just a fleeting instant, she also realized it would all be over in five short minutes. Such a brief, yet interminable, space of time. She dipped her head, checked her notes, and promised herself she would remember every second of the next five minutes as long as she lived.

Raising her head she said clearly and confidently, "Good evening. I'm Char Brody of CB Designs and this is my work."

Instantly the music swelled. The stage and runway were lit to daylight brightness as the first model materialized dressed in a stunningly simple dress of yellow organza, its high hem and wide, wide skirt creating the illusion of a flower in full bloom.

"For day," Char intoned, "buttercup organza. Leg baring. Full, full skirted. Capped sleeves. Sheer bodice with printed satin camisole."

The first model clipped down the runway as though her legs were on ball bearings. She swept, she danced, she posed, and postured and the moment she reached the end of the raised platform the applause began. Behind her two more women, even more exquisite then the first, began their sensuous prance down the elevated walk.

"For afternoon. Two variations on a theme . . ."

Char's voice picked up momentum, matching the cadence of the music and the mannequins. She was grinning as the energy from the appreciative audience washed over her. It was then she knew this feeling of success had to be a part of her life forever. Perhaps tonight would make a difference. Perhaps . . . perhaps . . .

Even as she heard her rehearsed commentary, Char's mind flew to the future. She was amazed to find that Fletcher and the future were one. He was out there capturing her triumph on film and she knew he could feel it too: the uniqueness of it all, the force in the air, the fullness of being she was experiencing.

The last words were out of her mouth before Char knew she had spoken them. She blinked. The models lined both sides of the runway clapping, waiting for her to walk between them and accept her kudos. She smiled grandly, accepting the applause as appreciation for her talent. It was over.

Backstage she supervised the packing of the show garments and arranged for shipping. Someone had kindly handed her a glass of chardonnay, but it did little to lift her spirits. She kicked off her shoes and sat atop a trunk, admitting to herself that the thrill of adulation was nothing compared to the crash. Then quietly, surprisingly, Fletcher was beside her. The hand he laid on Char's shoulder was warm and understanding. Instinctively her own covered his.

"It's hard when it's over. I felt depressed for months after I sold my company." He smiled gently without a trace of cockiness.

"At least you were the one to call it quits," Char said wistfully. "I only had five minutes. I never wanted it to end."

"You'll have more than five minutes in the sun if the applause was any indication of what people think of your work." Reluctantly Fletcher let his hand fall away as he stood up and stepped back.

Char raised her eyes, almost too tired to speak. Fletcher looked so wonderfully solid, as though he could wrap his arms around her, crush her to him, and make her vibrant once again.

"It takes so long to make good, Fletcher," she said sadly but without complaint. "For a minute, out there, I convinced myself that someone would be after me for the cover of *Vanity Fair* any minute." Char laughed lightly. "That's ridiculous, I know. But it felt right, being the center of attention, having people love my work. It felt so right."

"That's why it will all work out eventually. No

one's an overnight success, you know."

"You were," Char reminded him. "Or did you lie about being a computer whiz?"

"No, I didn't lie," Fletcher laughed, "and I never said I was an overnight success. I said I was successful when I was young. I put a lot of sweat into my business. But it doesn't really matter now, does it? It's a part of my life I've put behind me."

"I suppose it doesn't. And it was marvelous while it lasted."

"That's my girl," Fletcher said as though encouraging a favorite puppy. Immediately Char's eyes narrowed. Fletcher was being considerate, courteous, and downright compassionate. He hadn't even said anything suggestive. Something wasn't right.

Had she lost her allure suddenly? Was Paris and their passion atop the Eiffel Tower only a dream? Whoever said women were fickle hadn't met Fletcher Hawkins. Just when she was about to tell Fletcher that the field was clear, that Ross was no longer in the picture, to see if she'd get a rise out of him, Fletcher put out his hand and pulled her to her feet.

"Come on. You're too tired to think about putting one foot in front of the other, much less figuring out how come some people make it big and others have to struggle. Now I don't want any argument. I've been watching you give orders for the last two days. It's my turn. Slip your shoes on and we're off."

"But the banquet isn't over . . ." Char protested, "I don't want to go home yet."

"You're not going home. You're going to stay right here, in a room in the hotel, and get some rest. Don't worry, I wouldn't dream of charging CB Designs. This one's on me. What's three hundred a night among friends?"

Without another word Fletcher slipped her hand under the crook of his arm, pressed a key into it, and led her to the elevator.

"Fletcher, I don't think this is a good idea," Char objected quietly as they rode to the seventh floor.

How could she have imagined his interest had waned? This was so in character. Fletcher sees what he wants, waits for the opportunity, takes it, and makes his move. This was exactly the kind of behavior that had angered her on the beach — had left her breathless under the Parisian stars. Char could feel her heart beating in quarter time. She knew what she should say, but she couldn't seem to concentrate, not with him swaying against her as they walked, not with him holding her arm with such casual possessiveness.

"No. No talking. I refuse to hear anything but 'Yes, Fletcher.' Do you understand?"

"Yes, Fletcher," Char breathed, amazed that her assent came so easily. Exhaustion had melted away, every nerve in her body was alive with anticipation, waiting for Fletcher's next move. Would a hand slide across her back, an arm pull her into him for a kiss like the ones they shared in Paris? Would he slip the thin straps from her shoulders.

Would he . . . ?

And what would she do? She hadn't meant to feel this way about Fletcher. She hadn't wanted the anticipation, the attraction, the appeal to be so overwhelming, but Char couldn't deny the reality of her desire any longer. Not when they were together like this.

"Here we are. Seven-oh-two," Fletcher murmured, his voice as hushed as the deserted hall.

"Seven-oh-two," Char whispered, loving the sound of those numbers. They would forever be her lucky numbers, she was sure of it.

Suddenly she was no longer holding his arm. Instead her hands were clasped in his, the key between her praying palms.

"Are you going to be okay?"

His black eyes pierced her gray ones. His lashes were long and curling, his skin unblemished and perfect. Tonight he wore a tattersall shirt, the collar buttoned down, the sleeves rolled up. How easily it would slip out of his jeans, pop the shirt buttons . . .

"Fine, of course," Char answered, her voice small even as she tried to sound as nonchalant as he. She was, after all, an adult. She wasn't inexperienced, so there was no reason to be feeling the butterflies, no good reason that she should be trembling, and her knees feel weak.

"Good."

Fletcher slipped the key from between her clasped hands, looked at it thoughtfully for a moment, then turned and unlocked the door. Gently he pushed it open, then moved so that Char could pass by him into the grandly decorated room. Her gown rustled, her shoulders straightened, and even she was aware that her scent trailed enticingly behind her. She hesitated, loving the drama of it all as she waited for Fletcher to come to her, touch her. Then, just as she was about to turn, a seductive smile, small, and perfectly formed, on her lips, the door closed behind her as Fletcher said:

"Sleep well. I'll be in seven-ten if you need me. You were great tonight."

Fletcher Hawkins had left her alone! To sleep! Alone!

Without thinking, Char found her shoe in her hand, raised above her head, ready to let it fly. Thankfully she came to her senses in time. It wouldn't do to put a dent in the door when it was Fletcher's head she wanted to bash. He was probably stretched out on his bed right now laughing like a madman. He knew *exactly* what she expected. He was the same old Fletcher: arrogant, egotistical, thumbing his nose at every convention. Why had she ever thought him unusual, thrilling, mysterious? He was nothing more than overgrown adolescent leading her on like an unattractive A student, then dropping her for the prom queen.

Well, she would show him. Two could play at this game. She could be just as cool as he. Flipping off her other shoe, Char plopped herself on the bed, switched on the television, and tried to figure out a way to get even.

"Mr. Crown? There's an urgent call for you in the lobby."

Louis Crown dismissed the young man by turning his attention to his table companions. "One's work is never done in this business is it, my darlings?"

The fashionably dressed people at the table gave a general twitter of concern, interest, approval, and acknowledgment before the West Coast editorial director of *Women's Wear Daily* took his leave. Behind him, at another table, the editorial director of *California Apparel News* watched with interest, then excused himself and followed Louis Crown to the bank of telephones outside the hall.

Picking up the receiver, Louis was disappointed to find Melinda Pasternak had taken him away from the banquet. Though he had only met her once, the reporter bothered Louis. She always looked quite the mess, so how could she report on fashion? There was, after all, an image to uphold in this business.

"Louis," she said, "I don't have time for your attitude tonight, so shut up and listen." She cut him off short, the only tactic that ever made him sit up and take notice. Louis cursed her mentally but did as she asked. He waited for her to continue. "Isn't CB Designs showing at the banquet tonight?"

"You know they are. It was in my weekly report."

"Good. I need you to get to the designer."

"Char Brody?" Louis sniffed. "It was a lovely little show but I think interviewing her is going a little overboard. *Women's Wear Daily* is a bit beyond a local designer . . ."

"Find her, Louis. I want a comment from her for a special insert. Tomorrow's edition. Now this is what I need you to get from her . . ."

Suddenly Louis was all ears. The moment he hung up, he headed backstage, holding Char Brody in high esteem after what Melinda had told him. Still at the phone banks, aware that something was up, the editorial director of *California Apparel News* called his spy at *Women's Wear Daily* and told her to check out any late-breaking news.

By midnight in Los Angeles, Louis was exhausted and had given up trying to find Char Brody. The insert would have to run without comment from the nymphlike designer. A staff writer at *California Apparel News* was already finishing a bio on Char. And Char Brody herself was sitting in a hotel room watching a rerun of *Dragnet* unaware that the most powerful trade papers in the fashion world had just decided she was the next Chanel.

Chapter Six

She was actually chewing her nails! This was as ridiculous as the pacing she had done an hour ago and just as stupid as cracking the door, peeking into the hall toward room seven-ten.

The more rational she tried to be, though, the crazier her behavior became. But Char knew her logic was buried under annoyance, exasperation and aggravation at Fletcher's abandonment. She'd been alone long enough now to come to terms with exactly what she was feeling. Much as she disliked proving Ross right, Char knew she was angry because Fletcher's ardor had cooled. Suddenly he was all business, snapping away while she fitted customers, asking pertinent questions about her business, flitting off to shoot someone else for his layout. He was so smooth. She was such a fool giving him credit for his sensitivity. Thinking he was only waiting for the right moment to cross that thin line between the professional and personal. Well, there was no shame in falling for him, the only shame would be if she didn't regain her dignity. He was no gentleman and she was no lady to be trifled with.

Throwing her legs over the side of the bed, Char picked up her right shoe. When the left eluded her, she tossed the right on the bed and left the room without either, her mermaid gown trailing with a swish that sounded suspiciously like whispery laughter.

"Seven-ten. Seven-ten," she muttered, marching down the deserted hall until she came to the right door.

It looked like all the rest, but behind it was the man who had made her feel like an idiot. Determined, Char raised her hand, made a fist, and knocked the way people do who really want an excuse to leave before their resolve is tested. Deciding confrontation was more effective in the light of day, Char knew she should go back to her . . .

Then her heart stopped. The door was open. Fletcher held it close to him, silhouetted by the feeble light creeping through the heavy drapes. She saw the fine cut of his muscles as they shaped his broad shoulders and corded his arms, the breathtaking slimness of his body, the beautiful sheen of his hair. She smelled the scent of sleep and felt the waves of warmth his skin still held. Char almost weakened until she realized he'd been sleeping like a baby while she spent a sleepless night. Suddenly she found her voice.

"Fletcher, we need to talk. Now."

Straight-arming the door, Char walked past him, ignoring the fact that he seemed neither surprised nor worried by her visit at this early hour.

"Come in," he said, a chuckle in his voice as he closed the door and reached for the light switch.

"No," Char stopped him, "no need for lights. This won't take long."

"All right. Mind if I sit down? I'm a little chilly without clothes."

"Of course not." Char nodded toward the bed but kept her eyes averted as he slid between the sheets.

"Okay. I'm fine now. Go ahead."

Char gritted her teeth at his nonchalant directive and forged ahead. "Well, I want you to know that I'm not a person who likes confrontation, but I think something really must be said here about your behavior. I've allowed you to follow me around. I've given you access to every inch of my studio and my home—well almost all of my home. I've made room for you in my life, and you're treating this whole thing like it's a game. I just don't think it's very professional of you, nor do I think it's nice at all. Basically that's about all I had to say."

"I see." Fletcher's voice floated toward her softly, his tone almost concerned, almost hurt, but not quite. "Well. I agree. You've been overly generous with your time and your work and your knowledge. But could you just be a bit more specific about what it is that I've done to make you feel as though I've been unprofessional." He added quickly, "I just want to know so I don't ever do it again."

Char crossed her arms petulantly. "Well, it's your attitude. It's disconcerting."

"Okay?" He drew out the word, raising his hands to urge her silently on.

"Oh, come on," Char flared, her arms flailing as she took a step toward the bed. "You know exactly what it is you're doing. You come all the way to Paris, you pursue me as if I'm the most desirable woman in the world, you convince me to let you into my life. Then we get back here, I turn everything topsy-turvy for you, now you act as though I'm just a—a—thing. You shut the door on my back. You gave me a key. You got a room. I think that we're finally going to . . . tonight . . . we're going to . . . and then you do that. I mean, really!"

She turned her back once more, her arms vice-like across her chest as though they could keep her hurt and angry heart bottled up inside her. What she'd forgotten was the lovely invitation her dress presented. The beaded fabric glittered in the shadowy light, her skin glowed gold beside it. Her backbone was a shaded trail dipping gracefully into her waist, then suggestively dropping beneath the beaded cowl.

"And what did you turn upside down for me?" Fletcher asked quietly. Absorbed in her anger, Char didn't hear the rustle of sheets behind her as he got out of bed.

"I told everyone in the work area to give you

114

what you needed. I let you photograph me in the morning, at night when I was too tired to see straight because I was working on the accounts. I . . . I told Ross I couldn't see him seriously anymore. And you didn't do a thing about that. First all that talk of being made for each other, then I make room for you, then you don't want it."

Fletcher heard the tiniest sob invade her voice and his heart went out to her.

"But you didn't tell me about Ross. How was I supposed to know the coast was clear? The way he looked at me when he came to pick you up at the airport, I figured he'd have you in a chastity belt by nightfall."

"You should have known," Char answered with a sniff, her head raised just enough so the hot tears behind her eyes would stay put.

"Actually I did know," Fletcher admitted, close enough now to put his hands on her bare shoulders. He let them lie there, waiting to see what she would do. Her body trembled. He smiled, wanting to laugh with pleasure and adoration. Such a woman, this cropped-haired, strong-willed, creative lady.

"You did?" Her voice was so small he could hardly hear the question.

"I did," he answered, his lips close to her ear, his breath warm on the crook of her neck.

"Then why did you leave tonight? Why did you only take pictures?"

"Because, my darling woman, I had no way of knowing what it was you wanted. You told me

115

you had a commitment to Ross. When I realized he hadn't been around in a while, I figured you'd need your space." He leaned closer, his lips almost touching her hair. He could smell the scent of flowers and spice still clinging to her from her triumphant evening, and it was enough to drive him to the brink. "I don't make assumptions. I may be bold, but I don't force myself on people. Especially those I care about."

"How could you not know that I wanted you to . . . you know." Char's voice was hardly a whisper in the dark room. They stood close together, yet still their bodies didn't touch. Only his hands anchored her to him, prolonging the anticipation, heightening the curiosity she was feeling now. "After Paris. The way we kissed . . ."

"You said it was a dream in Paris. Nothing to be ashamed of, just memories. You said all those things."

"But the way we kissed . . ." Char reminded him. "How could you not know?" Slowly he turned her toward him. Uncertainly she lifted her face to his. Their eyes met. Her generous lips parted as she asked again. "How?"

"I knew," he murmured, "and I remember, and I want so much more now."

Then his lips were on hers, his hands sliding over her shoulders, pushing the thin straps of her gown away, and pulling with them the silk and the beads. Flesh met flesh as Char and Fletcher melted together in sweet discovery. Words were spoken and cut off before their meaning was clear.

Words were unnecessary.

This was Paris without the stars, without the city lying at their feet. This was memories of meeting and memories in the making as Char and Fletcher discovered one another in the way only true lovers can.

When finally he held her, asleep in his arms, as he buried his lips in the silkiness of her hair and breathed in the scent that was her, Fletcher reaffirmed that a life filled with freedom and creativity was a wonderful one. That same life filled with love would be a perfect one.

Fletcher's eyes opened to the subdued but insistent ringing of the phone. Raising his head by half an inch, his free hand was reaching for the receiver when Char stopped him.

"Don't answer it," she mumbled, her long fingers curling into the hair on his chest. For good measure she cuddled closer, vying for his attention, sure she could beat a telephone.

"I hate a ringing phone," Fletcher moaned as his head hit the pillow and his arm wrapped around her again.

"It's a mistake," Char answered sleepily. "Nobody knows we stayed over."

"True. And the Four Seasons is not exactly where my friends would expect to find me."

"Is that so?" Char's head popped up.

Her hair was sleep tousled, her makeup forgotten the night before, was still evident in surprisingly attractive smudges around her deep-set eyes. Char's long neck arched as she listened to the low ringing. She tipped her head, narrowed her eyes, and the ringing stopped.

"See, I told you so," she murmured, her lips making their way slowly up Fletcher's body until she was able to roll atop him, winding her hands through his long black hair as though she couldn't get enough of it.

"How did you do that?" Fletcher drawled, his hands spanning her naked back, measuring it before he let them slide down to her waist.

"An old trick. Now kiss me before I realize what I did last night and run out of here screaming."

"Your wish is my command, Ms. Brody," Fletcher answered, abandoning the marvelous nether reaches of her body to cup the back of her head and pull her lips toward his. Just as they touched in the most tentative of kisses, just as Char remembered all the sweetness of the night before, the phone began to ring again.

"Oh, Lord!" Char rolled off Fletcher, grabbing the sheet on her way down, and pulling it over her head.

"I better get it. Maybe management wants to reimburse us for your room since you didn't use the bed last night." Fletcher chuckled, paying no attention whatsoever to the mumbles coming from beneath the sheet as he answered the phone.

"Morning," he said cheerily, cradling the phone as he joined Char in her makeshift tent. "Uh-huh. Yeah. She's here."

Frantically, Char waved him away. She didn't want anyone to know she was in Fletcher Hawkins's room at . . . What time? She didn't even know what time it was. But Fletcher was pressing the receiver into her hands and there was nothing to do but answer.

"This is Char Brody."

"Char, it's me, Robert."

"Robert, how on earth did you find me? I didn't even tell the studio I'd be staying over."

Char rolled her eyes. Robert Browning was the best independent rep in the business. He'd managed to sell her one-of-a-kind gowns into some of the best boutiques in California. She'd always said he knew everyone and everything, but this was ridiculous.

"Hey, Char, who're you talking to?" Robert asked. "I'm the man who can add. They haven't seen you at the studio. It's one o'clock . . ."

"One o'clock!" Char shrilled.

"Yeah. One o'clock and that's p.m., babe. In the afternoon. So anyway, you don't answer at your house. I work backward and start at the most logical place. You didn't feel like driving home after last night's festivities. I call the hotel and ask for Char Brody."

"But, Robert, I'm not in my room."

"But, Char, I've seen that photographer who's following you around. You think I don't have eyes like everybody else?" Char slid, deeper beneath the sheet, letting it cover her face like a shroud.

119

Everybody saw it coming. God, had they all been on conference call making bets about how long she'd hold out? "But listen, babe, that's neither here nor there. Just thank your lucky stars I got a good memory for names. Otherwise I wouldn't have remembered who to ask for after I couldn't get you. Now listen, sweetie, I gotta know what it is you've been doing. I mean, if we're going to work together like partners the way we planned, I can't be having these surprises."

Char sighed, resigned to the fact that the word privacy was not in her vocabulary these days and asked: "What are you talking about, Robert? And make it quick. I've got a two-hour drive back to Coronado."

"Hey, no problem. I've gotta be quick anyway if I want to free up this line. It's been ringing off the hook since I opened shop. So tell me, Char, how come I'm sitting here with three million dollars worth of orders for CB Designs? *Three million,* Char."

Chapter Seven

"What!"

Char bolted upright, tightening the sheet around her, almost strangling Fletcher in the process. She fought the cover away with no regard for Fletcher floundering beside her.

"Char, what are you doing?" He demanded as he too batted his way to the surface. But Char wasn't listening. She had jumped out of bed as though it was on fire, holding the phone to her ear like a lifeline. Fletcher sat back, propping himself on the pillows to watch Char pace. His lover was gone, replaced by an executive in the buff who was oblivious to everything other than whatever the man on the other end of the phone was telling her.

"Robert. Talk to me, Robert. I thought you said you accepted three million dollars worth of orders for CB Designs."

"I didn't say I accepted them. I said I got 'em, and more are coming in. Now just what is it you want me to do with 'em?" Char could feel him chomping on the end of his unlit cigar. Only that almost imperceptible sound betrayed his excitement.

"I want you to fill them. Don't be ridiculous!" Char cried, a barking laugh, a disbelieving giggle, punctuating her orders. She had come to an abrupt halt then, as suddenly as she had stopped, her pacing began again. Her beautiful bare body was all determined motion at the foot of the bed, turning this way and that, her head, her beautiful breasts swaying. Her expression was a whirlpool of emotion. Fear and disbelief and joy and amazement swept over her fine features until she looked at Fletcher. Then the only emotion on her face was one of unadulterated love. Char held the receiver above her head and gave a whoop, ran to him, and planted an incredibly firm kiss on his lips. He reached for her but she eluded him, forgetting him so easily in her excitement.

"Char! Char!" Robert hollered, in no mood to put up with her shenanigans while wholesale history was being made.

Happily she returned to the business at hand. Once Robert had her attention, he launched into the lecture he'd been planning since this bizarre run on CB Designs started.

"Char, think about this a minute. If you want me to fill all these orders, then I gotta have merchandise and, unless a whole lot's changed in the last few weeks, I don't think you've got three million dollars worth of wholesale hanging around that rabbit hutch you call a factory."

"Oh!" She blinked as though doused with cold water on a hot summer day. How horrible to be confronted with reality when a dream was unfolding in front of her. Twirling the phone cord, stalling for time to think, she muttered, "Oh, you're right. Absolutely right."

Suddenly everything came into sharp focus. Fletcher watching her with an amused and desirous grin on his face, her nakedness, the chill of the receiver cradled against her shoulder. She was grateful at least that Fletcher's camera was out of reach.

"Robert, hold on a minute," Char pleaded, knowing she couldn't think like this. Still holding the receiver, she grabbed her discarded gown and stepped into it, slipped the straps over her shoulders. She whipped the receiver back to her ear, ignoring the open zipper, never thinking she looked even more alluring now than when naked.

Fletcher, realizing a seduction would not be forthcoming, followed suit, leaving the bed and stepping into his pants before grabbing his camera. As was his way, he faded into the corner to photograph Char Brody. Instinctively, without hearing the other end of the conversation, Fletcher understood the import of what was happening here. Perhaps the news wouldn't transform the world, but the woman he had loved the night before was changing before his eyes.

Her energy was overwhelming, her exhilaration over Robert's news made Fletcher an accessory in the room rather than the focal point of it. That was not a thing a man was happy to perceive. But Fletcher forgot his bit of hurt feelings as he watched. Char was firmly attached, via telephone, to the man on the other end. Fletcher felt it all: the swelling of her interest transforming itself into sheer, utter excitement before becoming intense curiosity and finally dwindling to concern. God, how contagious she was.

He wanted to be a part of it, wanted to meld into Char during this moment, so that he could experience what she was feeling, hear the news in the exact same way she was hearing it. Accepting the impossibility of his wish, he settled for visually recording the minutes as they ticked by.

"Okay, Robert, don't panic. We'll work this out. What is it we're looking at? Gowns? Daywear? What? Everything! No way. You're serious?"

"Damn serious, kiddo. And I think it's great. I just don't know why, where, or how this is all coming down. I hope you can get it together in time to ride the wave. This is the big one. Your ship's come in, Char."

"Oh, Robert," Char admonished, her voice quivering, "I will get it together or die trying. I've been waiting for this all my life. I'll have you riding a Rolls to work for this, Robert."

"Wish I could take the credit," the man said with a verbal shrug. Robert, who liked to remind everyone that he just peddled "rags," still had a soft spot in his heart for that fairy tale success. Especially when Char Brody was the princess and he the only white knight in sight. He'd represented her one-of-a-kind gowns for eight years and had a modest success placing them with a handful of stores. But this . . .

"Well I sure can't." Char stood still, racking her brain for an answer to this mystery. "Do you think this is a backlash from last night?"

Robert snorted. "All this from strutting your stuff at the design awards? Nah. Nobody'd order this fast because of a local show. Especially Neiman's and I've got an across-the-board order from them."

"Neiman's. Oh, my God. You're right. Well, it doesn't matter how it happened, only that it did. I've got to think. Got to figure this out. There's no way I'm going to let this get away." Char sat on the edge of the bed but jumped back up again. Her muscles, every nerve, her skin, her entire body was tingling. If she could have run back to Coronado, stitching the entire way, she would have.

"I can get fabric on the daywear and the casual line, no problem. Those are all domestic suppliers. I think Maggie can find me at least a dozen seamstresses without too much trouble. But where am I going to cut? What about machines for the seamstresses? We can't do it by hand in this quantity. I'll need a new facility and fast. Machinery will have to be ordered . . ."

"Whoa, Char. I think you've forgotten one small thing. You haven't got the money yet," Robert reminded her, "This is the paper, know what I mean? These stores are the pits when it comes to making good on the invoice. I'll have to wait the full thirty days even if we offer 'em a great discount on payment in ten."

"I'll borrow against orders. And I'll have Alana get on anybody in arrears. I'll . . ." Her mind spun into the financial maelstrom without a thought for the danger of overextending herself before bouncing off onto another tangent. "This is all for cruise season, right?"

"That's what they say. Most of 'em anyway. Some want immediate delivery on the gowns."

"Okay, we'll work it out. Three million dollars! Good grief, Robert! I can't believe it. That's a hundred percent markup on wholesale. That means I'm a . . ."

"Millionaire," he answered for her, "and from the looks of things we're going to be able to qualify that with the word 'multi' real soon. Now I can't quite believe it either, but I guess we better start acting like this is the real thing. So you want me to confirm? You think you can pull it off?" Char didn't hear the twinge of concern in the man's voice. The question was moot. How could she not pull it off? This is what she'd been working for, planning for, her entire life. It was meant to be.

126

"I'll manage even if it kills me, Robert. You have only just begun to work your tail off for CB Designs. I'll be back in Coronado by three. Fax whatever you've got to the studio with the absolute latest delivery dates starting with casual wear. That line will be the easiest to turn around fast."

"You got it. Listen, I've got to run. Myra is swamped trying to get the phones. Talk to you later." Robert rung off.

"Later," Char whispered back, letting the phone drop to her side. Her attempt to dress while she was talking had been forgotten. One slim beaded strap hung off her shoulder, her feet were bare, and her hair still sleep tousled. Stunned, she suddenly felt heavy and tired as she realized that Robert's wonderful news could be the worst she ever had.

Here was her window of opportunity, her brass ring. The straws of her career were lying within her reach waiting to be spun into golden threads, but Rumpelstiltskin was hanging around, too. Unless she could deliver, the dream and the reality would vanish. And what if it slipped away from her no matter how hard she worked? What if this were her one and only chance?

Suddenly chilled, just a bit frightened, Char sat heavily on the bed staring into space until she heard her name called as from across an incredible distance. Shaking her head, she finally tore her eyes away from the absolutely fascinating pattern of the carpet and faced Fletcher.

Yet when she looked into his eyes, she felt as though she wasn't really seeing him. For a moment, she felt so alone that her mind had reached out to someone who was miles away, not the man who sat inches away. Color rose to her cheeks as Char looked into Fletcher's loving eyes and realized it was Ross she had been thinking of. Ross who would be able to guide her during this critical time and not Fletcher who could love her through it. Fletcher, as Ross pointed out, had left business behind too long ago. His success was in another time, another marketplace.

"Char?"

Fletcher's voice hung in the air. His verbal hesitation matched his physical one. He wanted a sign from her. Just a smile, a softening of her eyes, a hand raised toward him to include him in this moment. When she finally focused on him, it was not to offer an explanation or an invitation but to ask him a question.

"Do you believe in miracles, Fletcher?"

He didn't hesitate. "After last night, you bet."

"I do, too."

Char looked him straight in the eye and Fletcher saw that the softness of her mist gray eyes had a new edge to it. Her face was set in a look of such deep concentration. Strangely Fletcher thought he saw her age before his eyes. A chill ran down his spine as he looked at her, half dressed, her gorgeous body so still while her spirit ran off to tend to more important things than

128

love. There was nothing more he could say, nothing more he wanted to say, so he did what came naturally, the one thing he knew he must do.

Click.

Char was out of the car before it stopped. She ignored the mid-afternoon shoppers staring at her as she bolted across the sidewalk in her beaded gown. The drive from Beverly Hills to Coronado Island had been made in record time, and Char couldn't wait a moment longer to find out what was happening at the studio. She ripped open the back door and stepped into a madhouse. Behind her, Fletcher locked the car before following and, as unobtrusively as possible, slipped in behind her.

Char had explained the wonderful turn of events to him as they dressed. Her initial paralysis evaporated, only to be replaced with a frenetic stamina that was amazing to see. She had explained everything again as they waited for the parking attendant to bring around the car, then continued to explain and exclaim and take deep breaths to calm herself the entire time they drove.

During the drive Char had squeezed Fletcher's hand, reassuring herself that he was real and sitting beside her. She had leaned across the gearshift to kiss his cheek. She loved him and told him so. In between her recitation of the news of her surprising orders, Char told him how happy she was that he had been with her. Together they speculated on the whys and wherefores of the situation until, finally, they concurred that it was only the world coming miraculously to its senses that had driven the market to give her her due. Laughing, both admitted they had no answers.

Fletcher, as perplexed as she, was delighted with her odd stroke of fortune. Luckily he kept his head, realizing Char's high color and her taut body were signs that life's little necessities would be forgotten until the excitement wore off. Though she protested, not wanting to waste a minute of time if they stopped for food, Fletcher insisted they eat. He drove her through McDonald's.

Burgers, fries, and soft drinks in hand, Char insisted she couldn't eat a thing, yet the fries were gone before they managed to get back on the freeway near San Clemente. The burgers disappeared not long after. Fletcher didn't point out that Char had forgotten to give him his lunch, eating both burgers without blinking an eye. He only smiled without saying a word. His job was to drive and listen and let her fill his heart with her joy. He remembered all this—so well. What a thrill when the world validated your work by saying it was worth millions of dollars. He had no idea what triggered this madness and he didn't care. It was happening. He only hoped that when the work began in earnest, Char would still be able to enjoy her success. He hadn't managed that part too well.

Now, though, there was no doubt that intoxicating thrill was going to last through the day, the night and, maybe, beyond. Char's employees were running around the studio like a small army preparing for an attack.

On a rickety ladder Maggie, the head seamstress, was rifling through a wall of fabric, pulling out bolts of silk and cotton, linen and wool. Beneath her, Carol, Char's assistant-cum-pattern-maker, was shouldering them before laying the bolts out on the room-length cutting table. Carol barked yardage estimates, making notations on a clipboard to her right before accepting another load. Through the doorway Fletcher saw Olivia and Theresa, the two women who patiently beaded Char's intricate designs. Their fingers were flying, their lips moving a mile a minute as they talked about the strange turn of events. To their left, in the same room, Ilsa sat at her sewing machine, listening through the whir of the needle to every word. At the far end of the main room Alana, the part-time bookkeeper, was handling both phone lines and looking as though she was ready to tear her hair out. Her overwhelming relief when she saw Char walk through the door was too much for Fletcher. He pointed his camera her way and captured the moment forever on film.

"Char, my God, where have you been! I've got *Women's Wear Daily* on the line and *California Apparel News* has called three times, not to mention buyers from some of the biggest stores in the country *and* some rather bitchy steady clients who rang up wanting to know why they weren't told before this hit the papers." Alana shoved the phone into Char's hand. She was obviously not enjoying the hubbub. "You know I'm not paid enough for this. Three days a week. Books only. No tax stuff. That was our agreement. This truly is ridiculous. I've been here since nine and I haven't even looked at the receipts and invoices yet."

"Alana," Char wailed, her hand covering the mouthpiece of the phone. "I'll be happy to pay you an extra day's wage, I'll send you on a vacation to calm your nerves. I appreciate your help, everything you've done, and I know that none of this was in your job description. But for God's sake, would you please give me a clue as to what it is *WWD* wants. Or what any of them want for that matter!"

Alana threw up her hands, Maggie stopped pulling bolts, Carol quit jotting notes. Ilsa stopped the sewing machine in mid-seam. Even Olivia and Theresa looked up, needles held above the chiffon they were beading. Everyone waited, their breath held in disbelief. Char Brody didn't even know what had happened to CB Designs because of a celebration a continent away.

Alana, put upon as always when things of import were left to her, snatched up a tabloid-size paper, snapped it open, and handed it to her em-

132

ployer.

"It's hard to believe that you missed this!" Imperiously she sniffed as though Char's ignorance was insufferable and inexcusable. Thankfully she was a fabulous bookkeeper, otherwise Char would never have been able to have kept her around as long as she had.

Char held the phone against her hip with one hand, taking the copy of *Women's Wear Daily* with the other. The picture was marvelous. Stunning, in fact. The women were of a class and breeding foreign, but adored, by those in the U.S. Char, of course, recognized the gown. The beautiful white dress with the silver-tipped beads she had lovingly displayed in Pilar's boutique. But it wasn't until she read the first few paragraphs of the story under the headline "Lil Out-Fashions Foxy Di" that her hands began to shake and she truly understood what had happened.

There on the front page of the country's fashion bible was a picture of Lillith Prescot, an English duchess who had the honor to rival Princess Diana's beauty and fashion sense. Lillith was, perhaps, even more of a fashion pacesetter than her highness the princess. Where Diana was restricted by certain royal restraints, Lillith could do as she pleased. Her daring was as unquestioned as her taste. When Lillith wore something new, the impact was swift and sure for the designer. Success among those in the know was instantaneous and, inevitably, the influence filtered down to the

133

ready-to-wear market. Certainly it was Lillith Prescot who had made Bracco and Michael Hall. Now she was waving her magic wand over Char Brody and the fairy dust, as it fell, was blinding.

For a moment Char's mind was a blank. The word "how" kept running around inside her head until she thought it was careeingn off her skull like a pinball. Then it all fell in on her again, the recollection that had flown out of her mind a moment ago was once again crystal clear.

Straightening, perching herself on the side of her desk, her gown trailing to the floor, Char put the phone to her ear. She was ready to talk to anyone who wanted to listen about CB Designs.

"I'm so sorry to have kept you waiting. This is Char Brody. How can I help you?"

"Ms. Brody," the reporter oozed, "I hope you won't mind answering a few questions . . ."

"I'd be happy to."

And so it began. The questions and answers she had rehearsed for years were finally being asked and answered. This was the interview Char had always imagined and she gave *WWD* everything she had.

Of course she was delighted that the duchess had chosen her gown to wear to the queen's anniversary ball . . .

Naturally she would continue to create as she saw fit, and if the duchess enjoyed her designs, she would be thrilled . . .

No, there were no plans to create a special

wardrobe for the duchess . . .

No, she hadn't heard whether or not the duchess might wish to work directly with her . . .

Yes, of course she realized, how unusual it was for a woman of her rank to purchase outside a couture showing, but it certainly wasn't unheard of . . .

She knew Lillith Prescot enjoyed patronizing new talent . . .

Wasn't it thrilling that the lady's taste was not confined by convention or rank . . . ?

Plans for expansion? Those plans had been in the works for some time. It was evident that CB Designs had a much broader audience than the one it had been catering to. *Of course, I only wanted to be sure that an expansion was planned with an eye toward staying power. My history as a private designer is a long one and my future in ready-to-wear will hopefully be successful, too. Yes, I would describe my work as enduring yet flippant. Perhaps witty. Interpretations of classic silhouettes. Color and handwork are the foundations on which I build my designs. There is no sense in shocking for the mere joy of it, or decorating simply because one has the option to do so, isn't that right? Yes, I believe there is almost a geometric quality to my work. I create, sometimes starting with something as simple as a lace inset . . .*

Well, thank you. I'm glad you like my work. I'm thrilled that the duchess will be wearing my gowns and, I hope, she'll give some consideration to a wardrobe of casual wear and daywear. No, there are no plans to license at the moment. I'd like to concentrate on this next phase of my career without losing the personal touch that has made CB Designs so successful in Southern California. Thanks. Thank you. I appreciate your comments. Anytime. Yes. Lunch? Of course. I'd love to. Call anytime . . .

"Char." Carol didn't give her boss time to breathe. She was on her before the phone was in its cradle. "Robert faxed us this list of orders. It's only a partial since Myra hasn't had time to type a full one yet. I don't know how we're going to do it, but I managed a few things before you got back. I've called Merry Lee Distributors. They say they can get us three hundred and fifty yards of that mocha patterned silk we used for number 1580, the little tea dress. We can also have about two hundred yards of the white piqué and the striped blue and red piqué to get that romper in the works, four hundred yards of cotton sateen for the blazer, three hundred yards of the twill for numbers 1622 and 1624, those pant silhouettes. We have enough interlock on hand to do the camisoles. We can fill Nordstrom's order if we . . ."

Carol was closing in, shoving a three-page, single-spaced typed list into Char's hands. Red check marks and blue dots were the code of the day. Char had instinctively reached for the list, fully

136

intent on studying it. But Carol's excited voice faded for just a moment as Char felt something more compelling than the sound of her assistant's voice. There was a force surrounding her, pulling her forward, even while she remained stationary. Char could feel the intimacy of it, as though a spirit had entered her body, filling her mind with memories. It was as though this sprite could block out the world or send it off to the land of slow motion.

Powerless to resist it, Char raised her eyes trying desperately to pay attention to Carol while seeking the source of this magnetism. Slowly, sensuously her lashes were raised, her eyes moved upward, her lips parted, ready should words be necessary to banish this distracting phantom.

But this was no spirit that called to her, this was no supernatural force that threatened to defeat her purpose. This was only the pull of love and desire, flesh and blood. This was Fletcher's heart reaching out to wish her well as he silently conveyed his admiration. And, in his black eyes, there was also a reminder. Patiently he held Char's gaze while she struggled to understand what it was he wanted her to know. When finally she understood, when he smiled and she grinned back, when they silently communicated with pandemonium between them, Char's heart fairly burst with loving him. This, she knew, was the language not only of love but of tolerance and respect. Fletcher was reminding her of such a fundamental business courtesy that Char was embarrassed she hadn't thought of it herself. Silently she thanked him for his help as she realized she had a lot to learn.

"Carol," Char said quietly, laying her hand on the young woman's to curtail her rapid rundown of what had happened in the last six hours. "I think I better do a couple of things before we get into this."

"But, Char, every minute counts," Carol objected.

"Yes, it does. That's why I can't neglect this any longer. It's okay. I promise. By the end of the week we'll be on our way, Carol, and nothing will ever be the same again. But now, this minute, I have to do what I should have done the second I saw that article."

"But —"

"Please." Char's tone left no room for argument.

Carol sighed, "Okay. I'll keep checking on our supplies."

"Thanks. Alana?"

"Yeah, Char."

"Can you wrap up that call. I need that line."

"But it's a buyer from . . ."

"We'll call them back. Just as soon as we can," Char said firmly.

Five minutes later Alana was off the phone and Char was sitting behind her desk waiting, listening to a ringing phone. Finally she heard a sleepy voice.

"Allo?"

"Pilar?" Char whispered, tears welling in her eyes when she heard her friend's voice. Fletcher's smile deepened in appreciation. Char's voice gained strength. *"Merci beaucoup,* Pilar."

It was then Fletcher walked out the door. He had taken the picture he wanted. He caught the crystalline teardrop of joy just as it faltered in the corner of Char's beautiful eye, before it fell, and wound its way down her cheek. He wasn't needed in the studio. Char had thanks to offer and work to do. But he would be back. Of that there was no doubt.

"I have done nothing!" Pilar insisted. "Nothing."

The drowsiness had vanished from her lovely voice. Char envisioned her sitting cross-legged in her antique sleigh bed surrounded by the satin pillows in every shade of green, in every conceivable shape and size. More than likely she was hugging one of them to her marvelous chest the way another woman might hug a child.

"You've done everything, Pilar. Don't try and tell me differently. Now tell me all about it starting with Lillith Prescot walking into the boutique. Did you hog-tie her and make her buy my stuff just so you could be sure I'd supply you?"

Pilar's lovely laugh came tripping over the wire, sounding as though she were minutes, not continents, away.

"Non, ma chère. I only spread my arms wide offering her whatever she desired. She desired what you had made. Ah, Char, she looked so grand in the white gown. I was right. The beading had to fall perfectly over the breasts. Though I must say I think the duchess has not always had the breasts she had that day. She carried them too proudly. They were paid-for breasts."

"Pilar! I don't care a thing about her chest! I care about what else she took with her when she left," Char cried, laughing through her mock indignation. Her feet propped atop her desk, she shut her eyes and imagined Pilar in the room with her. She could almost feel her friend reaching out with her long, strong arms to give her a hug for luck. Since that was impossible, Char settled for her chatter and all the news.

"The duchess took only all that I had from you, a Saint-Laurent gown, a Chanel suit and three bags—oh, two pairs of shoes and a belt of purple calfskin with a charming buckle of gold and silver."

"No, Pilar, not her entire shopping list. I only want to know what of mine she's going to be photographed in. Now, specifically what did she buy of mine?"

"But I have told you, *chérie.* She has all that you left with me," Pilar insisted.

"All? The daywear? The wraps? The play-wear?" Char repeated incredulously.

"Oui. Oui. Oui." Char heard the incredible, absolute, unselfish delight in Pilar's voice and blessed her for it. "Ah, *chérie,* you are going to be so great a designer. You are going to own the world."

"We are going to own the world," Char corrected. "Pilar, she bought all this at your boutique. I can't imagine the Parisian press hasn't picked that up."

"Oh, *mais oui.* I have had a few customers because of the duchess. Only those who understand how to shop in small, unique boutiques of Saint-Honoré, of course. I would not let in the others," Pilar said as though it were little more than admitting she had won a Nobel prize.

"A few customers. Hah," Char prodded.

"Franchement, it has been very good for business. I only wish I could have reached you when the lady left. I was so excited then. But you were not to be found. I'm afraid now I am only tired."

"I'm sorry you couldn't get me," Char answered, thinking she would leave it at that. But Pilar was her friend and Pilar was her confidant. Char couldn't help confessing to her. "But you'll be happy to know why you couldn't reach me."

"Ah, Char. Fletcher?" Char heard the tease in her voice underlying the hope.

"Fletcher."

"I am so happy. You are silly not to have done the same in Paris. But this is just as good. It

141

was — how do you say it? — *nécessaire*."

"No, it wasn't necessary," Char laughed. "It was inevitable."

"But of course. A strange word and the same to be used for your success. It, too, was inevitable. Now I must sleep, Char. I will dream that you and Armani and Yves and Christian are all making beautiful new things just for me before you go off to the Riviera for a rest."

"There won't be any jetting for a good long while, Pilar. But dream away. I'll have Carol ship you off some other things right away to replace what the good duchess took away. Now, get your rest. I'm going to need all the help I can get."

"No. You need only your mind and your heart. All will be well. *Félicitations, ma chère!* Congratulations."

Char hung up, wishing she could be with Pilar, needing a woman to talk to who understood the emotional tie she had with her work. With Pilar, Char could look at a face and form that provoked grand inspiration. Vachel had banished Pilar, not realizing that the beauty of her aging, the maturing of her wit, the ripening of her look would continue to fire him toward ever greater heights. He let her go because she spoke the truth when she said he had given up using his soul and his mind. She angered him when he should have been grateful for her courage. He should have understood how useless it made her feel that he wouldn't listen, how she finally had to give up trying to help him. Char would never forget the lessons Pilar taught. Hopefully distance wouldn't dim Char's understanding of her friend's wisdom.

But Pilar was soon forgotten as the afternoon continued to bubble and boil with anticipation, work, interest, and concern. For the first time since she opened the doors of CB Designs, Char actually held an honest-to-goodness meeting. She called her small work force together to tell them what all this would mean to her and to them. Char asked for their commitment, she thanked them for their help, for giving her designs life and substance. Even Alana caught the fever, her quick mind adding and subtracting figures until she had a good idea of the profit structure this small company could achieve if everyone pulled their weight and luck was with them.

At five o'clock Carol took Robert's last fax off the machine and laid it in front of Char. Five women looked at the sixth with awe and wonder. Never in their wildest dreams had they conceived of such a day. CB Designs had been a special place, meaning something different to each of them. Each of them could probably have made more money with a larger firm because their talents were unique and their professionalism unquestioned. But they stayed with Char, liking this little community they had built, liking the fact that they shared in Char's success. Each one as if, somehow, she had helped Char with the creative process. Now, their attention riveted on their boss, Char read the bottom line from Robert's final message of the day.

"Total orders . . ." Char intoned, hesitating and raising her smoky eyes to her employees, her daily companions, "bottom line, wholesale . . ." she teased them, adoring the drama of the moment. She saw them lean forward. The silence extended a beat. "Five—million—dollars!"

The women squealed and hugged each other. From out of nowhere there appeared a bottle of champagne whose cork Char dutifully popped. Styrofoam coffee cups materialized and each was filled to overflowing. They all sipped and giggled and talked of what had to be done first and last to meet the demand for CB Design's coming season. Each of them swore they knew this day would come. Theresa wondered if any of them would ever sleep again. Alana insisted the first priority must be a computer system. Ilsa wanted ten more seamstresses, preferably with an equal number of sewing machines. Maggie wanted the suppliers to send reps to see her instead of her trekking to their warehouses.

Through it all Char laughed and praised them and patted herself on the back. The warmth of their camaraderie was marvelous, but it was also wearing. There hadn't been a moment during which Char was alone to regroup, yet she would no more dream of banishing her thrilled crew than of running out on them. It was early evening when she finally had time to collect her thoughts.

By seven everyone had gone, all smiles, wrapped in their secure cloak of enthusiasm, not realizing yet the challenge that lay ahead of them. Even Char couldn't fully grasp the enormity of their task, nor did she admit to herself that she was flying by the seat of her pants. The dream that had dogged her for so many years was, in reality, a deadly undertow that had pulled many a designer before her to their creative death. One wrong step, one piece of machinery that didn't give a solid return on investment, one bad collection that turned away her fledgling customers, could destroy her forever. Too many people had proven it before her: fashion was fantasy. Once the dream was shattered, no one gave you a second chance to re-create it.

But in the dimly lit workroom, in the silence that surrounded her, Char didn't think beyond the moment. She wandered through her "factory" touching everything. The long table she had found at a jumble sale and used for pattern cutting would soon be gone. In its place, she knew, would be the best cutting tables money could buy. Not just one, but many. They would be steel and wood, perfectly balanced for the optimum scoring. A robotic marker would imprint patterns she designed in every conceivable size. She would have every gadget, every new machine, the best fabrications, the most fabulous accessories — everything her heart desired to make CB Designs dazzle the fashion world with its foresight. CB

Designs would grow to magnificent proportions under her caring eye.

She would move from this little storefront. Soon, beyond executive offices decorated in blue and cream, there would be a warehouse bustling with men and women making her designs reality. Her gorgeous clothes would be bagged and tagged and moved along automated racks that crawled, mazelike, on the ceiling. And the clothing would find its way to boxes and the boxes to the best stores in the country, so that every woman of taste could own a CB Design. Soon, Char knew, she would walk down the street and see women she didn't even know wearing her clothes. Her designs!

She would have a public relations director and a person who did nothing but work with customs on overseas orders. She would jet to New York, where her showroom would be the talk of the garment district. She would open her own boutiques, not to rival Pilar or any of her steady customers, but to present a united front to those women who would come to rely on CB Designs for their complete wardrobe season after season.

And always, Char would have the fabric. In her new factory there would be a special room. From floor to ceiling she would create the most exact shelving to hold bolt after bolt of sample fabrics. Huge rolls would lie on specially made tables ready to be automatically unrolled and straightened as the self-operating cutters precisely clipped and trimmed. Visitors would stand in awe, wondering how Char could possibly envision a finished garment from a piece of fabric that had only the slightest bearing to a jacket or a skirt, a dress, or a gown. And, through it all, she would remain serene, forward-thinking as only a designer of worth could be. She would say the words that others had said before her:

"I felt I needed to grow, to create on a larger scale."

"Women today need someone to interpret their lifestyles."

Char giggled, the sound of her laughter echoing in the empty little rooms. She felt as though she were liquid, her body just an extension of her senses. Through her skin she could feel the texture and smell the dye and hear the rustle of the fabric she rubbed against. The scent of dye, undetectable to anyone else, was headier to her than any perfume. The sound of silk stirring in the wake of her touch was comforting, the feel of everything was titillating. Char ran her hands across the bolts the way a boy drags a stick along a picket fence. Her fingers touched the crispness of the cotton, then trailed to the cool, slick silks and onto the warmth of the woolens. This was where she lived, here with the fabrics and the threads. Faux jewels glinted in workboxes as they waited to grace a neckline or dance around a hem. Faux pearls waited to be strung around a waistline. Lace and braid, trim of every description was catalogued, begging to be the thing that inspired Char next.

When the phone rang she wasn't disturbed. It only underscored the intimacy of the silence in these two rooms she called her factory. Three rings and the answering machine clicked on. She heard her own voice, realizing she must change the message. This one sounded as though she were too eager to please. Definitely not the right image for a designer favored by royalty. She giggled. In a few months she'd have a receptionist, not an answering machine.

Char rolled her back against a bolt of ebony charmeuse and wrapped the ends of it about her shoulders like a shawl as she listened to the familiar voice that responded to her mechanical invitation to leave a message.

"Ross here. I just heard. Kudos, Char. Call me. I think I can help. I'll be waiting to hear from you. Love you."

The line went dead. The machine beeped. Ross's congratulations were recorded for posterity. Ross was congratulating her, thinking her quite marvelous and that alone felt wonderful. Finally, he was taking notice of her business.

Char let her cheek rest on the silk that lay over her shoulders. Slowly she turned and picked up the bolt, intent on carrying it to the cutting table. But it slipped through her fingers before she could lay it down and fell to the floor. The blackness of it as the lengths unrolled mesmerized her. She had never known there were so many shades of darkness: pitch in the folds, jet where the light caught it, raven on the long luminous sweeps. So many shades of black just like—Fletcher's eyes. Char held the fabric out—a beautiful vampire in a cape of silk. Slowly she draped it over her body from head to toe, walking away so that it unraveled behind her, a long train behind the queen of design. Fletcher had been out of her mind too long. Now that he was in it once more, she realized she couldn't bear another moment without him.

As though their souls were mated, her mere thought his command, Fletcher materialized. Char looked toward the open door just as the last syllable of his name rolled lazily through her mind. He was there, taking pictures, smiling sweetly at her as he lowered the camera before raising it one last time.

Then the camera disappeared and other things were held in his hands as he came quietly into the studio. Char smiled, inviting him in, knowing by the look in his eyes that she had never looked more beautiful. There was color in her cheeks, she could feel it burning. And the shadows that hooded her eyes were intriguing not foreboding. The light that caressed her wide lips was so gentle they seemed to sparkle with diamond dust. Looking at Fletcher, she felt his appreciation, through his eyes every delicious sensation was heightened until she was almost drowning in awareness. He was close now, bringing with him an aura of uniqueness that enfolded her. He held up both hands, his lips parted, his eyes never leaving hers. She saw amusement and exhilaration in his expression. She smiled back.

"Chinese," he said. "You need to eat."

Char remained silent wanting to remember this time, wanting to remember when love came fully into her heart. He stood there so full of pride, so full of desire, that Char was both overcome by his emotion and strangely equal to it.

"And roses," he added, holding his right hand higher, watching intently to see if his gifts met with her approval.

"And lilies, and daisies," Char whispered. "You've brought too much."

He shook his head slowly, "I don't think so."

She inclined her head. Neither of them moved. Outside, the world went on; inside, time stopped. He had waited so patiently for her and now, once again, time was hers to command. There was no one else she wanted. He alone understood the enormity of what had taken place, but she confided in him despite his knowledge. "I'm a success, Fletcher," she said quietly, awe tingeing her voice.

"Yes."

She stepped forward, trailing the black silk behind her. Slowly she went to him. He didn't reach for her but waited on her pleasure.

"I'm rich, Fletcher."

She was grinning now, holding out her arms, still in her gown of blue and green beads. There had been no time or thought given to her clothes as the future opened up before her. Time had sped by so quickly there was not a moment to change her clothes even while her life was changing.

She was almost on him when he said, "I know."

Char didn't hear the note of sadness buried deep in that acknowledgment. Fletcher wasn't even aware he had spoken with such melancholy. He was thrilled for her. The adventure was so great and he remembered it so well. He also remembered the moment he had to let it go. How difficult that had been. He'd had misgivings then. Now he had none. His life was fuller, richer for his decision to leave it all behind. He was sure of that. Wasn't he . . . ?

Char was very close, her face tipped up just a bit, her lips invitingly near, her skin — ah, her skin.

Never taking his eyes from hers, Fletcher put the bag of food on the worktable. Carefully he plucked a rose petal, rubbing it gently between his fingers as though to gauge its softness. Without hesitation he drew it down Char's throat, slowly, cautiously, past her collarbone, down her chest to the point where her breasts rose above the beads of her gown, tempting him with their fullness.

Char's arms lengthened, holding out her silken cape as her body trembled with controlled ecstasy under the touch of the petal. She threw her head back, her eyes fluttered closed, a gentle moan bubbled from her throat. The exquisite simplicity of the petal against her skin brought her almost to the breaking point of ecstasy and, when another was drawn across her shoulders and down her arms, Char could no longer contain herself.

In a moment she had wrapped Fletcher in a mantle of black silk. Her mouth was on his, probing, insisting that they now finish what he had begun. His arms were around her, the bouquet dropped at her feet. Without hesitation he crushed her to him, her body pushing into him as though they could be one by sheer force of will. Then his lips were on her flesh, following the trail that a single rose petal had blazed, following it with exquisite accuracy. Weakened with desire, Char's legs gave way beneath her. Her breath quickened, her body was driven, her mind was closing to everything but the charge to remember each sensation. With the grace of a well choreographed ballet they melted together, collapsing in a cloud of black silk on the cold, hard floor.

Around them the fabric billowed, covering them for a moment before losing momentum and settling beneath them, becoming nothing more than a lovely hindrance to their lovemaking. Fletcher pulled at Char's dress, peeling it off her body, aware of the sound of a hundred tiny beads ricocheting off the walls around them as the delicate threads snapped.

Char writhed beneath him, anxious to have her turn. She pulled at the buttons of his shirt, needing to feel his skin against her nakedness. It was an interminable exercise as they struggled, but each conquered zipper and buckle, each button and belt mastered heightened their desire, until finally they were naked. Fletcher put his hands about her small waist and pulled her toward him, devouring her, needing her, wanting to keep her only with him so she would never feel the pain of failure or the emptiness of true success.

Then they cried out together, small and insignificant sounds in the room filled with fabric and jewels, but meaning the world to the two people who uttered them. It was over—the celebration, the uncertainty, the hope for the future. Their minds were wiped clean of every thought save the one that mattered most. Both knew their lives would never be the same without one another.

Chapter Eight

"Carol, get in here. Now!"

Char released the button on the intercom wishing they had opted for the voice-activated model Ross suggested. But what was done was done. Pushing a button wasn't hard work; it was an annoyance when there were so many other things she needed to be doing with her hands.

"Yes, Char?"

Carol poked her head into Char's new office. True to plan, it was decorated in the most appealing shades of blue and cream. Huge photos of her latest designs, a copy of the original *WWD* article, and one of Fletcher's more inspired pictures of Char were framed in gilt and hung strategically on the walls along with bulletin boards of fabric swatches and sketches. Char stood behind a desk that looked as though it had been carved out of alabaster, she pointed to a chair that could have been made of ivory. Carol sat down and waited. Char's lips were moving silently as they so often did now. Carol knew Char was talking to herself, trying to remember exactly what the next thing was on her calendar.

Gone were the long lazy days where Char would simply sit and sketch. Now she had to worry about the next interview, schmooze with the buyer from a major department store, and deal with all the details for the new showroom in New York, not to mention the investment bankers that seemed to come out of the woodwork to make suggestions for investing the millions of dollars that suddenly belonged to Char Brody. Carol moved in her chair, impatient but not angered that she should be kept waiting.

"Sorry," Char said when she finally put the last swatch block in her new briefcase. "I just wanted to get a rundown on the shipments for Nordstrom's before I head out. I'll be in Oregon at their headquarters for part of the day tomorrow, then I'll be doing a trunk show at the main store before heading off to New York. I'm going to check on the showroom and talk to the last candidates for showroom manager. We're going to have to get that showroom up and running fast. After Fletcher's article there seems to be more interest than ever in stocking CB Designs. Now, do you have the figures I need?"

Dutifully Carol gave Char a rundown. She was a natural, able to keep the most intricate scheduling straight in her head. But she was tired and overworked and had more on her mind than the Nordstrom order.

"We've shipped to the Oregon store. The one in San Francisco has evening and daywear but no casualwear yet. We're at eighty percent for Nordstrom, one hundred percent for Neiman's. We're still waiting for credit approval for Carter Hawley Hale. Bullocks locally is all shipped. We've got the factory on overtime."

"Great. It's amazing what's happened. Five months and I'm almost shipping on schedule. Nobody thought I could do it, but I did." Char snapped her briefcase shut, pulling a stack of letters toward her. Glancing at them, she shoved them across the desk to Carol. "I've got a dozen letters to answer. I've kept the ones that need personal attention. Could you take care of these for me while I'm gone?"

"Sure, Char, no problem."

Carol made no move to take the stack of mail. Instead she sat quite still screwing up her courage, trying to remember it was only Char she wanted to talk to, not the president of the United States. Funny it had never been hard to talk to her employer before. Now it was one of the biggest challenges she had ever faced.

"Something else, Carol?" Char asked with just a trace of impatience. Two little lines of peevishness that had recently begun to mar Char's beautiful face appeared as if by magic.

"Yes," Carol began then changed her mind, but it was too late. Now that she'd started to talk, she couldn't seem to help herself. "Well, no, not exactly. I mean it doesn't have anything to do with the orders."

"Can we talk on my way to the car. I've really got to get going." Char picked up her briefcase, hoping her tight schedule would deter Carol.

"No, it can wait."

Char blinked. Carol had gotten the message but her tone of voice made it rather obvious it was not well received. Char sighed and put her bulging briefcase on the desk with an overdramatic thump.

"Obviously it can't." Both women flinched at Char's unusual shortness. Chagrined, Char apologized. "I'm sorry, Carol. It's already been a long day and it's going to get longer. Forgive me."

"Sure. Okay. Well, it's just something I want you to think about." Now that the floodgates were open, Carol jumped in with both feet.

"Shoot."

Char checked her watch without even realizing what she was doing. Carol ignored what had now become an annoying habit of her employer. She wondered if Char even saw the hands on the face of her beautiful new diamond-studded watch, or just looked at it to make sure it was still on her wrist. Carol cleared her throat.

"All of us—those of us who've been with you since the beginning—well, we've been working our tails off, Char, and none of us can say we have anything to show for it. I don't want to sound ungrateful, but the last few months have been the most exciting time, the greatest professional experience, I've ever had. I think the others feel the same way. But we also feel as though we've out-lived our usefulness. We can remember a time when we were a team. Now it doesn't seem we even warm the bench."

Char's eyes widened, her mouth dropped. "Carol, how can you say that? We've got a company to show for it. New offices, new machinery, a warehouse that's filling up with garments on an hourly basis. Five months ago we were working out of a factory the size of this office. Carol, we've got plenty to show for our hard work."

Carol shook her head, "No, *you've* got plenty to show for your hard work. It's not like it's tough to notice, Char. The jewelry. The new car. All things you deserved, for sure. I mean that clunker you drove forever and a day was about ready to bite the dust anyway. And I think it's great that you can indulge yourself with jewelry and stuff. But, you see, we all feel as though we were more than just bodies around here. We thought you re-spected us as friends and professionals."

"Carol, don't be ridiculous. Of course I do. If I've forgotten to thank you, I'm sorry. I'll talk to Ilsa and Alana and Theresa and Maggie and Olivia—everyone—just as soon as I get back."

"It's more than that, Char. This company stepped into the big time, but you've left us all behind. We haven't had a raise, even though we've doubled our output and our hours. We've worked so hard to make CB Designs what it is, just like you have, but we're not sharing the rewards.

"We all want to stay here, Char, but we're not

going to let you hire people who have experience from New York and put them above us in jobs we used to do. We're the ones that made this happen. All of us who kept sewing and cutting and lugging bolts of fabric around when you were nobody. Alana spent half her free time looking into warehouse space and checking out the cost of machinery, setting up the books for an expanded work force. Then we all helped move this stuff because we knew that the money wouldn't come in until we started delivering some of the big orders.

"Well, we delivered them. On time. And the stuff is selling like hotcakes. And the money is coming in, Char." Carol sighed. Tears were swimming in her eyes. She didn't know if she felt resentful or embarrassed to have to ask for what she felt was due all of them. Then she looked at Char's stricken face and realized her boss was as crushed by what she was saying as Carol was by what Char had omitted. "I know you've been running fast, but it's time to take a look at us now that things are going more smoothly. Can you understand?"

"I've been a real idiot, haven't I?" Char sat down heavily in her chair, picked up a pencil, and began to tap it on the top of the desk. Shamefully she noticed how uncomfortable Carol looked. Char was horrified that the young woman had been put in this position. But her second thought pushed away the first and left Char almost shaken.

She felt anger, pure and simple. Carol had chosen the worst possible time to bring up a subject as important as this one. Char's nerves were shot just thinking about the publicity schedule that lay ahead of her. She had hardly had time to do more than kiss Fletcher goodbye in the morning before flying to her first appointment. Half the time they never even connected. If there was anyone who needed attention, it was Fletcher, not Carol and the others.

It was also obvious they had no idea what the actual state of affairs was at CB Designs. Well, Char would just have to set her straight. They were friends and colleagues, yes, so Char would speak to her as one. Carol would understand and be able to explain it to the others.

"Carol, I'm sorry. I truly am. I had no intention of snubbing you or making any of you feel as though you weren't appreciated. I do think, though, there are a few things you have to understand. Ross has explained this to me, and I'll try to explain it to you."

Char held her hands wide then dropped them in her lap as though to say it was painful to have to be so direct.

"Yes, things are going extremely well, and yes, I have picked up a few things for myself, but all of them are necessary for the more public work I'm doing now. An image has been established and I have to live up to it. The few things I've purchased—the car, the jewelry—are minimal compared to what I've poured into the company. The machinery, the long-term lease on the factory

160

space, the advertising agency and public relations agency are all costing a fortune. Whoever said you've got to spend money to make money wasn't kidding."

Char smiled but Carol sat quietly waiting, not as charmed as Char had hoped she would be. Char's eyes flicked away from Carol's. Her momentum was tripped but she continued on, knowing she had to wrap this up and head to the airport fast.

"Look, Carol, here's the bottom line. I've made a lot of money overnight. I've put most of it back into the growth of this company because I had to deliver merchandise fast or there wouldn't be a company. If there was no company, you wouldn't have a job and the subject of raises would be a moot point. You also have to remember that I've got to be careful what I commit to now. If I raise everyone's salary, I have to be able to meet those new commitments every two weeks. Until I have a good feel for our cash flow, that's going to be a bit tough. We have to have consistency in our sales before the benefits can be consistent.

"Meanwhile I'm expected to come up with a new season of designs and get that in the works too. It's not like the old days when a client would come to us and we'd have six months to work on one gown. We've got to have salespeople who know how to show a line. Showrooms. Samples. Right now the accounts are coming to us, but that deluge may not last. We're running one step ahead of being put right back where we started. So until there's a higher confidence level, I'm afraid . . ."

Char leaned forward a knowing smile on her lips as she pleaded for understanding. But Carol saw the impatience in her gesture. Char wasn't really thinking about the five original employees at all. She was wishing she was headed to the airport.

Carol wasn't off base in her assessment. Char did want to be on her way. She wanted to be on a plane with a glass of wine and time to think. Luckily, she also realized that it had taken a great deal of courage for Carol to come to her and she was right. Char hadn't really thought about her original staff in a long time. They had so easily assimilated into the larger picture, it was difficult to remember that, at one time, they *had* been CB Designs. So, the rejection Char was about to issue melted in her mouth, and instead she allowed herself a moment to look at the individuals and not the company.

"You're right, Carol. I haven't been fair. I think fifteen percent would be possible for the original employees. Fifteen percent and an apology. We'll see what happens in a few months and talk again."

Carol stood up, smoothing her skirt. It was a CB Design.

"Thank you. I think we'll all appreciate both" was all she said, the muscles in her jaw tightening. Fifteen percent was like a slap in the face. It was nothing compared to what some of the new executives were making. Desperately she tried to quell her resentment. Char had obviously thrown out the first figure that came into her mind. It was better than nothing, but not by much.

Char was on her feet instantly, pulling her briefcase off the desk while she waited for Carol to leave. She didn't want to appear impolite by rushing past the woman, but she wished Carol would hurry up. Though Carol had been given what she wanted, something had changed between them. This wasn't the happy and triumphant moment Carol had expected, nor did Char feel the relief and appreciation of being brought back to earth by an old and trusted employee. There was a splinter now in their affection for one another and it made them both uncomfortable.

"Is there anything else you want to talk about?"

Carol smiled at Char and shook her head saying a quiet "No, and thanks again" as she left the office, closing the door behind her. Heading toward her desk, Carol did an about-face in front of the public relations office and walked quickly through the warehouse to the factory. There she whispered to Maggie, who left her fabric inventory to tap Ilsa and Theresa and Olivia on the shoulder, while Carol went to find Alana. Soon they were all settled around one of the large tables in the lunchroom.

"Fifteen percent for all of us," Carol said flatly, shooting a quieting glance around the table the moment excited chatter erupted. "Fifteen percent, which is a pittance, and a half-hearted apology about not paying enough attention to us. For the most part I got a bunch of talk about how the money has to go back into the business right now. The message was pretty clear. This is a onetime thing. If we're all going to have jobs in the future, we're going to have to be just like everyone else around here. The game plan is set and we're in our little spaces."

"Ross. That's Ross talking," Alana commented. "I've heard him advising her. If she keeps listening to him, we'll be forgotten by next year. He's right out of the sweatshop school of finance. Spend like hell on the equipment, pay slave wages to the underlings and big bonuses to the guys at the top. He's tough, but I never thought Char would fall for that stuff."

"She hasn't." Theresa spoke without looking up from the work she had brought with her. The other women gave her their undivided attention. Theresa didn't say much, but when she did, it was worth listening to. "You forgot Char still has stars in her eyes. She can't see anything but her good fortune. It's like getting married. You don't care if anyone else has a date Saturday night because you've got the best man in the world and you're sleeping with him, see?" Theresa shrugged as though everyone knew what was coming next. "By the first anniversary you still like him, but he's getting to be a lot of work. The whole marriage is a lot of work and it isn't exactly fresh, but you have time to look at all the little things you got to do to keep it going."

She let the piece of beaded chiffon fall to her

lap. "It's like Char just got married, that's all. It won't be this way forever. Let her get all this I'm-the-boss nonsense out of her system. I say she deserves it. She was never late on my paycheck even when things weren't so good. She sent fabric home for my kids' school dresses. I had the best-dressed kids in school because of her. When I couldn't work because I slammed my hand in a door, Char paid me anyway."

"That's all well and good, Theresa," Carol interrupted, "but look at what she's done to us now. She's hired people at great salaries to do the things we did for minimum wage. Heck, some of those people replaced us. I mean, how come Alana isn't controller? How come she's still the bookkeeper and there's some guy making four times her salary in the big office?"

"Because Char is listening to the people who advise her and hiring people who have experience with big business. I haven't made a dress company before—have you?" Theresa ignored her work now and looked around the table. "Any of you said, 'Here's all my money. I'm going to make a company and pay everybody top dollar'? Nah! None of us are taking the risks. She's doing the best she can. Hell, I'd be scared if I were her, I can tell you. I bet she's scared now. We just don't see it under all the hoopla."

"Maybe you're right," Maggie muttered, pursing her lips as she considered everyone's opinion. "Besides, fifteen precent isn't bad. It could be better, but it's something. Maybe if we wait awhile longer, give her a full six months to settle down and look around at things, she will reconsider our status. If nothing happens, we talk to her again. Maybe all of us should talk to her."

"In six months if I'm not head of a department making comparable money to those people she brought in from New York, I'm walking." Carol stood up abruptly. She was hurt and she was angry. Fifteen percent was like buying pencils from a beggar even if you didn't need them. "If Char can't remember who it was that helped her without being reminded, then I don't want to work here anymore. Mark my words, it's going to get worse before it gets better if Char doesn't snap out of it soon."

Carol stalked off. There seemed to be nothing left to say, so one by one they drifted away. The only thing they could do now was get back to work and try their best to make the impossible deadlines in front of them.

Ten minutes later, Char rushed through the bustling factory, her head bent as she strode purposefully toward the back door and her car. Theresa watched her until she disappeared. Char hadn't even nodded to the guard, nor had she mumbled her usual thanks as he opened the door. Theresa shook her head.

"Scared" was all she muttered before going back to her work. It was the most beautiful dress she had worked on yet. This one was bound to make lots of money for CB Designs. Once Char Brody understood her business better, she would be

166

back. She would remember who it was that helped her and who she was.

All that hurrying only to wait. Char glared at the board. The Oregon flight had been delayed and her righteous anger did nothing to change the information. Sighing, she flopped into the nearest chair, draped her garment bag over the one next to her, and placed her carry-on at her feet. It was hot inside the terminal, so she slipped out of her short red jacket, adjusted her saffron silk blouse, and crossed her legs with little regard for her cropped pants. For an instant she let her eyes run over the exquisite purple wool of her slacks. The color of royalty. It was a beautiful length of fabric and so exquisitely expensive.

The last thought reminded Char there was work that could be done while she waited. Digging in her carry-on, she found what she wanted, then settled back to work. She didn't get much done. Ten minutes later she was interrupted.

"Can I see?"

Char, engrossed in what she was doing, was unsure if the man was speaking to her but looked up nonetheless. His voice had a familiar ring, his presence a familiar aura.

"Fletcher," Char sighed with contented surprise, happy to see him and wondering how he had found her.

Her smile was his invitation to sit beside her. He accepted happily. It had been too long since he'd seen her luscious lips part in so genuine a welcome, too many days since he had seen that look of complete concentration turn into one of unadulterated pleasure. Even in her sleep — when they were lucky enough to be together — Char's brow furrowed with some emotion he couldn't fathom.

She didn't seem to be worried. Just the opposite, really. Everything appeared to be going extremely well. Char reveled in her newfound fame without a trace of regret for her lost privacy. No, Char Brody didn't seem to have a worry in the world, yet she still seemed to bear the weight of it on her shoulders. At night she moved and mumbled and, if Fletcher looked very closely, he could see the hint of dark circles under her eyes when she woke. He wasn't sure why, but that annoyed him a bit. She had it made, yet she looked so driven. Her operation was going smoothly, she called the shots, she was . . .

Then her lips were on his and his arm was coming around her, feeling the incredible sinewy strength of her muscles beneath the silk of her blouse. Instantly he lost that odd, discontented feeling that seemed to sneak up on him more often than not these days.

"That's a nice hello," he whispered, letting his forehead rest against hers without regard for the curious looks from Char's fellow passengers.

"That was a thank-you for coming to find me. I appreciate it. Not to mention the fact that I needed a touch of love just now."

"I'll have to remember to surprise you more often. It might be difficult, though, since these days I don't have a clue where to find you half the time. Carol filled me in today. I'm lucky the flight was delayed or I would have missed you. Now," he kissed her lightly again, "are you going to let me see?"

Before she could say a word, Fletcher had the pad of paper in his hand. Char watched his smile falter. Though he quickly hid it, Char saw his disappointment. He'd been trying to hide it for months now, but she saw it in the twitching around his lips, the fading brightness in his eyes that spoke so eloquently of disillusionment. Char took the paper away. She slipped it into her bag wondering why she felt as though she had just been judged and found lacking.

"I thought you were sketching. I haven't seen you do that in a long time." It was only a comment, but Char found it put her off a bit. She didn't have four hands, after all. What did he expect?

"No. I had some paperwork to catch up on. I needed to work out the allocation of these three items so we don't deluge this market with one silhouette."

"I guess that would be a disaster," Fletcher drawled.

"Do I detect a note of sarcasm?" Char asked, ready for an offensive move.

"No, honey. Not at all. I'm sorry if it sounded that way."

Fletcher leaned back in his seat and rubbed his eyes. He'd heard it, too, and he was ashamed. Sniping at Char wasn't going to make things better. The problem wasn't hers, it was his, after all. Or at least he was willing to take the blame. She certainly wasn't. In fact, Fletcher wasn't at all sure she realized there was a problem between them. "I was only thinking it's a shame you have to deal with that kind of thing. You should be sketching, creating. You should be doing what you love."

"What makes you think I don't love this?" Char asked, taken aback that he assumed she disliked these chores. "You must remember how fascinating it was to watch your company grow by leaps and bounds. I need to see it all, Fletcher. It's not as though I've abandoned the creative side, you know. I'm still designing. It's just there isn't the leisure anymore to do it all day long. Someday I'll be lolling about with nothing on my mind but the question of how to make black wool look perfect on every woman's figure. Right now, I've got to see this company through its first year. Nobody else knows what it should be. When everything's put together, it will run itself. But nobody else can decide what's best for CB Designs but CB herself. Fletcher, I'm surprised at you."

Fletcher smiled at Char. What that smile lacked in warmth it made up for in tact. "You're right. Of course, you're right. I was out of line. I'm sorry." A child chased a ball past them. Fletcher watched him as though it was the most interesting activity he'd ever seen. Char slid her eyes toward the little boy just as he caught up with his toy, then crossed her arms before fixing her eyes on the toes of her shoes.

"That doesn't sound like a convincing apology," Char pouted. "I thought you, of all people, would understand what it takes to pull off something as big as this."

"I do understand it, Char, and I said I was sorry. I guess I'm just feeling sorry for myself. A little left out. A little forgotten." Fletcher nudged her with his elbow. He didn't smile and there was a husky longing in his voice. "We need some more time together, Brody. That's all there is to it." Fletcher was silent for an instant, then he slid down in his seat and crossed his arms to mimic her. Leaning toward her he suggested, "Maybe I could help. Maybe I could step in for a bit. I could watch over the factory and keep an eye on shipping to give you some time to . . ."

"No," Char said too quickly, caught herself, and tried to soften her rejection. How could she explain to him that he was too new in her life to share in this, that she found him so overwhelming personally she couldn't take a chance that he might overshadow her in business? Besides, he'd already had his time in the sun and he'd made it on his own. This was her time, she would call the shots. "You've been out of manufacturing for a long time, Fletcher. I know you hated the grind. Besides, you have that new assignment to worry about. It was *Life* magazine, right?"

"Yep. Nice of them to come up with a project

that keeps me in San Diego. I just wish I wasn't working so many nights. But documenting illegal alien border crossings isn't exactly something that happens at high noon."

"See," Char said, a bit too brightly. "There's no way you could possibly help me out at the factory and work nights. And that is only the half of it. I just don't think fashion is your forte."

Char plucked at his football shirt. He looked marvelous with his jeans worn to the peak of perfection, his sockless feet covered by a pair of Weejuns, his football jersey soft, well washed and tucked into the slim waist of his pants. Yes, he looked wonderful, just like Ralph Lauren. But he wasn't Ralph Lauren, and her factory was no place for him. He had to see that.

"Okay. You don't want me around the factory. I guess Ross's advice is good enough, you sure don't need mine."

Fletcher looked away and studied the people milling around the terminal. All were anxious to be on their way and none more anxious than Char. Suddenly she was just like a thousand other people, her mind wrapped around the prospects and the problems of keeping the money she had and making more. A few months ago, she would have spent the day in bed sketching while he showed her contact sheets for his article. Now, she was scheduled every minute of the day and he resented it. The only problem was he wasn't sure why he did, since any free time she had was spent with him.

Fletcher honestly believed he felt indignant because he missed her. The wonderful time they shared when they first met had set the stage for a relationship unlike any other he'd ever had. From the moment they met, the book was being written and Fletcher had devoted his entire being to watching each chapter unfold.

But then someone had changed the plot. A woman with a title walked into a small boutique an ocean away, and that was all it took to put the wheels in motion. The change had been so gradual he hardly noticed it at first. In the first heady weeks of Char's venture, Fletcher had been a part of it. They had stayed up until the wee hours of the morning, planning, talking, dreaming. Then, like an engine picking up steam, Char moved ahead, leaving him behind and picking up Ross on her uphill charge. Now it seemed she was so far away, she was almost out of reach.

"Fletcher, why are you trying to pick a fight?" Char asked gently, laying her hand on his arm, pulling him away from his thoughts. "Ross had shared this dream with me for years and yes, he does have up-to-date information I need. But I know this has nothing to do with Ross or with you wanting to spend time in the factory. And I'm damned sure this has nothing to do with the fact that I wasn't sketching when you walked up. Now, do you want to tell me what's going on?"

Fletcher shook his head. "I'm just tired, babe. I'm coming down now that I've wrapped up the photos on the project you were a part of. Came out nice, don't you think?" Char smiled weakly. Yes, the few photos he had chosen of her to put in his article about the quiet wealthy had been lovely, but hardly explained the need for the hundreds he had taken of her. Still, she had to remember she'd been an afterthought in that article, not the focal point, so the five he had used were more than she should have expected. Someday she must ask to see all the others. So many others.

"I guess we're both exhausted and I miss you," Fletcher said. "I miss all that planning and scheming we used to do when this first happened. I miss you next to me every night in bed." He smiled but there was a sadness to it as he drew his finger down the side of her face.

Char tipped her face into his touch. "I miss you, too. We both knew this was going to be rough. You were the one who warned me, if you recall. Now you're the one who's taking the brunt of all this. I'm gearing up and you're finishing up. Listen." Char shifted in her seat and leaned closer to him. Fletcher could just see the rise of her breasts beneath the light fabric of her blouse. How he wanted to touch her, make love to her. How he wanted to listen to her excited talk about what the future would bring instead of a recitation of her agenda. He forced a smile, hoping she wouldn't see that it was just a wee bit false, while she talked. "I know a way we could see each other and I'd still get a lot of work done."

"What? Move your office into my bedroom?"

Char slapped his arm playfully, grateful his

good mood was returning. She had enough to do now without worrying about Fletcher and his male ego. Fletcher was self-sufficient, he didn't need her to be at his beck and call. He just needed some quality time. That was one of the things she loved about him. Funny how at one time she worried his wanderlust might be a problem. Now she wished it would grip him again, give him a project to attend to that was as all-encompassing as her business had become.

"Don't be absurd. What if — now don't say no before you've had a chance to think about it — but what if, now that you're free during the day, and can find a bit of time for fun, you come to work for me? Not in the factory, of course, but on the creative end. You could shoot all of our ads. The agency hasn't shown me anyone's portfolio to match the quality of your work . . ."

Fletcher threw back his head and laughed, not so much from amusement as from incredulity. He could hardly believe his ears. Char was handing him a job and he didn't even have to fill out an application. He felt like a poor relation. Or worse, he was sleeping with the boss and she had to find a place for him.

Ignoring the insult, assuming Char didn't really understand how rude her offer was, Fletcher answered: "I should hope they haven't been able to show you anything that matched my work. Char, I'm not a fashion photographer. I haven't any interest in shooting pouty-lipped, anorexic women on a daily basis."

"You shot me on a daily basis. If you remember, that's how we got ourselves involved in the first place."

Fletcher chuckled and shook his head. "This is nothing like that. I was working on a journalistic pictorial. You're a beautiful woman, but you're a far cry from models who make their living preening for a camera. If I wanted to spend my waking hours with that kind of woman, I sure as hell wouldn't be hanging around you. Or at least I wouldn't be trying to hang around you."

"I'm making it tough, aren't I?" Char screwed up her eyes as though waiting for a painful blow. What came was a gentle reprimand and an admission that lifted a weight from her shoulders. "No, you're just not making it easy. But you're making it no more difficult than I would have done if the tables had been turned. I suppose I would be just as single-minded if I was chasing a story. I must admit, though, I don't think I'd ask you to carry my camera bag."

Char let her fingers play over his wrist before clasping his hand in hers. "You know, Fletcher, your honesty is one of the most attractive things about you. Do you know how many men would never admit something like that?"

"I'm glad you approve." Bowing his head slightly, Fletcher squeezed her hand. "But for all our philosophical mien, we're still back where we started." Fletcher lowered his voice and tugged at the low neck of her blouse for emphasis. "How are we going to get to see each other more without the factory tracking you down every hour, or you hanging out with me at the border when you do take some time off?"

"Well," Char teased, lowering her eyes as she flirted with him, "there is one other option."

"Which is?"

"Move in with me," Char answered. "The place is small but I'm going to be getting something bigger one of these days. Meanwhile we'll see each other every spare minute. You won't have to be running back and forth between my place and yours or me to you."

Fletcher's caress stopped mid-stroke. He opened his mouth but shut it, knowing he should think before he spoke. His gut tightened, hostility burning its way through his body. Words were forming in his mind and he didn't like what he was thinking one bit. How many times did he have to listen to what she wanted? Hadn't he just spent the last twenty minutes making a very simple request. Make time for me, Char. Was there something really difficult to understand in that? Char sounded as though she were offering to keep him, and that sent his blood pressure skyrocketing. Love her he might, but she was beginning to overstep the bounds of an equal and loving relationship.

"Char," he began, only to be interrupted by the flight announcement.

Both of them looked toward the gate. Char had forgotten their discussion. Fletcher could feel her spirit slipping away as her body bent to retrieve her hand luggage. Suddenly his anger was gone.

177

His interpretation of her offer now seemed petty and he didn't want her to leave just yet.

"I have to go, Fletcher. You'll think about what I said?"

She was grinning at him even as she slung her bag over her shoulder and stood up, hardly able to contain her anxiety about the flight. Fletcher stood up, too, and took her by the shoulders.

"I don't think so. I like my place. I think we both need some space, but we've got too much right now. How about we compromise?"

"I'm open for suggestions," she said brightly.

"You're back when?"

"Day after tomorrow. Fletcher, I've really got to go." Char took a step toward the gate. He caught her hand and pulled her back as he looked over her shoulder. People were queuing up to enter the plane, but the line was hardly moving.

"You've got plenty of time. Don't worry. What time's your return flight?"

"Ten. I'll be here at ten."

Fletcher knit his brow, rummaging through his schedule as best he could without a calendar. "That's rough. I'm supposed to hook up with the reporter from *Life* and cover the Mexican consul's meeting with the head of the border patrol . . ." He narrowed his eyes, obviously racking his brain for some solution to this dilemma. Then he made a decision. "The heck with it, Char. I'll meet the reporter and have him do his thing. Somehow I'll get the bigwigs together another time . . ."

"Fletcher, I can't let you do that," Char objected, wanting to check on the progress of the line behind her but worried she might hurt his feelings.

"I can and I will. Thursday, noon. You and me. Cancel every appointment you've got for the rest of the afternoon that day. I'll fix lunch, then you and I are going to the beach. We're going to take pictures and walk and eat and talk, and if *Life* doesn't like it, they can damn well find another photographer. Then we'll make love as though it were the first time. Promise me that Thursday is ours."

He took a step closer, his fingers tightening on her shoulders. His whisper was at once cajoling and adamant. Char, mesmerized, felt the world slipping away for an instant while he held her in thrall. She knew how much this assignment from *Life* meant to him and he was putting it jeopardy just to spend time with her.

Yes, the moment had been right for everything to come together. She had breathed in as if to speak, but found herself speechless instead. She smelled the scent of him, felt the warmth of his hands through the thin fabric of her blouse. She had meant to check the gate, looking over her shoulder. Instead, she realized that light coming through the floor-to-ceiling windows had caught the deepest, darkest strands of his hair and bathed them in an unearthly glow, making her forget her intention. For just that small window of time, every plane of his face, each sparkle in the depths of his eyes was clarified and Char was drowning

179

in the sensations of love he created.

"Yes," Char answered in a small voice, her eyes locked to his. "I'd like that."

"We can't let it slip away, Char, this thing between us. We can't work it away, or wish it away, or let it die from neglect. It means too much."

"I know, Fletcher. It means that much to me, too." Char let her fingertips rest on his lips. She felt his lips move to kiss her, a small gesture that created a world of longing in the most private part of her.

Slowly his fingers relaxed and he realized he had been holding her too tightly. But Char hadn't noticed. She didn't understand that Fletcher harbored a fear inside him. He was terrified that it was he who was sabotaging their love. She had no idea that he was begging her to make everything right again and ease this reasonless indignation, this nameless dread that he was about to lose the best thing that had ever happened to him.

It was then he crushed her to him, kissing her as though there were no tomorrow. And Char kissed back, melting into him, forgetting about the showroom and the interviews and the airport.

"Thursday?" Fletcher insisted when they finally parted. Char nodded, dazed by the intensity of their kiss and the passion in his voice. "Noon. My place."

Reluctantly Fletcher turned her toward the boarding gate, still holding her shoulders. He smiled. From behind Char looked less like a fashion mogul and a great deal like an extremely well-dressed college student. Her short hair bared the vulnerable nape of her neck. She was loaded down with carry-on luggage, her red jacket wound around the strap of one. He was about to give her a playful push toward her plane when he pulled her back against him once again and buried his lips in her hair.

"I love you, Fletcher," she whispered, turning her head ever so slightly so that he was the only one to hear her confession.

"I love you, too, Char Brody. Oh, how I love you."

Then she was gone.

As Fletcher watched her plane rise into the sky, he couldn't help but wonder why loving her was beginning to hurt more than just a bit.

Chapter Nine

Coronado Island is attached to San Diego by an arcing sweep of bridge. The mere fact that it's an island lends an exclusive and elusive air to it, as though only those native to the place truly understand the workings of it. There is a naval base hidden by miles of wire fencing, and resort hotels of the highest calibre stretch south toward Mexico, catering to the wealthy who come to the island for business and pleasure. Bungalows for the working people are built close together on the interior of the island; manor houses for the wealthy are leisurely spaced, with views of the beach. The very wealthy live in Del Mar, La Jolla and San Diego, coming to Coronado Island to enjoy the quaintness they miss by living on estates the size of the island itself.

The tiny shops that dot the main street have deceptively simple names like "Oriental Furnishings." Inside the modest-looking shop though, are Chinese antiques, half of which could have come from the Forbidden City itself. A door or two down is the local liquor store that sells as much Dom Pérignon or Cristal as it does Perrier and Pepsi. Clothing boutiques for men and women, exclusive children's shops and jewelers are sprinkled about for good measure between the bank, real estate office, and pharmacy.

Rolls-Royces, Jaguars, and Range Rovers are as common a sight as well-kept, beautiful women, tanned and fit men who wear their wealth casually, and children who have never heard the word no. So hardly anyone looked twice at the white Mercedes parked brazenly in a red zone in front of a small store. Almost no one paid attention to Char sitting behind the wheel staring thoughtfully at the For Lease sign in the window of the empty shop until Marge Hudson startled the driver.

"Open up!" She mouthed, tapping on the window.

Surprised, Char dutifully rolled it down with a push of a button. Just as automatically, she smiled. For the last two days, smile was all she had done. Smile at this reporter, this customer, this buyer. Smile. Smile as if life is grand and energy is as unlimited as money and creativity. Char only wished she felt as happy and confident on the inside as she appeared to be on the outside.

"Char Brody, I could just kill you!" Marge scolded, leaning into the car.

"I hope not. I've got a lot to do today."

Char laughed, pushed the button that unlocked the door, and invited Marge in with a wave of her hand. The plump blond was seated in the blink of an eye, leaning over to kiss the air in the general vicinity of Char's cheeks. Dutifully Char leaned close, making all those small sounds that constituted a greeting among a certain group of people.

"You certainly must have more than enough to do. I haven't heard a word from you. Not an announcement that you moved. Not a phone call to gossip about all the wonderful things I've been hearing about you. Nothing!" Marge's lovely little finger waggled under Char's nose. A huge diamond on another finger blazed in the morning light, sending a prism dancing in the car's interior. "You know I've been in Europe for six months hiding out while I had my face and tummy done. Then of course after that, I thought I might as well relax, so I stayed a few months longer. I think I deserved it, don't you? And I'd met the most delightful countess, who took to me instantly. I understand the woman had been a recluse for years, but I was able to bring her out of her shell. I took her with me on my little side trips and she seemed like a new woman."

Char indulged herself with the first completely amused and sincere grin she'd given anyone in the last few days. More than likely Marge had run into the local con artists who used her gullible American friend to stay in the best hotels and eat at the finest restaurants for a while. Well, Marge

184

could afford to be taken for a million or so. It didn't matter one way or the other. Her wealth knew no bounds nor, to be fair, did her generosity.

"I'm happy you could help her. I know how that pleases you," Char commented absentmindedly, unable to give Marge her undivided attention, her eyes wandering to the For Lease sign. The black print seemed to get bigger and bigger, as though the words accused her of abandonment. She shook her head, trying to banish the feeling, doing her best to concentrate on what Marge was saying.

". . . And of course I couldn't believe my eyes. There you were, splashed all over the Italian edition of *Vogue*. But, my dear, I was so pleased for you. I must say you photograph beautifully. So I tell my friend, the countess, that you are a very dear friend of mine and, indeed, I've brought some of your things with me. I wore that peach colored pajama—you remember the one?—to a dinner with a most unusual man who owned a very large yacht. I never did quite figure out where his money came from." She knit her almost creaseless brow and thought as hard as she could before realizing it didn't really matter at all. "He seemed quite common, but I did look stunning in those pajamas you designed for me. Everyone said so."

Marge sighed and let her small twinkling blue eyes roll toward the window, where she seemed to envision herself, Madonna-like, dressed in peach

185

pajamas, surrounded by a halo of beauty. Then she clucked and the present was her concern once again.

"But of course I don't want to kill you because of those pajamas. I was just so disappointed that you moved. I came back. I came here, and look what I find. A For Lease sign on your shop. Oh, Char, you've abandoned us!"

"Marge, I haven't!" Char laughed, amused that the woman would put so much energy into her theatrics.

"But you have. Nothing is the same now. Jennifer says that you've moved to some awful factory on the other side of the bridge. A terrible working-class area."

"Marge, it's a business area. Do you think I could find warehouse space on Coronado Island? I haven't seen a working warehouse in all the years I've lived here."

"I understand, darling. My last husband always said you had to get quite dirty to make a lot of good clean money. Or something like that. Anyway," again the hand waved and the rainbow of sparkles sprinkled the inside of Char's new car, "I don't really understand where we're going to have to go for our fittings. Char, dear, I don't mean to be awful about this, but I don't want to be fitted in a warehouse. I just wouldn't feel comfortable."

"Marge, I'm so sorry. You won't be able to be fitted anywhere but Bullock's or Nordstrom or one of your favorite stores. I'm not doing custom work any longer. I've expanded to ready-to-wear and one-of-a-kind gowns for the couture departments at the larger stores."

"But that's outrageous, Char!" Marge cried, her indignation heartfelt. That surprised Char more than anything else she had heard in the last few months. "But we were the ones who made you, darling. We're the ones who love you. You can't just forsake us."

"I'm not abandoning you, Marge." Char's smoky eyes narrowed with concern, her brow furrowed. She leaned closer to this woman who had never made more than polite chitchat during her fittings and who now professed, and actually seemed to be, hurt by what she considered Char's snub. She had no idea Marge ever thought twice about her. "Marge, my business is just growing. By leaps and bounds, I might add. Now you'll be able to get CB Designs at any of the stores you like."

"But that's the point. If I can do it, then anyone else with the money can do it, too. It won't be special like it used to be. I know what will happen. All those lovely unusual things you used to make for us all will turn mundane. You'll have to design with an eye to the masses. It won't be the same at all."

"You make it sound as though I'm dying. I promise. My line will be even more lovely, more luxurious. Now that I have the money to manufacture for the mass market, I'll be able to put more into the upper-end items. Believe me, you'll love the new things."

Marge sniffed, unconvinced despite Char's assurances. "I don't know, Char. I think mostly I shall miss coming to this little place. Somehow it seemed so wonderful, a little hideaway where all us girls could go and order something wonderful and have a little talk. I used to love it when you ran from the back room to the front, then back again while you had an inspiration. You always picked the most lovely fabric for me. You held it to my face and draped it over me in a way that I knew, whatever it became, it would be just exquisite. I suppose I loved my CB clothes because they were only mine. I always knew that even if you made the same look for someone else, it would never be exactly the same. Your little establishment made me feel—special."

There was a silence in which Char felt so removed from Marge, as though suddenly the other woman had disappeared, kindly allowing Char the time she needed to think. Her eyes flicked back to the storefront. Now she knew why she had stopped here so suddenly. She was looking for the comfort she once had, the feeling of place she couldn't seem to enjoy anymore.

The last months had been, if nothing else, a shock to her system. It was as though she had suddenly been thrown into a foreign country without resources or knowledge of the language. The experience was at once challenging and frightening. First there had been Fletcher, so loving, so unexpected, everything she wanted in a man. But before she had a chance to work through the stages of new love, all the rest had happened, leaving her nothing if not confused.

The world was a wild place, undulating and changing around her, demanding things from her she wasn't sure she could give. Creativity. Energy. Beauty. Time. Gentleness. Love. Decisions. Choices. The great "they" wanted her to predict the future. They wanted her to satisfy them, even though they didn't know what it was that would make them happy. Fletcher wanted time. Ross wanted to run by her side to the end of this incredible marathon. Carol wanted position and money. Marge wanted exclusivity and Char wanted . . . What did Char want?

Sighing, she realized Marge was right. There had been something so special about the little shop and the outrageously exquisite clothes and the gossip that came from another world—one Char thought she would never be a part of. But now she was.

Money poured in every day. Expenses were met easily. People were hired and paid and there was more left over than she had ever imagined there would be. Then why was she so . . . afraid? Why had the thrill, the challenge, suddenly become a terrorizing contest without an end or a winner? Shaking her head, remembering her companion, she took Marge's well tended hands in her long-fingered ones.

"It was a special time. You and Jennifer and all the rest made me feel like an artist. But what good is working if you don't work toward a goal?"

Marge leaned over, her blue eyes twinkling, "I don't know, darling. I've never worked a day in my life."

Char's shoulders dropped, the seriousness of the moment was gone. Marge Hudson was not exactly the person to be talking to about any of this.

"Now listen, Char," Marge went on oblivious to the younger woman's puzzlement, "I fully intend to badger you until you promise that you won't cut us off completely. A few of the girls were talking, and we think you owe it to us every once in a while to design especially for us."

"We'll see, Marge. Give me a few more months. Let me get settled. I can't think about anything now except getting this business up and running."

"Do what you must, dear. Just don't forget about the locals. Actually, I have the most marvelous idea." Marge clapped her chubby little hands together. "I won't let you forget about us. Let me give you a party. Oh, I think that's just the thing. Something small. Fifty or sixty people. And all the ladies will wear their CB Designs. Now wouldn't that be special? Let me see, when shall it be?" Marge dug into her Gucci purse as though it were a shopping bag, rifled around, located her planner and flipped the pages. "Here we go. Yes.

How about two weeks from tomorrow. That would be a Friday. A perfect time for a little dinner party. I think it's the least you can do. Come to a dinner in your honor."

"I think that would be lovely." Without hesitation Char accepted the invitation. Always invited to parties as a colorful addition to the guest list, suddenly Char was to be the honored guest. It seemed amassing a small fortune did amazing things for her social standing. Immediately she was sorry for that mocking thought. She was actually quite touched by Marge's gesture. Not to mention the fact it would be wonderful for business. Maybe she could even get the press to cover it. Every woman at that party would love to see herself in the pages of *Women's Wear Daily*.

"Then it's settled. Two weeks from Friday. Oh, but I feel better."

With that, Char was kissed once again and Marge Hudson went about her business. Char watched her walk away, feeling a twinge of pain deep inside as if Marge had taken something when she went. She shook her head and laughed. All this melancholy was ridiculous, brought on by jet lag and nothing more. Oregon and New York in less than two days was enough to do anyone in.

Starting the little white car, Char put everything in order: the window was rolled up, the CD player turned on, and the engine brought to life. Without a backward glance at the corner shop, she pulled into traffic and headed toward her destination. She had a date she couldn't miss.

The apartment Fletcher leased when he had come to the southern most part of Southern California was wonderful. Fully furnished, it was owned by a businessman with exquisite taste, a small but well equipped darkroom just off the kitchen and the beach below the balcony. When Char came into his life, Fletcher was glad he liked this place since his lease would obviously have to be extended.

So it was Char he was thinking of as he laid the balcony table with his landlord's china and crystal. It was Char he imagined living here with him someday, until they could decide where to build the house that would be their home base. Maybe they would buy this co-op. The landlord seemed less interested in the space now that he had married. His young bride, it seemed, preferred the rarefied atmosphere of a mansion in Corona Del Mar. Fletcher laughed, thinking how awful it would be to spend one's life with a partner who was more concerned with the size of their house than the love they put in it.

Every now and again Fletcher looked down at the beach, splaying his hands on the balcony railing as he leaned out to look at the sparkling ocean or turn his head to stare toward the Hotel de Coronado. He could barely see it from where he stood, but his mind's eye remembered how beautiful the classic hotel had looked decked out in Christmas lights a few months ago.

God, but this area was beautiful. San Diego, Coronado, Corona del Mar. They were cities that embodied the best of all worlds as they combined the elegance of wealth and the psyche of Southern California casualness. There was an idleness about the place Fletcher liked. Businessmen made deals while playing tennis on private courts and eating crab cakes made by personal chefs. There was a certain style to women who dined on tacos and enchiladas dressed in the linen shorts and silk Ts, dripping with understated gold and baubles studded with informal jewels. There was a marvelous synergy between the world of the quiet wealthy that he had documented and the world of those who served in it.

Shirtless in the May sun, Fletcher breathed deep and stretched. His muscles rippled. He felt a deep satisfaction as though waking from a long, lovely sleep. A woman swept by on Rollerblades, dressed unabashedly in a thong, just as Fletcher checked his watch. Char was five minutes late and it seemed like five years. He chuckled, realizing he was acting like a soldier on leave disappointed because his lady wasn't waiting to greet him at the train station.

Running his hands through his hair, Fletcher flipped it behind his ears, grabbed his shirt and buttoned it halfway. While he tucked it into his jeans, he wandered through the place. Flowers were on the coffee table and two bottles of wine were chilling in the fridge. The house was spotless thanks to the services of an agency that specialized in once-a-week quick fixes. The bed was freshly made and he hoped it wouldn't stay that way for long.

He missed Char so much; missed her laughter and her chatter. He missed watching her when she didn't know he was looking. He loved the way her bottom lip disappeared for an instant beneath her top one when she was working; the way her eyes went from misty gray to silver when she put the finishing touches on an idea that had to be sketched at that moment and not a second later. Laughing, Fletcher remembered the first time he had awakened to find her sitting stark naked behind the bedroom drapes, trying to sketch by the light of the moon.

"Char," he had said sleepily, raising himself on his elbow when he saw she wasn't there. Then the drape parted and he saw her silhouetted, beautifully bare, her sketch pad on her lap.

"Here I am, Fletcher. I didn't mean to wake you," she whispered apologetically.

"You left. That's what woke me. What are you doing?"

"I had an idea. I needed to sketch it."

In the darkness Fletcher smiled. "You could have gone to another room and turned on the light."

Char shook her head. "I couldn't."

"Why not?"

"Because you're part of my inspiration now, Fletcher."

The simplicity of that remark that had changed so much. It was then he realized her observation held true for him, too. She was now tied to everything he was, everything he did, everything he created. So he had slipped out of bed and gathered her up just as the silvery light came into her eyes, and she held her sketch up for his approval. He had pulled her close, flesh to flesh, his only comment to toss the sketch pad on the bed and entice her to follow it. That night they had made inspired love. Not the most passionate nor the most inventive, but the kind that first kindles a flame, then carefully fans it to a blaze. Between them there was no need for plots and strategies. For Char and Fletcher, there was a love not only of body but of mind and spirit.

Longing for her now, Fletcher turned on his heel and headed to the darkroom. Carefully he gathered up recently developed photos of Char and carried the bunch into the light. Settling himself on the sofa, Fletcher laid them on the coffee table, deftly nudging them about, assessing his work, looking for the one photo that would focus the very essence of Char Brody in his mind.

But his smile of anticipation faded, replaced with an unsettling look of displeasure. The shots were no good. The light hit her wrong, making her skin look unnaturally taut in one. In another he had caught her scowling, her full, full lips almost a caricature of beauty. Yet another showed her bending over a piece of machinery like a farmhand. The entire batch was wrong, unusable. Fletcher shoved them away, as though they had offended him. Once more the feeling of sublime anticipation at seeing Char was replaced with an uncomfortable tightness in his gut.

Without looking, Fletcher gathered up the photos and tossed them onto the worktable in the darkroom. Now was not the time for introspection. One of these days he and Char would sit down and he would tell her about this odd emotion he experienced so frequently. She would tease him and kiss away any misgivings he had about life and love and her. Maybe today would be that day. Char would work that magic she had worked on him so many months ago, and they would start again, bright eyed as they looked about their world, wanting to create it differently each day.

Fletcher checked his watch again. She was really late now. Concerned, he picked up the phone and checked with the airport. Her flight had been on time that morning. She must be on her way.

Opening one of the bottles of wine, Fletcher poured himself a glass, wandered out to the balcony, sat down in a chair, and propped his feet on the railing. Thankfully there was nothing cooking.

196

Crab salad and bread could keep until she arrived. So he settled back and waited for her to come to him.

"You didn't touch your cheesecake. That's not like you."

Ross sipped his coffee, watching Char pore over the printouts in front of her. To say they terrified her was an understatement. Take away the last three zeros and Char could have handled the figures without a problem. But she was looking at debt in the millions. Somehow the fact that the balance sheet indicated assets, including a hefty cash reserve, in the same millions didn't ease her mind.

"I don't know, Ross," Char said quietly.

"What's there to know. The cheesecake here is marvelous. You've always loved it."

Char scowled at the beautiful slice of creamy cake, the satiny strawberries, the crumbling graham cracker crust. It was about as appealing as a scoop of ice cream on a potato. Nothing seemed to tempt her these days. She was losing weight, looking ever more lovely in her clothes, but knowing if she lost much more, she would look like a hanger instead of a walking advertisement for her own designs.

"I'm not talking about the cheesecake, Ross. I'm talking about this balance sheet. I don't like the debt to be so deep. I always paid everything off immediately and owned it."

"This isn't then, Char. This is now. You're not designing wedding dresses for the likes of Jennifer Cory. You're president of a fast-growing, very attractive, privately held company. You need the leverage for tax purposes. Do you know I've already had inquiries about you selling out?"

"Don't tell me," Char moaned, burying her face in her hands before peeking through her fingers at Ross. He was smiling into his coffee cup, thoroughly pleased with her, her situation, and his part in its success. Ross loved nothing more than being at the helm of a going concern, even if only as a consultant. "Have you really?"

He nodded. "Yesterday morning. I promised you, when I agreed to act as your consultant, I would tell you everything straight. They're willing to make an offer today. Want to talk about it?"

Char thought for a moment, then shook her head, "No, I don't even want to think about it. I haven't had time to enjoy what's happening. If I'm blinded by the thought of tripling my money, I might just take their offer and run. I'd never know whether I could have made it on my own."

"Char," Ross drawled, the coffee cup settling back onto its saucer as he leaned toward her, "you mean you might consider selling out? I never knew money held that kind of allure for you."

"It doesn't," she reassured him emphatically. "It's the fear that I might fail. That makes me think I should take a buyout offer. That way I could always say it was an offer I couldn't refuse. It would be the coward's way out."

"A lucrative business decision," Ross corrected.

"Business decisions are what we're here to talk about, remember? Nothing else. So no more talk about selling out, okay."

"As you wish. Now, what is it that's bothering you about the balance sheet and the marketing plan from the agency?"

Char pulled the piece of paper close to her and peered at it as though profound concentration might change the numbers. But they remained indelibly printed on the paper.

"It's the debt. I can't reconcile myself to owing so much for machinery and committing so much money that I haven't even made yet to advertising. I'm not sure it was a good idea to start advertising right away or commit myself so deeply to this agency."

"Okay." Ross's voice took on that studious, singsong quality he used when he was about to explain clearly and carefully why the other party didn't know what they were talking about. "The debt is necessary to counteract the income for tax purposes. You'd have no idea what you would be paying in taxes if you didn't have depreciation and loan interest to write off. You need to give that machinery as long a life as possible. If you own it, you haven't the advantage of the interest on the loan payments.

"Now, as for the advertising agency. Remember,

your profit comes from quantity now, not quality. If you tried to give top-of-the-line quality, you'd price yourself out of the market. Word of mouth will, of course, create some interest, as will the store promotions. Remember Jordache? They didn't even have product until they established interest. They used advertising to push through the idea that everyone had to have the name Jordache on their rear end, and people believed those commercials. You're a step ahead. You've got inventory now you need to create an image and sell that inventory. Don't worry about it. Advertising and public relations are a business expense. You write that off, too."

"But the agency is talking television," Char challenged. "Have you seen the productions costs, not to mention the airtime commitment?"

"Okay." Ross shrugged. "Maybe you don't need television. Let's talk to them about a co-op program with the stores. You produce a spot, the stores buy the time. Everybody benefits and you're not out a couple of million."

"That's a great idea. Why didn't the agency suggest it?"

"Char," Ross laughed, his hand covering hers without a second thought. "You are such a babe in the woods. No agency in their right mind would suggest that. They wouldn't get the commission from placing the time. It's economics, that's all. Production costs are a pittance compared to the commission they get when they place space or time."

"And all this time I thought they had my best interests at heart." Char sighed, rolling her eyes for emphasis. Ross grinned at her, thinking he had never seen her look more lovely. She was exciting, this new flinty edged, sharp eyed, questioning Char Brody. It was as though he had seen her a thousand times yet just now fully understood what attracted him to her.

"No one has your best interests at heart anymore, Char." Ross tightened his hold on her hands, his expression becoming serious.

"Does that include you?" She asked quietly, cockily.

"Probably. Not right now though. Now this is a grand adventure. A start-up is much more exciting than a buyout. Besides, I care about you. But then you've known that for some time, haven't you?

"Ross . . ." Char objected gently.

"What? Is it such a bad thing to tell you that? I've always cared about you. Before Fletcher Hawkins, you cared about me, too. I keep thinking that fling is going to end soon and you'll come to your senses. Until it does, I'm still in the game because I have what you need. I'll give you my knowledge, everything else . . . well," he shrugged with confidence, "I'll wait until you come to me for everything else. And you will, Char. Your life is changing, you're changing. I think you're becoming more like me everyday and, may I say this

201

newfound savvy, sits well on you."

Ross drew a finger down her arm as though testing the quality of the linen in her jacket. His hand was beautifully manicured, his shirt cuff starched, his suit of wool so buttery Char wished she could take it off him if only to study the delicacy of the weave. Her eyes flicked up to his, but he wasn't looking at her. Ross kept his eyes lowered. A lock of wheat-colored hair fell over his forehead. The noise of the late lunch crowd seemed to fade into the background when he began to speak again.

"You know there are people out there who want you to fail, Char. Fashion editors who are frustrated designers. Designers whose inspiration had dried up. Buyers who don't want to have to worry about how to fit a new line on a rounder. Then there are those people who are pulling for you. But even those people have reservations. They say 'Thank God, it isn't me' because they know, that the probability is you're a flash in the pan. Finally there are those people who want you to fail because they hate to see anyone succeed. They want to be important. They want to be lauded. They want their fifteen minutes of stardom. That's why I'm here for you. I may be the only one who is really pulling for you, Char . . ."

"There's Fletcher," Char reminded him softly.

Ross raised an eyebrow. "Is there?"

She was so taken aback, Char could do nothing more than listen to her sharp intake of breath. Of course there was Fletcher. And just as Ross began to speak again, a stab of conscience pierced her consciousness. Something about Fletcher. But then he was driven from her mind as Ross's words sunk in.

"As I was saying, I may be the only one who is really pulling for you, Char, because I love you . . ."

Char's mouth fell open, her hand under Ross's went cold, and a shiver traveled up her spine. But before she could find the words to tell him that she didn't think she could ever love him, before she could even fully process what was happening, hands gripped her shoulders and she heard a voice from above.

"That's funny, I thought that was my line."

Tipping her head back at the same time Ross looked up, Char realized that Fletcher, standing behind her staring at her luncheon companion, looked as though he could quite possibly kill Ross Parnell.

Chapter Ten

"I'm glad you made it home. I checked. Your flight wasn't late. I guess you just got caught up in business and forgot we had a date." Fletcher let go of Char and stepped around her, flipping at the papers on the table. "Cheesecake. I see you already had lunch. Funny, I could have sworn we were supposed to dine together at my humble abode. The allure of Mr. Parnell here and his expense account lunch was just a bit too much of a temptation for the new Char Brody, fashion celebrity. Hard to come off the New York glitz back to a quiet lunch on a balcony above the beach."

Char buried her face in her hands for an instant muttering "Damn" before reaching for Fletcher. He let her hand lie on his arm as though her touch was of little consequence.

"I forgot. Fletcher, I honestly forgot. I'm so sorry. I got back this morning. I knew I had something on the calendar. But then I stopped at the factory and found out that a shipment of silk had been delayed and the striped jacket wasn't translating to any size larger than an eight, so I had to work with the new pattern maker. Then Ross called with the balance sheets and suggested lunch . . ."

Char looked frantically to Ross for help. Fury engulfed her when she saw his smugness, but she needed his corroboration, so she held her tongue. He had to help her. He owed her this. To Char's great relief, he came through.

"She's right. I'm afraid the factory was frantic when I called. She needed to go over these figures for the agency, so I did suggest lunch. You know how that can be, don't you, Hawkins?"

"I'm not sure I do. Usually when I make a commitment, I stick to it. Especially if the other party has gone to considerable lengths to rearrange their schedule."

"Sometimes breaking a commitment says more about the importance of that commitment than sticking to it," Ross answered.

"Ross," Char hissed, warning him he was on thin ice.

"Sorry, Char. Just an observation. Listen. I think we've gone over everything we had to."

"Maybe more than she wanted to know, Parnell," Fletcher interjected.

"I think that's for the lady to decide, don't you? Besides, I wouldn't be too quick to offer advice, Hawkins. You gave Char a bit of publicity in that article on the wealthy just as she was shipping her first major orders, but you've been out of center ring too long. Things have changed. I'm not sure you could have kept up with them from behind a camera." Ross raised a challenging eyebrow, stood, and shot his cuffs before leaning down to kiss Char on the cheek. "You have any questions, I'm at your service." He let his gaze linger on Fletcher for emphasis. "Day or night."

"Thank you, Ross," Char murmured. Head down, she waited in silence until he was out of earshot before trying to explain what Fletcher had overheard. "There was nothing to that, Fletcher. Ross and I have known each other a long time. When he says he loves me, he means it. As a friend, as a longtime companion. I didn't see any need for you to be so rude."

"Rude?" Fletcher laughed incredulously. "Me? Char, where were you during that conversation? Didn't you look at his face? Didn't you listen to the tone of his voice? Don't talk to me about rude or crude or any such thing. I think your *friend* has me over a barrel when it comes to those virtues."

"I see." Char let her hand slip off Fletcher's arm. She sat back, considered her napkin, then plucked it off her lap and folded it carefully in front of her before speaking again. "Then I suppose I'm included in that assessment, too. I mean I was the one who forgot about our lunch date. I was the one who so crassly, if subconsciously, chose work over pleasure."

"Don't be ridiculous," Fletcher scoffed.

"I'm being as rational as you are," Char retorted.

Fletcher's head snapped to the side as though he'd been slapped. His dark eyes perused the restaurant and Char saw exactly what he did.

The Crown Room in the Hotel del Coronado was elegant. One of the finest restaurants on the island. Here, in this one room, was everything Fletcher had left behind so many years ago. Here were people of wealth and power, lunching quietly while they made decisions about millions of dollars. Char could feel a passionate resentment emanating from him. How he could hate what once meant so much to him was beyond her. She reached for him again. At first he resisted, giving in only when she insisted, winding her fingers through his, and holding his hand tight.

"I'm sorry. I'm so, so sorry, sweetheart. I know you were counting on this being our day. I know we need time together, but it happened and there is nothing I can do about it now."

Fletcher looked back at her. For an instant she thought tears welled behind his eyes, but it was only a trick of the light, a sliver of a silver beam piercing the darkness.

"Char, I cancelled a very important sitting today because it was necessary for us to be together. It was an unprofessional decision, I admit it, and I asked you to do no more, no less. In fact, your appointments were actually easier to cancel than mine. I'm reliant upon the good graces of people I want to document. So my question to you is, if you know we need to work on us, why are you making it so difficult? Do you really want to be together?" Fletcher asked seriously, hurt still burning in his heart as he heard Ross's declaration ringing in his head.

"Of course I do . . ."

"Char, wait. I can't have this conversation here. Let's go to your place or mine. I really need to be alone with you. No prying eyes. No busybodies trying to figure out why Char Brody has just exchanged rather well known luncheon companions at the Crown Room. You know how this island is."

"Fletcher, the conversation won't be any different there than it is here," Char insisted.

"Oh, that's fine!" He threw up his hands and immediately a waiter appeared. Fletcher waved him away. The service was too good at this place. He lowered his voice. "That's just fine. Now you don't even want to be alone with me."

"Fletcher, what has gotten into you? You're acting crazy. It's the middle of the day, I've got fires to put out and you're angry because I don't want to waste half an hour getting back to my apartment so we can argue there?"

"Gosh, Char, I wasn't aware that breaking a

promise to someone you supposedly loved was considered fine and dandy, but being hurt and disappointed by that was considered a completely ridiculous reaction."

"Lord, Fletcher, you're really soaking this one. Even if I'd called you to cancel, you couldn't have made your appointment in Mexico. You're trying to blame me for something that was beyond my control."

Char pulled her hand from his but he pulled back, forcing her close to him. She felt the warmth from his skin they were so close. She saw in the outline of his dark eyes the depth of his anger.

"Listen to me, Char. I'm not asking you for anything I'm not willing to give back. For months now I have played second fiddle to this business of yours. I've waited patiently, gone about my business, encouraged you on every front. I've tried damn hard to arrange assignments that kept me in the area because you're that important to me. Sometimes, like today, I've put my professional reputation on the line. I call a halt to all proceedings when you tell me one thing and do another. We were supposed to spend the entire day together. We're supposed to be adult enough to realize that life is more than just work. Now you're telling me you're too busy . . ."

"There are major problems I didn't anticipate. There has to be flexibility. I have to take care of them. If I don't do them, who will?"

Fletcher took her hand and pounded it lightly on the table for emphasis. "Those hotshots you hired to run the company, that's who. It's their job, damn it!"

"It's my company. If it is going to survive, and if it is going to be the kind of business I have always dreamed of, then I am the one responsible for every aspect of that business."

"Responsibility is not making every single decision, it is not putting out every single fire on your own. It is not living and breathing CB Designs. Look at yourself, you've got enough money now to last the rest of your life. If you really wanted to, you could run off with me to Tahiti and sketch. You could leave every decision to someone else. You'd still have a company and still be a multimillionaire. I know, I did it. Then I turned into a walking, talking Dow Jones ticker tape."

"Fletcher, I don't think you're listening to what I'm saying," Char objected, frightened not only by his anger but by his suggestion she relinquish her control over CB Designs. Had she come so far just to turn it over to people she hardly knew?

"I'm listening a hell of a lot closer than you are, babe. I've been there, remember. I had exactly what you've got now." Fletcher sat back, releasing her hand. There was no comfort in their contact.

"Then take what I'm doing and saying seriously," Char spat back.

There was no need for him to bring up ancient history. She'd heard it all before. Fletcher made it sound like he skated to success on the smoothest pond. Well, it wasn't like that for her and he better damn well understand that. She was dancing as fast as she could, and if he didn't like the steps, then tough. He could sit this one out.

"I do take what you're doing seriously," Fletcher said. "I understand what it means to be in your position. But I am just a little bit tired of being an afterthought. I try to give you the benefit of my experience and I'm locked out. It's as though I'm invalidated because I don't make decisions based on computer printouts anymore. Have I lost brain cells somewhere?

"And what about my schedule, Char? Could it be that you might not take my business as seriously as you should? I rearranged a long-standing shoot schedule so we could be together. But somehow the import of that has gotten lost in concern over your television schedule.

"Am I only good as an occasional lover but not good enough to become involved in the things that worry you, that you're working toward, that you want to create? Well, if that's the case, then why don't you make an appointment with me when your schedule is free. We'll just have a quick roll in the hay. That should satisfy you. And I promise, I won't be too busy to keep that appointment."

Char was on her feet. The chair she was sitting on toppled and fell. For a moment, in the time when everyone stopped in mid-conversation to see where the noise came from until they resumed talking, Char was riveted to the floor, her indignation evident for everyone to see. Without a word, her movements measured, she picked up her purse and turned to leave. But something stopped her.

She couldn't leave like this. Her heart was breaking. This wasn't the Fletcher she loved. He was acting like a child when she needed his constancy. He had chosen to discard whatever it was they had meant to each other. There was no concession she could make, it seemed, that would satisfy him.

Over her shoulder, her voice low and confessional, she said: "You have an odd way of loving someone, Fletcher Hawkins."

Head held high, her heart shattered, Char left the restaurant, gulping the clean ocean air as she strode across the parking lot. Even when she heard him behind her, running toward her, even when she felt his hand on her arm and felt her body twirling into his and her lips being crushed beneath his, Char couldn't stop the misery that coursed through her. From head to heart and beyond, she ached. Even when her body betrayed her and she clung to him, wishing he would make all these new and strange feelings, all this fear and confusion, go away so she could be herself once more, hurt and anger overrode need.

"You think that's all I want from you, Fletcher?" she asked, her tone as dull as her mind when he finally released her. She stepped back, speaking with sadness. "Maybe when we met we misread each other. I saw a man with a lust for life, a direction that was all his own. You looked out from those wonderful eyes of yours and saw the world, not just a part of it, but the whole crazy thing all twirling around in its own special universe. I'd never known anyone who could do that. Now I find that it's the little things that you like to focus in on really.

"The fact that you could get this upset because I forgot our date just shows how wrong I was about you. You haven't found the secret of contentment. You only like people to think you know what it is. You're just as petty and grasping as the next man, only you don't lust after money. You lust after control and it's me you want to control."

"That's unfair and you know it, Char. I don't want to control. I want to share with you equally. I want to share the responsibility for this relationship and the benefits. I just want to love you, Char."

There was the underpinning of a plea in his voice as he reached out to her once more. Looking into her eyes he saw that they were the color

213

of a storm. Not the lovely gray of an April shower sky but the metallic, ashen shade of the sky before it opens up and destroys what's beneath it. But there was no lashing in her voice, no fight, only resignation. She didn't want to be swayed by what he had to say because it was too complicated. To really listen would mean that she would have to make more decisions. Already there were too many.

"I think my assessment was extremely fair. As equitable as your assessment of my motives for loving you. A roll in the hay is the way I think you put it. It's a good thing you don't make your living with words, Fletcher. You'd starve."

Char pulled away from his tentative touch and stood back. The sun caught the thin gold threads that were woven through the cotton dress she wore. The color snapped out, a glittering point of bright beauty in this moment of sorrowful desperation.

"It's time you figure out what you want, Fletcher. You want to be a citizen of the world, then do it up right and don't lay all this pedestrian morality on me. Whatever is bothering you is more than me missing a date, or you finding me having lunch with Ross, or the dent put in your professional reputation. Ross wasn't a threat to you before, but he may be now. At least with Ross I know where I stand. I don't even know what you want anymore. Half the time you sound like you're frustrated and angry

214

with me because you don't think I'm handling the company right. The other half you're begging me to run away and ignore the whole shebang so we can sit on an island and make love. What exactly is it you want, Fletcher? Give me a clue and I'll try to make it happen. But don't expect me to guess. Don't expect me to take the time to figure it out for you. I don't have that kind of time anymore. My life's changed. Maybe the problem is yours hasn't."

Fletcher looked down at her. He had never loved her better nor been more afraid for their love than now.

"You're right on both counts. Your life has changed immeasurably. Mine hasn't because I choose for it not to change further. Making room in my life for you was the only change I wanted. Then CB Designs took off and I was happy for you because you had dreamed of it so long. You see, I thought all this success and all this money would enhance the things I loved about you and enrich our life together. I thought we would simply go on as we were but with a heightened perspective, a new lease on our creativity. I never imagined all this would make you calculating and selfish. You're different, Char. If you can't see it, I know you can feel it.

"When was the last time you sketched? The last time you had an inspiration? When was the last time the mere feel of fabric sent you into ecstasy? I remember when you used to unroll bolt after bolt of fabric just for the sheer pleasure of feeling it. Now all a bolt of fabric is to you is a wholesale statistic, a pattern thought out to appeal to the lowest common denominator, not designed with ultimate artistry in mind."

Fletcher half turned from her and ran his hand through his hair as he searched for the words that would make her understand how he felt, how useless his presence in her life seemed to be, and how little regard she had for the importance of his.

"Char, if that's the kind of change you had in mind — selling out for cash and fame — then I'm afraid we are further apart than even I thought we were."

"Fletcher," Char said sadly, "you can't see the forest for the trees. You sound so godlike, standing there telling me how I'm losing my creative soul. Well, I'm here to tell you I'm doing no such thing. I am being a responsible businesswoman. I have employees to worry about, a new company to ground. You may have forgotten what that kind of responsibility entails. It's been a while since you've been responsible for anything other than getting the next roll of film to the developer.

"I'm not walking away from this the way you did your company, and I'm not going to spout off about creativity. What I am going to do is make a go of CB Designs. You see, I still believe in dreams and when they come true, I don't want to wake up."

"That's funny. I felt the same way, only I guess I was dreaming about the wrong thing. I was dreaming about loving you and mutual respect and a meeting of mind and soul and body that comes along once in a lifetime. I was dreaming about loving you forever."

"Oh, stop, Fletcher," Char begged. She felt tears in the back of her throat. He looked so sincere, so hurt, so lost. It was almost too much to bear. But Char wasn't going to be swayed. He was talking about control and she was talking about growing. "We're not communicating. We're not going to resolve this in the parking lot of a restaurant. I'm sorry I forgot about our date. But that's all I did. I didn't hurt you, I didn't go out of my way to make you feel left out or forgotten. It was an honest mistake and I think we better leave it at that for now. I've got to get back to the factory. Let me work the rest of the afternoon and we'll talk tonight, okay?"

"Sure. Whatever."

Fletcher shoved his hands in his pockets. He could feel the clench of his jaw, the tightness behind his eyes. He wanted to cry out just to hear the sound of his own frustration. He hated uncertainty, hated the fact that he was not in control—not of Char—but of his own emotions and his own destiny. He needed to get away from her to sort out what he was feeling. Then her hand was on his arm, her long fingers tightening just a bit, as if trying to reassure him he would not be alone. But he knew she was already walking away.

"I'll call as soon as I get home. Unless you'd like to . . ."

"No. That's fine. I'll talk to you later. I've got to go."

Raising a hand, he laid it on the side of her face. It felt so small to him, the high ridge of her cheekbones, the length of her jaw. He let his thumb glide over her lips and saw that she pursed them as though to kiss his finger before thinking better of it.

Without another word, he let his hand drop and left. He didn't want to see her leave. He didn't want to see the beautiful little white car or the way she held the wheel as though she had been born to such luxury. Fletcher didn't want to see the sun shine on Coronado or another woman in her daytime diamonds.

Turning south, he headed to the beach, slipped out of his shoes and ripped off his shirt. Then Fletcher Hawkins began to run. He ran the length of beach, the cold water lapping at his flying feet, until he veered away, exhausted, and trudged up the deep sandhill to his apartment. By the time he was inside, he knew exactly what he had to do. It was the only thing that could save them.

Showering quickly, Fletcher felt the load on his heart lighten. The moment he was dressed he

218

picked up the phone and dialed Char's apartment, knowing she wouldn't be there. He couldn't hear her voice, nor could he talk to her yet. He was leaving. Not running away, only looking for answers. He didn't know when he would be back. He left the message on her machine.

"Mais non! I do not accept that!"

Pilar paced the length of the boutique's back room without thinking, just as she had done each day for the last two weeks. Five steps one way, three the other, veer slightly to the right on the way back to skirt the worktable where the seamstress's sewing machine silently waited for a bit of work. But there would be none. The seamstress had been gone a month, the work a bit longer.

"I want to talk to George, *tout de suite.* He cannot be so busy that the phone cannot be picked up. I must have another few pieces from him to fill out my selection of sweaters."

Pilar listened, rolling her eyes as the woman on the other end of the line gave feeble excuses why George could not possibly ship a small order at the moment. The woman was kind, she was solicitous, her voice dripped honey, and Pilar knew she could not wait to hang up the phone. Well, Pilar would be more than happy to oblige her. With a cry of frustration the tall cocoa-skinned woman slammed down the receiver and fell into the delicate Louis XIV chair. Char had sat in the same chair a few short months ago while Pilar basked in adoration only a room away.

Now the party was over. Inventory was low. There were few customers and even less hope. It was bad. Pilar buried her face in her hands. All this time Vachel had been battling with her and she didn't even know they were at war.

Pilar could hardly remember how it had all begun. A little rumor here, a whisper there. Vachel was unhappy that Pilar's "little venture" was so well received. What on earth did anyone see in her selection of only the most mundane fashions? Pilar had been ungrateful for his help. Hadn't he made her what she was? Yet she carried none of his designs in the boutique the English duchess found so fascinating. It hurt him. It dismayed him. She was disloyal.

Little whispers, small confidences in the right ears and suddenly Pilar noticed that this lady or that had not called when she said she would. This one or that had cancelled a long-standing appointment, sending a note or having her secretary ring. All so civilized. This supplier or that could no longer deliver such a quantity or could not accept Pilar's credit. It must be cash now, one said, a message echoed by another and another. She was new, after all. No track record.

Yet Pilar had thrown back her wild mane of

hair and thought nothing of it. She was Pilar and Paris knew her. Paris loved her. She never thought that Vachel would demand fashionable Paris to choose between them. By the time she understood he was bringing pressure to bear on her suppliers and her customers, it was almost too late. But not quite. Vachel liked nothing more than to be made to feel grand, and Pilar was not above a bit of play-acting.

So she sent him a note and he responded. Come to dinner at the chateau, he insisted. We shall talk over old times, he cooed. Pilar held her tongue until, dressed in silver lace and black velvet, she sat at his table ready to say whatever it was he wanted to hear, ready to beg to be released from the prison of his vengeance.

"So," the great couturier said sweetly just after dinner and while the brandy warmed. "It has been too long, Pilar. How is it with you?"

"Ah, Vachel, you know better than I. I think you've been playing games with me, only you didn't tell me the rules." Vachel's eyebrow lifted in mock surprise. He was amused beyond his wildest hopes by Pilar's ignorance.

"What would I know of you, Pilar? Since you left me, I have only been working harder than ever. Have you seen Larrisa, my protegée? She is so fair. Her blond hair is a marvelous contrast to my fall line, don't you agree?"

"She's lovely, Vachel. Truly. I'm happy you've found someone to give you inspiration again,"

221

Pilar answered cautiously. She had seen that look in Vachel's eyes often when she was the favored one. It was the look she hated, the one that entered his eyes when he wished to hurt for the pleasure of causing pain. "But, Vachel, I don't think you remember well. *Mon Dieu,* it was you who released me from my contract, was it not?"

"Darling, how on earth could you remember it that way? You left me. First your soul, then your body. I saw you looking bored when you were fit. You were no longer impressed with my genius. For that I could not forgive you, Pilar. Without you body and soul I was drowning, there was no inspiration until Larrisa. Now I can go on. My collection is better than it ever was. I am grateful you left me. I am grateful you have given me another chance to be magnificent."

Pilar had heard enough. He was playing cat-and-mouse, his silly little game that had driven her to distraction over the last year they were together. She may have been a foolish child, ready to adore him, when he first singled her out from all the mannequins at his disposal, but she had grown in knowledge and sophistication. Now Pilar saw him for what he was: a self-serving, self-possessed egomaniac. Let others fall at his feet. She would not do it any longer.

"Then," she pondered, "if you are so grateful to me, why is it that you are wasting your precious time making sure my little shop must die a thousand deaths? Why is it, Vachel, one so great has an interest in something so small?"

The hateful glint in the little man's eyes deepened. In his hand he held a silver fork with which he would delicately coax the garlicky *escargots* from their shells. Considering the way the polished surface shone under the light from the candelabra, Vachel seemed to also consider his answer carefully. He spoke without looking at her for a few moments.

"You were so bright, Pilar. Such a gem in my collection. Never had I seen my garments transformed the way they were on you. You gave them life, a reason for being other than simply the beauty of the cut or the fabric. And everyone adored you. Everyone. No one has ever adored me. My talent yes, but I know I am not cared for."

He raised his eyes to her as though it were a great favor.

"Actually, I have no desire to be loved, only recognized and appreciated for what I am. Yet it was you who became more the symbol of Vachel than I. I couldn't have that. You had to leave my runway, my life. This silliness with your boutique on Saint-Honore. Well." He shrugged, put the fork down on the linen tablecloth, and tented his fingers, resting his chin on them, looking daggers at her now. "It was nothing to me at first. Then I saw your name. I heard about you. I heard the praise for you—your taste, your style, your wit. You were on everyone's lips. You and that hovel you held up as a salon of elegance. It was so ridiculous, really. But I needed to know that it was still I who controlled you. I who had the power. Even just a bit.

"So I called here and there. I made inquiries. Sometimes it is best for those who make the style not to jump too quickly into a new venture, to allow our names to be linked with that which will not last."

"But your name was not linked with mine, Vachel," Pilar reminded him. Her shoulders remained squared and strong, her eyes never wavered from his. He would never know that she was afraid in front of his sentence of failure.

"That, too, was a mistake, Pilar. Perhaps had you asked. Only inquired, mind you, whether I would deign to offer one or two of my garments . . ."

Pilar was up now, throwing her lace trimmed napkin onto the table. It was cold in the cavernous dining room of the sixteenth-century villa Vachel called home, but she was warm with indignation.

"You talk out of both sides of your mouth, Vachel. You wanted me to keep my name separate from yours, you wanted me to beg you show your gowns in my shop. You must make up your mind what it is you want. You must give me an opportunity to strike back."

"I will give you nothing, darling," he answered, leaning back, lounging in his velvet covered chair. "I don't want you any longer. I thought I did, but I was wrong. I only want you out of my way. They took to you so quickly, didn't they? All the fawning people of the press, all the ladies with the money. Even the duchess. It must have been exciting for a moment. But it's over now. Paris still understands where the power is, and it isn't behind the pretty face of a shopkeeper."

"There are other designers, Vachel," Pilar whispered, "who do not fear you."

He laughed. "Not like me, Pilar. Not like Yves or any number of others who I can sway with a phone call. I would suggest that it is time you looked for a wealthy husband to take care of you. I will never let you manage on your own. Never."

Pilar let her eyes wander over the exquisite room in which she found herself. She had been there so often, laughing, talking, alone with Vachel as well as surrounded by people who, when they moved, made the fashion world tremble. She had been so impressed to be loved by this talented man — not in the way a lover would, but as a man who respected her talent and her bearing. She had been thrilled to be the most beautiful of the beautiful. Now she saw it all for what it was.

Vachel, so much talent yet no obsession with

his craft. That had been lost long ago. He created now for power and money. He designed for anyone who could pay his fee. He befriended anyone who thought him godlike. Thank the Lord she was no longer a young girl but a woman who could challenge him.

"You are a sad man, Vachel," was all Pilar said. Regally she turned to leave. Just before she walked through the doorway, she heard him say, "And you are a stupid woman, Pilar. You are alone." Pilar chose not to acknowledge him, she chose not to turn back.

Now she sat isolated, unmoving, remembering the hopelessness of that night, remembering the days and weeks that followed. Vachel had been right. Her admirers had fallen away like petals of a dying flower. The customers still came—some of them—looking for something new, looking for advice. But what could she give them? Dresses that had hung too long against the wall? Belts and scarves that were no longer seasonable? She must write Char again. It was so difficult to get her on the phone. She was so busy. Perhaps Char could . . .

All thoughts of Char and Vachel and her problems were curtailed when Pilar realized the small light announcing a client had brightened and was blinking at her to get up and attend to business. Quickly she brushed at the tears that had appeared so suddenly. She sniffed and drew herself up to her full height, then glanced in the

226

mirror, assuring herself that she was Pilar, she was the last word in fashion. Bravely she smiled, first at her reflection, then wider as she rounded the corner and stepped into the showroom to greet the gentleman who was examining the window display. With one quiet, tremulous breath, Pilar composed herself.

"Monsieur. Vous désirez?"

Turning toward her, the man spoke, "If that means, can I help you?, the answer is I certainly hope so."

"Fletcher Hawkins," Pilar cried, just before she threw herself into his arms.

Chapter Eleven

"Vous êtes une super nana."

Pilar laughed, a healthy, happy laugh as she winked at the man who threw the compliment her way. Her hair, a riotous black halo that fell to her shoulders and beyond, caught the breeze as she watched him go. She let the laughter fade to a giggle, caught her hair, and wrapped it in a rope over her shoulder. Breaking off a piece of her warm *baguette,* she offered it to Fletcher. He accepted without coaxing. Munching thoughtfully on the crisp crusted morsel, he watched the late afternoon shoppers head home.

"What'd he say?" Fletcher nodded to the fast disappearing lothario between mouthfuls.

Pilar chuckled again. The loaf was almost gone, the breeze was chilly even for May, but she didn't care. Sitting above the Seine on the cool concrete balustrade with a friend while busy Parisians milled about was the best medicine in the world.

"He said I am a fabulous babe," she answered with a haughty toss of her head.

"Well, he's got that right. I'm not sure I agree with the poetry of his observation though. What ever happened to French as the language of love?"

"Before love there is always lust," Pilar reminded him, holding up the last piece of bread. Fletcher shook his head and rested his elbows on his thighs, letting his clasped hands dangle between his legs. Pilar popped the last of the *baguette* into her mouth, chewing pensively as she let the silence between them lengthen. Fletcher was a comfortable man to be silent with, so this was no hardship.

"I feel terrible that you closed up shop, Pilar. You didn't have to do that because of me," Fletcher said finally.

"But it is a holiday when you come all this way to see me, Fletcher." Pilar rearranged her swing coat, paying particular attention to the way it swept out behind her. Once a mannequin, always a mannequin, she supposed. The diversion, in any event, was far preferable to answering any more of Fletcher's questions. He had noticed the lack of inventory, accepting but not thoroughly believing her explanation that a new shipment was due. Better she take advantage of his rather evident misery. For certainly she could see such pain in his eyes when he first looked at her. She swore she could feel the jagged edges of

229

his heart as they embraced. "But I don't think you have come all this way just to see how I am doing."

Fletcher shook his head. "You're right, of course. Not that Paris doesn't hold a greater allure since I've met you."

Pilar inclined her head. "You are too kind, *monsieur.*"

"I am too selfish, mademoiselle," Fletcher answered honestly. He swung his head toward her, considering how beautiful she was with the late afternoon spring sun bathing her in its golden light. But she was not beautiful enough for him to forget Char.

Each time he thought of Paris, he thought only of his love for Char Brody. It was here that Fletcher realized his heart could not feel, or his mind think, or his soul exist without Char as the focal point of his psyche and emotions. She was open and honest in a world too often inaccessible and corrupt. There was nothing hidden in Char and that was what he loved. He wanted her and he was afraid he was losing her. This woman beside him was the only one he knew to turn to for help. With a deep sigh he put his hands on his thighs while he considered the sidewalk. There was no other way to put this than simply.

"Pilar, things aren't going well, and I've come to you hoping you can show me the way to make them right. You see, I want from you the one thing I can't seem to do myself. I want you to make things clear for me. I hate being confused. More than that, I hate the fact that I don't have a clue how to fix what's wrong because I can't see the problem clearly."

"Char," Pilar said simply.

"Could it be anything else?" Fletcher held out his hands in the sign of helplessness all men understood and all women found charming.

"She is not doing well with the company?" Pilar held her breath waiting for the answer. If Char was faltering, then she could not be Pilar's savior. All would be lost.

"On the contrary. She's doing fabulously well. She's delivering on time to the largest stores in the United States. She's hitting every market except toddlers, I think. A perfume company has approached her about licensing, as well as a firm that manufactures handbags. Char's making money hand over fist and things are awful—between us, I mean."

"I didn't know," Pilar muttered, trying to find a middle ground in her heart where she could feel for Fletcher yet rejoice that Char was doing so well.

"Which didn't you know about, us or the company?" Fletcher asked with a little laugh.

"About either," Pilar answered. "I haven't spoken to Char in a very long while, Fletcher."

"I know, you've been awfully busy, too . . ." His voice trailed off as though to say he wasn't really expecting much help, only moral support.

"Non. Mais non, mon ami," Pilar assured him, clutching his arm. It hurt her heart to think of him being as alone as she. She understood how abandoned one could feel. "I'm only saying I haven't spoken to Char. I have left messages, but maybe she didn't receive them. She is so busy, and now she does not even answer her own phone like in the old days. So much for her to do. She is pulled this way and that."

Fletcher shook his head in disgust. "She's not that busy, Pilar, that she can't pick up the phone and talk to you. Nor is she so busy that she can't show me a bit of consideration once in a while. I feel like I've turned my world upside down for her, yet she can't find a moment to nurture what we were building. I photographed her, thinking she was an interesting subject, a woman I would enjoy being with. Then I fell in love with her, dammit, and it was so wonderful. She became my world. But how does she express affection for me? Or you for that matter? We're put off until her highness is good and ready to make time for us. What it really boils down to is that Char isn't thinking about anything but CB Designs. She's got tunnel vision."

Pilar, surprised by his outburst at first, found herself smiling gently as she wound her arm around Fletcher's shoulders and moved closer.

"Fletcher, you sound like a little boy whose mama hasn't enough time to make him cookies.

232

Is it that she doesn't have time to love you, or is it something else?"

Fletcher felt his shoulders sag. She had hit the nail on the head. It was something else and on the long flight to France he had defined the problem. He just wasn't sure he was ready to verbalize it to himself or to Pilar. All he wanted was to be reassured that Char's behavior was reprehensible, that his hurt feelings were absolutely called for. Unfortunately Pilar was not going to jump on his bandwagon. Now that he'd sought her out, it was going to be tough to take his toys and go home if she didn't want to play his way.

"You want to walk, Pilar?"

Fletcher hopped off the balustrade and held his hands out. Her slender body slipped into his, yet he thought only of Char. Chemistry was a crazy thing, but thankfully that was the one thing Fletcher could accept without question. Then Pilar was on her feet, easing her hand under the crook of his arm, offering him nothing more than a friendly ear and the European perspective on love and life. He was grateful and he intended to take full advantage of her wisdom. They strolled down the boulevard toward Notre Dame. The cathedral loomed ahead, the ultimate symbol of authority and faith. Fletcher nodded toward the buttressed edifice.

"You think maybe He's got the answer to my problem?"

Pilar laughed and shrugged, "I do not know what the problem is, but I doubt you will have to bother Him to find the answer."

"You're probably right. It's just so hard to explain what I'm feeling. Mood swings. Like the problem sometimes doesn't exist at all, then the next minute this difficulty seems to be all-encompassing. One minute I'm mad, the next I just want to take her in my arms and love her. I hate that part of it. Not being able to even decide what's really wrong between Char and me, or whether it's me or her to blame. I want it all to be her fault, this pulling away, this constant bickering. She can't even remember a lunch date because her life is a constant corporate crisis."

Fletcher stuck his hands deep in his pockets and raised his face to the breeze. His black hair blew away from his face. He was, indeed, a handsome man. His eyes closed for a moment, then fastened on the ground at his feet as he continued.

"Every time I turn around, Ross is hitting her up with some new financial mumbo jumbo and Char's buying into it. The guy is just putting the moves on. I know a startup is time consuming, but it takes on a life of its own. If Char has to single-handedly create the company, then it wasn't meant to be. She doesn't need to be worrying about most of the stuff Ross insists needs her personal attention. Sure she's expanding fast, but given the talent she's hired and as long as

234

her cash flow is decent, she's okay."

Fletcher put his free hand to his forehead as though trying to list his grievances in the proper order. Pilar tightened her lips to keep from laughing. Fletcher was so much a man, all complaints because he wasn't the center of attention. Certainly he should be, but Char was only doing what anyone would in the same situation. She was being overwhelmed. The next moment, Fletcher was launching into another criticism, so Pilar looked seriously at him, giving him her full attention.

"And why isn't she designing more? Qualified people have been hired to oversee shipping the garments, showing the collections, manufacturing. Fiscal esoteric idiocy is not her forte. If she can't provide the product at the same level that brought her to the attention of the world, she might as well chuck it. Nobody's going to care about her balance sheet if she's recycling the same styles two seasons in a row. I've been there. I know. Hell, I didn't worry about a huge factory or decorating offices. I didn't hire fancy executives until my company was grossing over twenty mil."

Pilar tapped his arm, taking on the role of devil's advocate to keep Fletcher from getting carried away. "And you don't think there is a difference between the fashion and the computer, Fletcher? Perhaps Char thinks there is an image she must make already to help her business. So

235

she designs offices and makes big business to keep people interested. Mystery is part of the equation."

Fletcher shook his head like a father absolutely refusing to believe his sixteen-year-old daughter had made a valid point. "If she just keeps doing what she does best, she'll be fine. But Lord, Pilar, the woman is acting like she's president of AT&T. It's all so ludicrous."

Fletcher walked a step or two ahead. Pilar dillydallied behind. In the center of the plaza a group of tourists listened intently as their guide talked about the extended construction of Notre Dame. They were as rapt in their attention to the guide as Fletcher was self-absorbed in his thoughts of Char. When Pilar reached him, her hands were dug deep into her pockets, a frown marred the lovely planes of her face. There was so much she wanted to tell him, but she wasn't at all sure he was ready to listen.

She wanted to shake her finger at him, tell him to go home and help Char, love her no matter what. Success was a wonderful thing compared to seeing all your hopes snatched away by a vindictive little man. Wasn't her life the one that had turned upside down now? Her money was running out, suppliers wouldn't ship to her and Vachel would not be completely happy until he saw Pilar reduced to begging. That was something to worry about, not whether an office was decorated, or Char wished to play the executive,

236

or she forgot to go to lunch, or she had meetings with Ross. But Pilar said none of these things because she loved Char and understood that first blush of victory.

When Vachel fell at her feet begging her to show exclusively for him, when she was the eighteen-year-old toast of Paris and all the fashion world, hadn't she forgotten her manners just a bit? Hadn't she spent money like water and never once worried that it would all end someday? Hadn't she thought only of herself and not of hurting the feelings of her friends? Maybe what Char was doing was the right thing, worrying about her future, though Fletcher thought she was only making herself important. And perhaps there was something else to all this, too. She cast a sidelong glance at Fletcher and moved up closer.

Seeing his handsome troubled face, Pilar decided not to tell him of her own misfortunes. Together they would make such a sad pair that she would cry, and she didn't know him well enough to do such an intimate thing. But this she did know. Fletcher was a good man with a giving, hurting heart. Yet he was full of pride and wouldn't admit that he might be at fault, too. So he stood behind the wall of his reason and righteousness.

But wasn't that the way with men. Just as it was the way with women to cling to the one thing they fear to lose and ignore the one thing they should be protecting. Pilar sighed. Looking at the setting sun she thought it would be nice to sit in the nave of Notre Dame and say a small prayer for herself and for Char and Fletcher, too.

Knowing there would be plenty of time for that, Pilar moved that final step closer and spoke to Fletcher softly. His head was bent so that he could hear her, but he looked as though he was listening for his absolution. Though gentle, Pilar would not be completely generous.

"Fletcher, my friend," she began, "you are being too hard on Char. She has done nothing all the rest of us have not done, *non?* She is excited. She is frightened. She looks for help but she wants to make all the decisions herself. It is like having a baby. The baby cries and drives the mama crazy, but the mama does not want anyone to walk the baby through the night but her. She will be the only one to raise the child. So, if the child turns out good, the mama can say with pride that she made it possible; if the child turns out bad, the mama takes the blame on her shoulders. You cannot condemn Char for taking care of her new baby. Sometimes the mama forgets the other people she loves. But that is natural, *oui?*"

"Pilar . . ." Fletcher laughed gently, taken off guard by her unusual approach to problem solving. She held up her hand. It was her turn to speak.

"But there is more, Fletcher? You know it is not all Char that bothers you. What is it inside, Fletcher, that makes you so angry?"

Asked so directly, Fletcher realized how ashamed he was of the true problem, his failing. But Pilar was a woman he instinctively trusted, one he wanted to be his friend for years to come. And so he confessed.

"I'm jealous, Pilar. I think I'm actually jealous of her and it's driving me nuts. I love what I do with the camera. At times I believe I'm making a contribution to humanity. I know that what I leave behind will be a permanent record of events that affect the history of this world, even if I'm photographing the faces I find in the ghetto. Each person, each face, means so much and tells a story in its own right. But business, the life it takes on, that's something fabulous to be a part of."

Fletcher chuckled, as though embarrassed to admit he could still get a thrill out of something he had so adamantly pushed out of his life.

"I thought I was beyond all that but, Lord above, I can feel it in my gut. She's calling the shots and I remember what that was like. It was an incredible power. The world moved forward on your say-so. It stopped because you held up your hand. I find myself wanting to be a part of it all again, but she's shutting me out. I resent the fact that Char has to work at all this. It should be second nature, all those decisions she has to make. There should be an excitement about Char's life, not perpetual tension."

Fletcher sighed and smiled, contentedly reliving those wonderful days.

"Funny how I remember the beginning so well, but I can't remember what it felt like to have it all end. I guess I don't remember the end because by then I didn't even recognize my own company or my product. I was the CEO. I was the chairman of the board. I sat in an ivory tower and people gave me money. My contribution had ended years earlier. I didn't make anything anymore, not really." He shrugged, remembering now the frustration of those final months. "Anyway, without that last memory, I crave the beginning again. I want to be in her shoes so bad I can taste it. Or at least I want her to turn to me for advice, not Ross. I'm equally, if not more, qualified than he is to help her. I want her to talk to me, listen to me, take from my experience, and let me be a part of hers."

"But, Fletcher," Pilar cried, "you cannot expect that. You were the one who insisted you left business behind because it was not fulfilling. You were the one who wanted to be something different with your camera. That is how Char met you. That is how she came to know you, as a man disdainful of everything she is running after now. Should she not have believed you? That this kind of life is of no interest? Perhaps

240

she is shy—no, I want to say worried—about bringing you into what is happening to her now. If she tries to make you too much a part of it, perhaps you will leave her the same way you did when it was your own success. Think, Fletcher, what you have told her. You have glorified everything that is not her success. It is hard for her to understand that you want to be a part of hers, *non?*"

Fletcher smiled sheepishly. "Yes, Pilar. It is hard for her, too, and I've been very selfish. I never thought that she might believe I would abandon her, but I can see how you could interpret things that way." He thought for a moment, then took Pilar by the shoulders and kissed both her cheeks warmly. "You are one wise woman, Pilar. If things don't work out with Char, how about you and I get together?"

"Vous êtes resté trop longtemps au soleil aujourd'hui!" She laughed, taking him no more seriously than he took himself. "You have had too much sun today, my friend. No model ever thinks seriously of taking a photographer to her bed."

Fletcher shrugged charmingly. "Then I suppose I must settle for Char."

"You settle for the best," Pilar assured him, her expression solemn.

And though she smiled, Pilar prayed—there in the square in front of Notre Dame—that Fletcher and Char would not be so foolish as to

241

let love slip through their fingers. No work was worth it. No gold, no silver, no material thing that life could provide. It was Pilar's one sadness that she had no one to love her as deeply, to feel as profoundly, as Fletcher loved Char.

But Pilar was a private person, so she did not share with Fletcher her fear, her hope, or her desires. She did what came naturally. She gave him hope, she offered him friendship, and she willed him to love Char well until her friend passed the first blush of success. Soon, she knew, Char would realize it was matters of the heart that truly counted: love, respect, and friendship.

"Come, Fletcher, I am hungry and I am a working girl who cannot afford a wonderful meal. You will buy it for me as payment for my marvelous advice."

"Your wish is my command. Though I hope no one sees me with a shop girl. What on earth would that do to my reputation?"

Fletcher teased her, taking her hand and putting it securely under his arm. Pilar tried to join in his laughter, but her chuckle was as half-hearted as her appetite. A shop girl is what she seemed destined to be if help was not forthcoming soon. Maybe before Fletcher left she would confide in him and ask his help.

Looking askance at her handsome escort, though, Pilar knew she would not impose upon him. His heart hung in the balance, and now he believed the scales were tipping in his favor. She would no more burden him with her worries than she would suggest the world would end before he lay in Char's arms again. How she hoped those arms were welcoming.

Putting on the face of the model, the face that showed no care, Pilar decided she would forget her troubles for just one night. Perhaps if Fletcher had good luck, it would follow her too. Bravely she matched his pace and banished her fears. She was Pilar and Paris loved her. Would that she were Char and had one man like Fletcher to love her.

The sun was incredibly warm. Char knew it had been a mistake to stretch out on the white cushioned lounge, but she couldn't resist. Ross had left her to wander on her own while he talked to the real estate agent. When Ross first suggested an outing, she had protested and squirmed and complained that the sample fittings for casualwear would take up most of her day. But her objections only seemed to make Ross more determined to whisk her away to parts unknown.

So while they zoomed away from Coronado toward Corona del Mar in his glistening Jaguar, while they listened to Vivaldi on the impeccable stereo system, Char filled him in on Robinson's offer of floor space to create a CB Designs boutique if she promised exclusivity for at least two years. She mentioned that she'd been approached to do a special line for one of the top catalogue retailers in the U.S. She pointed out that the rate of returns on merchandise had dropped in the last three weeks and productivity had risen substantially since implementing the new boxing system. She was so absorbed in her tales and the fabric samples she had brought with her, she didn't notice Ross grinning from ear to ear as he applied a bit more pressure to the gas pedal and the car flew down the road with exquisite abandon.

When they finally reached their destination, Char was unable to decide whether she was peeved with Ross's frivolity or pleased that he was forcing her away from the factory for a while. She settled on pleased. It wasn't as though she had anyone else to make her feel special.

Fletcher hadn't called after leaving the message on her machine. It was now five days after that silly mix-up at the restaurant. He was acting like a child and she missed him desperately. Preferring not to admit that to herself, Char decided to do as the song said and love — or at least enjoy the company of — the one she was with.

"What is this?" Stepping out of the Jaguar, flashing Ross a grin over the top of the car, Char looked around.

"This is your surprise. All work, Char, is not a good thing in your life. Even I have my boat and my cars. You need something to run away to. You also need to get out of that horrid little apartment and start living like the woman of means that you are. Come on, let me show you."

Hand in hand they walked up the shallow flight of stairs toward a magnificently appointed stucco home. Painted bright white, it sat above the ocean like one of the marvelous houses that dotted the hills of the French Riviera. She remembered a beautiful photograph Fletcher had taken of all the white houses . . .

Instantly Char pushed Fletcher out of her mind as she gripped Ross's hand more tightly, listened more intently to what he was saying.

Though not built on a grand scale, the place seemed palatial to Char. Without fanfare Ross opened the front door with the key he had obtained earlier from the agent. The foyer was marble, almost white but for shadowy veins of pink and gray running through it, attesting to the exquisiteness of the quarry from which it came. To her right was a living room boasting a fireplace of the same marble, with moldings that looked as though they had been lovingly reclaimed from an ancient temple and brought into the twentieth century specifically to grace this house.

The picture window in the living room faced west, toward the ocean. Today the sea was sapphire, tipped with diamondlike white caps. From a certain corner Char could even see the pearly froth spilling onto the beach. On the other side of the foyer was the sun room: glass roofed, glass walled, peppered with white rattan furniture pillowed with yellow chintz, the only room in the house that was furnished. There was a kitchen that could easily feed a party of four hundred, all the appliances stainless steel, oversized and spotlessly clean. Here the countertops were black granite. Above the cooking island hung copper pots of every shape and size. A maid's room and bath completed the ground floor.

Up the gracefully curving stairwell, Char found herself on a wide landing, illuminated by natural light coming through a huge leaded glass window above her. To her right was a guest room and bath, beautifully appointed in shades of green and peach. And to her left was a haven for her. Just for her and—well, Fletcher. She could no more imagine herself in the elegant master suite alone than she could imagine CB Designs existing without her.

Char smiled in appreciation as she ran her hand over the fine wood of the chair rail, then looked past the French doors and the wide balcony to the ocean. The lighting was recessed and the room huge. Through a wide hall there were two huge walk-in closets and the bathroom. Oh, the bathroom.

Along one wall ran a mirror that seemed to *be* the wall. Two hand painted pedestal sinks

246

gleamed in the dim light. The tub was claw footed, reminiscent of a French hip bath but deeper, richer, more modern in its indulgence. It sat in a glass room all by itself, swelling out like a balloon from the main room. Plants were everywhere: palms and dracaenas, ficus and orchids. Char knew that, lying back in sweet scented water, she would find herself transported to another world, another planet. A place where only she and Fletcher . . .

"What do you think?"

Char's lids fluttered open. She'd closed them during her daydream. Instinctively her hand covered those that held her shoulders. But the skin was too soft, the fingers not as long as she remembered, the voice all wrong. Looking over her shoulder she blinked, then chuckled. It wasn't Fletcher at all but Ross who had touched her and now pulled her back close to him. She smiled and shrugged.

"I think this is stupendous. I can't even imagine what this place must cost."

"That's going to bother you?"

"Ross, give me a break. You know I'm putting almost everything I'm making back into the company—salaries, equipment, inventory. I can't afford a place like this."

Ross twirled her around to face him and whispered through his lovely smile, "Don't be absurd. You could afford ten places like this. You're going to need the write-off. Start thinking the way a millionaire should, Char. Your life has changed. Let this," he tapped her head, "catch up with it."

Char grimaced, shrugging away from him. "Ross, this isn't a game, you know. This is my life, and I don't want it to all just disappear because I become overindulgent. Maybe I should wait for something like this. The car was enough. I . . ."

She let her objection trail off as she wandered about the master bedroom. Of course she could see herself living here. It had taken awhile, but now Char was really beginning to believe she was rich. Her new prosperous attitude was evident in the way she ordered fabric for the new lines, the way she ordered dinner, the way she bought a bracelet or a necklace or a ring without even looking at the price tag. She even moved through life differently.

There was a confidence in her voice when she spoke to buyers or reporters that had never been there before. She used to rely on her individuality, her good-naturedness to endear herself to these people. Now they sought her favor. Her old clients treated her as though she had always been a part of their set. There were invitations to dinner, lunch, tennis. In a house like this she could easily reciprocate. A place like this would be great for public relations. She could be written up in *Architectural Digest, Town and Country*. Char envisioned the parties she would throw.

Elegant and unusual, they would be the epitome of creative entertaining. And there would be quiet dinners she and Fletcher would enjoy on the balcony outside the bedroom—if he ever came back.

Without realizing it, Char walked out of the bedroom and down the stairs. She didn't even check to see if Ross was following. She wandered through the house. How on earth could she think about buying this place? Circumstances could change so quickly. Look how her life had been turned topsy-turvy in the last few months, not to mention the last week.

One day she was a good designer with a small clientele, the next she was the toast of the fashion world. One day she was seriously considering settling down with Ross, the next she was loving a man so unique she had to touch him to make sure he was real. Then *he* was gone. Leaving a message, hopping a plane and she didn't even know where it was he had taken himself off to.

Leaning on the railing of the veranda, Char looked over the side and saw the white tiled pool, the huge overstuffed lounges. That island of tranquility beckoned to her and she was powerless to resist. Suddenly she was tired of it all: making decisions, loving Fletcher, having him leave, wondering if her new collection would be well received, fielding Carol's persistent complaints about the original staff's treatment, living

249

up to Ross's expectations. It was all too much. So Char slipped onto the lounge, put her feet up, and tried to banish the one horrible emotion that seemed never to leave her anymore.

Not concern, not apprehension, but unadulterated fear. Only Ross seemed to have the power to ease her mind, to make her feel safe within her company as he advised her every step of the way. When they conferred, she felt in complete control. Never once did he question her ability or her commitment. He understood how money worked. If Ross said the world was right, then she clung to that assurance. Closing her eyes, Char let the sun ease her mind and warm her body, and that was where Ross found her twenty minutes later.

He announced himself with a kiss on her lips. It was light and wonderful and Char smiled, feeling attractive. She hadn't felt that way for so long.

"Taking liberties, are we?" She asked lazily as he sat down beside her. She opened her eyes, hardly able to see Ross for the blinding sun behind him.

"I thought they might be in order. If I'm the one who has introduced you to your Shangri-la, then I deserve a reward. I choose a kiss."

"Then, sir, I shall happily bestow it on you. I do think this might be my Shangri-la indeed."

Closing her eyes, Char waited for his lips to brush hers again. They did, for an instant. But

Ross decided he wasn't being given enough. He took her in his arms and kissed her without gentleness or hesitation. His arms wound around her back as he pulled her into him. Char's arms flew to his neck, more from the surprise of being pulled up than from passion. Ross chose to read something more into her reaction. He was lost in the feel of her, the warmth of her lips, the smell of sun in her hair and on her skin. His lips parted, his tongue darted between her lips and that was when Char decided enough was enough. She pushed back, her hands on his shoulders. With a gentle but insistent pressure, she held him away, still feeling the imprint of his lips on hers.

"Ross?" She asked quietly.

"Char, come on. It's not like we don't know each other," he insisted. "In fact, we've known each other a good long time. Too long for game-playing."

"Ross, I'm not playing games with you. I thought it had become extremely clear that I'm committed to Fletcher. You and I, we've only seen each other on a professional basis for months. I don't really understand what brought this on."

"Then I don't think you've taken the time to really look at yourself lately. Char, you're no more in love with Fletcher Hawkins than I am. He was a distraction. He fulfilled the side of you that was completely and utterly romantic. Face it, you're so much more than a sketch pad or a model for your own designs. That creativity of yours has spread itself over every aspect of your life. You design, you market, you manage. Char, don't you see? This was the missing link between us. All those months we went out, I knew you were very special to me, but for some reason I held back telling you. And it was because I felt there was something lacking."

Ross leaned back, holding himself erect while he considered her. Indeed she had changed. There was a beauty to her that hadn't existed before, a sharpness in face and form that was so alluring. She was like a runner pared down to muscle, every ounce of fat shed, so that she could run lean and mean. He smiled.

"Remember how we used to be able to leave each other without looking back? We were so casual. Now I can't fathom not being with you all the time. And, whether you want to admit it or not, I think it's the same with you. I'm always in your mind. Admit it, Char. You feel something bigger between us now. You've outgrown Fletcher. It's plain to see."

Char pushed herself up as she slung her legs over the side of the lounge. Her short skirt rode higher on her slender thighs. Ross reached out and touched her bare skin. She covered his hand with hers and closed her eyes, trying to find out if she felt what he said she did.

Yes, there by this exquisite pool, under a perfect sky, she couldn't deny he meant something to her. But what? Was it a serious emotional tie, or the contentment of convenience? Had she just stepped out of the clouds and into the real world where respect passed for love and affection for passion? Was an interest in making money, in being successful, the overriding reason to make a commitment?

Char stood up, letting Ross's hand slide away from her body. She felt him move on the lounge, she knew he was watching her. Was it his eyes that made her temperature rise, or did the sun blaze hotter for a moment? Was the weakness in her knees a delayed reaction from his touch, or was she trembling with a need to be away? Heaven help her, but she had no answers to those questions. The only true feeling she had was one of panic. Too many people wanted too much from her. The suppliers, the press, her employees, Fletcher, and now Ross. If what he said was true, at least one faction of her life would be settled. There would be no more worrying about love. Maybe Ross could do that for her. Maybe then she could stop racing just to keep pace with all the offers coming her way. She could slow down, feel at peace again. Maybe with Ross she could learn how to stop being afraid of losing everything because of her inexperience. He would be a business partner, a partner for life . . .

Suddenly her thoughts were interrupted by the

now familiar subdued ring of Ross's cellular phone. Glancing over her shoulder, she saw his ardor replaced with his "business" face. He almost seemed happier for it, or, at least, more like himself. Char smiled to herself while he gave his full attention to the call, then reluctantly held the phone toward her.

"Carol. For you." Char stepped toward him, took it, and turned her back, preferring the view of nature to that of the pool — and Ross.

"Hi, Carol. What is it?"

She listened. Then she felt it. Now she knew Ross couldn't have been more wrong if he tried. Char could no more love him than she could create a gown out of thin air. Inside her, in that place only the most beloved can touch, Char felt a warmth and a fullness she hadn't felt for a very, very long time. She smiled into the phone as she thanked Carol for tracking her down. She smiled as she folded the little phone together. She tried not to smile when she turned back to Ross, but couldn't help herself as she held out the phone and said:

"He's coming home. Fletcher will be here tomorrow."

Chapter Twelve

"There you are."

Char's voice fluttered over him like a summer quilt tenderly laid over someone on the verge of sleep. The party sounds in the next room had lulled Fletcher to a place far away from reality. Though he wasn't thinking, he knew he was reflecting with the greatest clarity. He wasn't removed from the celebration, yet he was not a part of it.

"You've found me out." Fletcher shrugged, offering a small smile as he held up his brandy balloon and cigar. "I've always wanted to play lord of the manor. Our hostess was kind enough to equip this rather male bastion with all the comforts. I don't know how she's gone through so many husbands if this is the way she treats them. A library all their own right out of a Sherlock Holmes movie. I'd say they walked out on a good thing."

Char lifted Fletcher's crossed feet, sat on the ottoman, then cradled them in her lap as she settled in. Sitting there in the light of the green shaded library lamp, the two of them looked like a portrait. Fletcher in his tuxedo was too ravishingly handsome for words. Char, her head turned just so, her long neck encased in embroidered lace that crept over the bodice of her white Swiss cotton dress, was a vision from another time. Strange how aware she was of her physical being. She could feel the fabric of her dress lying over her breasts; her hands felt fragile as they rested against the leather of Fletcher's shoes. Char was aware of the new, small lines at the side of her eyes, the deepening hallows beneath her cheeks. Slight changes but, oh, so noticeable.

When she looked in the mirror, someone who was "almost Char" looked back at her. The other was so close to the real thing it was frightening. But there was something missing in the reflected Char, and real one wasn't at all sure what it was. She prayed Fletcher didn't see the subtle transformation in her. Now that they seemed to be having a second chance, Char wanted everything to be the way it was when they first met. Thankfully the light was flattering and Fletcher seemed so content he wouldn't have noticed if she turned green.

"I'm glad you're enjoying Marge's home. But I don't think the library is the reason she's gone through so many husbands," Char chuckled, abandoning her self-analysis. Not tonight, she promised: no insecurity, no thoughts of work, nothing but enjoyment.

"I suppose you're right."

Fletcher puffed on the cigar, watching the blue smoke waft toward the molded ceiling, concentrating on it until it drifted away to nothingness. Char watched, too, then closed her eyes. She loved the smell of a cigar. There was something so — civilized — about the scent. The brandy, the cigar, a gorgeous man in black tie — the props were perfect, it was the play that was lacking.

Fletcher sat alone, away from the party. An actor refusing to step on the stage. Yet it wasn't his disappearance that annoyed the leading lady. The fact that she had no idea how long he'd been gone bothered her. There had been a time when she anguished over the minutes he left her alone while he poured a glass of wine.

"So," Char sighed, patting the shining patent leather of his bowed evening slippers, "who was it that offended you with their crass display of wealth, their disregard for the beauty of simplicity, or their complete lack of creativity in conversation?"

Fletcher chuckled. "You make me sound awful. Like a crotchety old man who has no patience."

Char raised an eyebrow as though challenging him to change her mind.

"I'm not that awful. I'm not, Char," Fletcher protested but even he knew better. "Okay, I'm a reverse snob. At least I didn't make a scene. I simply slipped out of that 'intimate' little dinner party in there and looked for a quiet place to digest my meal." He was silent for a moment, his eyes riveted on the celebration clipping along in Marge's immense living room. From the leather chair he looked across the walnut paneled library, past the black and white marble tile foyer, and into the high ceilinged living room that would have been called a ballroom in another time. "How does one ever feel comfortable in a place like this when there aren't hundreds of people about?"

Char looked around, her eye appraising the details of the room. "I don't know. I feel quite comfortable. I think it's a lovely place. So beautifully appointed. The craftsmen who built it were really something."

Char looked back to Fletcher and was surprised to find his black eyes clinging to her as though in amazement.

"What?" she demanded, a small, self-conscious laugh escaping her lips.

"It was just nice to hear you talk about craftsmanship," he said. "I expected you to give me an estimate on how much the gilt cost on the moldings."

Char stared at him for a moment, then hung her head, twisting it away from him. He might as well have slapped her. She pushed his feet off her lap and started to stand. But he pulled her back after discarding both cigar and brandy in one swift movement.

"I'm sorry," he whispered, tugging gently at her until she seemed to have no choice but to nestle on his lap in his arms. "I'm sorry. I forgot. No more snide comments. No more sniping at you. It's just this place, this party, and all those people. This isn't us, Char. Remember when we first met? The night we danced? How we laughed at all this? Remember how we were alone among all those people?"

"You have an odd memory, Fletcher," Char mumbled, spreading her long fingers over his chest, adoring the feel of the starched cotton of his shirt and the ripple of the exquisite tucks the designer had incorporated into the design.

"I have a wonderful memory, Char. I remember a fabulous looking woman who decided a solitary view of the ocean was preferable to the crush of well heeled humanity behind her."

"I didn't know many of the people at Jennifer's wedding. I mean, I knew them, but they weren't really friends. I wasn't . . . oh, I don't know."

Char fisted her hand and tapped his chest. How on earth could she explain all this? She was an outsider then. She was a curiosity. A single woman who worked for a living. A woman with style who brought it with her to parties that had, perhaps, become a bit boring.

Now she counted these people as friends. Now she stood toe to toe with them and even, in a way, above most of them. She rivaled their wealth and she had built her fortune single-handedly. Char knew there was more than one woman in the other room who envied her that thrill, that freedom.

But Fletcher would never understand. Fletcher could never fathom why economic similarity, beyond simply liking someone, could be the recipe for a solid relationship. He hadn't lived in a community in a long time. He had no desire to belong the way Char did now. She didn't want it all to disappear now, she didn't want to thumb her nose at this. Char, had lived on the fringes of this for so long that she now, quite simply, wanted it all: Fletcher, wealth, acceptance, and renown. It was a constant surprise that he couldn't see why she wanted to hold onto everything.

Beneath her cheek Fletcher's chest rose and fell with a tremulous sigh. She listened for the beat of his heart and found it. His hand stroked her hair. The silence lengthened, but there was little comfort in it. Char was the first to speak, asking the question she wanted to ask two weeks ago when she met him at the airport. But then they had been too busy touching each other, kissing each other, reaffirming their love for one another.

"Where did you go, Fletcher? Where did you go when you left me?"

Fletcher closed his eyes. He hadn't told her and never meant to. He wanted them to start clean and fresh, as though meeting for the first time. Char had accepted his return without question. He had never been happier than during those first few wonderful days. Now she wanted to know where he had found comfort after the hurt they caused one another. She wanted to know what he had discovered about himself and about her.

"I went to Paris, Char. I went to Pilar."

He felt her smile. She snuggled closer. "Good."

"You're not mad?"

"That's where I would have gone," Char admitted, almost adding, *if I hadn't had so much to do*. But she bit her tongue and hugged him tighter. "And did she tell you I was being an unreasonable child? That you should put me over your knee?"

"Hardly. She told me quite a few things, not the least of which was that I happened to have a few insecurities about all this stuff going on in your life myself."

"It's not stuff," Char objected, raising her head and granting him a glorious smile. She hadn't heard that teasing tone in his voice in so long.

"All right. All this marvelous, high powered success of yours. Basically Pilar suggested I give you rein to enjoy what it is you've earned. She thinks you need time to find out where you belong in this glittering world of money and power . . ."

"And?" Char prodded, poking her finger at his chest playfully when he didn't finish his sentence.

"And she suggested I face up to the fact that I'm a wee bit jealous."

Char's breath caught in her throat, as stunned as she was touched by this confession. She wanted to know it all, every detail of what he was feeling. But for some reason, she held back and didn't press him. Just knowing he didn't blame only her for the tension between them was enough to ease her mind.

"And did you do that?" Char asked.

"Sure. Of course I did." Fletcher answered. "I'm not a saint, Char. I didn't give up what I had all those years ago because I wanted to make a sacrifice. Some would say I didn't give up anything in the long run since I'm sitting on a fortune. I actually loved making things happen. But I left the corporate world because it was dangerous to believe that success really meant I was living. I needed to leave so I wouldn't believe my own press. I wish—"

"There you darlings are! My two most marvelous celebrities!" Marge Hudson's cheery little face poked through the open door, looking even cheerier with the scarlet blush the wine provided. Even from a distance Fletcher could see her blue eyes sparkling like two well polished diamonds. "Come along, then. This party is for you, Char. Everyone's been asking where you are. And, Fletcher, there are a few of the ladies who would love to talk to you about their pictures in that article you did on all of us. I think they want to know where they can get prints. You're so wonderful with a camera. But it's time to join the party. Come now . . . I won't take no for an answer."

"We'll be there in a minute, Marge," Fletcher said, but Char was already on her feet.

"We're coming now, Marge," Char called with a little wave before turning to Fletcher. "She's right. This is supposed to be for me. I should be out there. Besides, this is not the time to alienate my best customers. Come on, Fletcher, straighten your tie, come and have fun."

"I'll be out as soon as I finish the brandy," Fletcher said quietly. Char smiled even as she walked toward Marge, taking her hostess's outstretched hand.

She looked over her shoulder one last time and asked, "You won't be long?"

Shaking his head, he watched her disappear, happily swallowed up by her adoring public. All those women who swore they knew ages ago it was only a matter of time before Char Brody hit the big time. Fletcher considered the incredible gaiety. Char had left him without a second glance.

"You may have been wrong after all, Pilar. She has changed. Her, not me," he muttered.

Slowly he lifted the snifter of brandy and toasted his beautiful opponents—social position, power and, of course, wealth. He was almost ready to declare them the victors.

With receiver held to her ear, Char paced slowly back and forth on the balcony above the beach, her eyes riveted on the breathtaking sunrise as she listened to a phone ringing in an all-too-familiar apartment. Below her a lone jogger sprinted across the sand, sandpipers darted here and there following the flow of the lapping waves, poking their long slender beaks into the wave washed sand to collect breakfast. The water was blue, the sky was blue, the clouds so white and wispy they almost looked transparent. It was going to be a hot day, a beautiful introduction to the month of June. Funny how the promise of a perfect day made Char feel equally perfect.

"Bonjour. Boutique Pilar."

Char smiled and stopped walking, "Hello, yourself."

"Ah, Char," Pilar cried, feeling herself near tears at the mere sound of her friend's voice. "It has been too long. Have you not received my messages?"

"Of course I have, and I have absolutely no excuse for not getting back to you sooner. You have to forgive me just because I'm asking you, too."

"Mais oui. But of course. I am just so happy to hear from you. So happy, Char, you have no idea."

Char's brows pulled together in concern, "Pilar, are you all right? You sound absolutely frantic."

"No. Yes. I mean, yes, I am a bit. I have some trouble, Char, and I waited for you to call me because I was hoping you might help." Pilar's voice cracked and Char felt a stab of fear. She had never heard Pilar sound anything but carefree and confident.

"Of course, anything, Pilar. Why didn't you tell whoever took the message that you absolutely needed to talk with me?"

Char could almost feel Pilar waving her lovely hand in the air, swallowing her concern, as she said, "But it was only an emergency soon. I mean, recently. I am sorry, I forget the words sometimes."

"Forget the right words and just give me an idea of what's going on," Char insisted, leaning on the railing of Fletcher's balcony, looking out at the ocean and hardly seeing it. All her concentration was given over to Pilar. "Are you sick, Pilar? Is someone hurting you?"

"*Non. Oui.* In that order. I am not sick in the body, but in my heart. Vachel has decided I should not have my boutique. He has made almost all of my suppliers stop shipping to me. A few continue. They are not the couturiers, but they are good, respectable designers, so my clientele has changed just a little. But the shop is hardly stocked. I'm frightened I cannot keep it. My modeling contract has run out, so I'm no longer paid by Vachel and my savings . . ." Pilar hesitated just long enough for Char to get the picture.

"It's okay. Don't worry about a thing," Char answered immediately, her only thought to make things better for Pilar. "Vachel is not God, you know. Is it money you need? I can send you

265

money." Not only was this woman her friend, she was also the one who made Char's own success possible. She could kill herself for being so self-absorbed that she didn't return Pilar's calls immediately.

"You are so sweet, Char," Pilar laughed with relief. "No, I don't need your money. Who would take it with Vachel telling them not to ship to me? Only, could you ship to me your new line? I could not pay, but I might do this on consignment. I know it is so much to ask, Char. But if you could—"

"Don't think another thing about it," Char interjected, hating the fact that Pilar had to beg. Damn Vachel. Damn anyone who hurt Pilar! "I'll call the factory right now. What size structure do you want?"

"Char," Pilar breathed, her appreciation overwhelming, "you are so kind. I would like four to ten, if you could, on the gowns. Whatever you have available I will take in everything else. Thank you, Char. Thank you."

"Not another word. Consider it done," Char said in that tone her employees had come to know. It meant that no matter what, things would happen.

"I do, *ma chère,*" Pilar laughed. "I count on you to be my savior. Now, tell me good news. Tell me, how is Fletcher? Are you still so happy?"

"Now, Pilar, there's no need to play innocent. I know he ended up in Paris with you a few weeks ago. And I should have called you immediately—to thank you. Fletcher is well." Char turned to look through the open door, toward the bedroom where he was still asleep. The next question was harder to answer. Were they still so happy?

Yes and no. Certainly they were happier now that some concessions had been made. Fletcher was throwing himself into his project documenting Hispanic border crossings between Mexico and San Diego. No longer did he rearrange his schedule to try and meet hers. Char was sure that had taken some of the resentment he felt for her horrendous schedule. Char had curbed her all-encompassing interest in company business. On the nights they were together, they shared their day's work and their plans, but then found common ground on which to build the evening to its inevitable conclusion. And, though their time together was supposed to be only for them, Char couldn't resist cheating every now and again.

Sometimes, like this morning, she would rise early and call New York to check on fabric shipments, look over monthly progress reports from the field reps, or make fabric decisions based on the samples Carol always slipped into her briefcase along with pricing information. Then she would slip quietly back into bed before the alarm went off. Fletcher was none the wiser, she felt something had been accomplished, and all was well.

This morning, though, she needed to hear the

voice of a friend. And since Pilar was also business, she had dialed Paris. So here Char stood on
a balcony above a sparkling ocean, talking to her
dearest friend while her lover slept sweetly in the
room beyond. Were they still happy?

"Yes, Pilar, we are happy. There have been a
few changes. I had no idea Fletcher felt the way
he did about my overnight success. How odd to
think he envied me. I always thought he hated
anything to do with the business world."

"And you?"

"Me?" Char asked with surprise.

"Fletcher seemed to think you were being swallowed up by the snowball that was rolling."

"By the fact that my business was snowball-
ing?" Char laughed.

"Yes, that is it," Pilar replied happily.

"Let's put it this way, Pilar, I'm doing what I
need to do and Fletcher's coming around. But no,
I don't think I've turned into the raving maniac he
probably told you about."

"So, that is good." Pilar's familiar tone told
Char her friend had more to say, but would hold
her tongue until invited to do so. Char chose not
to make that request. In fact, she was a little bit
tired of Fletcher and his editorial looks; she didn't
need Pilar and her equally vocal silences. Char
was happy, Fletcher seemed happy enough, and
they were working on the rest.

"Yes, that is good, Pilar. Now, I really
do have to go. I just wanted to touch base,"

Char said perfunctorily.

"I am so happy you did, my friend. I've missed hearing your voice."

Softening, Char answered, "I've missed yours, too. I'm going to be coming over for Prêt-à-Porter. Perhaps you'll do me the honor of being my favored mannequin?"

"I don't believe that would do you much good in Paris now," Pilar answered sadly.

"Then Paris be hanged," Char said gently. "I'll see to the items you want."

"Merci, Char. *Merci."*

"Don't think a thing of it. Talk to you soon."

Char rang off, wondering if indeed she would seek Pilar out soon. Things hadn't felt quite right during their conversation. It was as though Pilar had lost some affection for Char, was perhaps passing judgment on her. Knowing she was just being silly, Char shook away her misgivings and dialed the factory. It was much too beautiful a day for worrying and the surprise she had for Fletcher would banish the last of her apprehension. The phone rang in the empty factory. She listened for the fourth ring, then the beep. Carol's answering machine had been an afterthought, and now Char realized she couldn't live without it.

"Carol. It's Char. When you get in would you please walk an order through. I need casual and daywear from the spring line. Also throw in a good selection of the fall chemises and five or ten beaded gowns. I want this shipped as soon as possible to Pilar's boutique in Paris. Do whatever is necessary to see that it's taken care of. The address is in the files. I won't be in today. If you need me, have me beeped. Bye."

Char hung up, realizing as she did so, that she had been unfair to Pilar. The woman was under incredible pressure. She shivered, trying to imagine what it would be like if someone wanted to destroy CB Designs. She couldn't even imagine how horrible that would be. Char was almost overwhelmed by panic just thinking about it. She wanted to rush into the kitchen, leave Fletcher a note, make excuses, and rush back to the factory just to make sure it was still there and functioning. Laughing at herself and the absurdity of her fear, Char shook her head. No one was going to take over CB Designs on a Tuesday morning in June. One day away from the office wouldn't make a whole lot of difference, especially since Carol knew where she would be, not to mention her constantly activated beeper. So instead of the note pad in the kitchen, Char headed to the bedroom.

Kneeling beside the bed, she stroked away a strand of dark hair that had fallen over Fletcher's cheek. With a swiftness that shocked her, Char felt her heart fill with an almost painful love for him. He slept the sleep of the righteous, deep in his dreams, untroubled by memories of wrong words or misdeeds. Had he indeed found the secret of contentment? If he had, Char wished he

270

would share it with her and banish the worry that was her constant companion. Only in his arms did her fretting subside, only during their lovemaking could she be lost to the world and think of nothing but him. Oh, God, how she needed him.

As if in answer to her heart's cry, Fletcher's eyes opened. He reached out his arm and brought her close, kissing her lips gently, smiling sleepily when they parted.

"Come to bed," he murmured.

"I have a surprise for you. You have to get up," Char whispered back, her eyes sparkling with laughter. He did make her feel so good.

"And I have a surprise for you," he answered, lifting the covers with one hand while he drew her into the warmth of the bed.

Char grinned and crawled in beside him happily. Her surprise could wait. It appeared that his could not.

"Almost there. Keep your eyes closed. Just a little longer. Did you remember your camera?"

"Yes. Yes. How many times do I have to tell you, Char. You know I really don't like to ride with my eyes closed. Can't I open them?"

"One minute. Just a minute!" She slowed the car, squinting behind her little round sunglasses, trying to identify the unmarked road she was looking for. Out of the corner of her eye she saw Fletcher lean forward. Quickly she pushed him

271

back. "That's enough. You promised. There it is!"

Pulling the oversized bill of her pink baseball cap lower, Char twirled the wheel. Her white Mercedes spun onto the private drive that led to the little white palace in the distance. Looking sidelong at Fletcher, she saw his eyes were still closed, but they wouldn't stay that way for long. Char stepped on the gas, scooted up the drive, and stopped the car. With a dramatic sigh she turned to him.

"Okay. Open your eyes. We're here." Char surveyed the property, her arms locked, her hands pushing against the wheel. When she realized Fletcher sat silently beside her, she turned expectant eyes to him. "Well?"

"Well?" Fletcher shrugged, unsure what reaction was expected.

"Do you like it?" Char prodded.

"It's beautiful. Whose is it?"

"Whose is it?" Char laughed and opened the door. "It's ours. I bought it last week. I saw it while you were away. Fletcher, it's absolutely perfect . . ."

She slid out the driver's side. Fletcher snatched his camera out of the back of the car before he did the same. Instinctively he pointed it at Char as she walked backward, her arms flung out, her face flushed with excitement while she pointed to the imposing structure. Slowly he followed, randomly snapping pictures, trying to listen to her, and trying hard to push away the bothersome thoughts that insisted on settling in his mind.

". . . You will absolutely adore the master bedroom. The problem with us was we needed to get away. You know, from your traveling and all your shoots, and me at the factory. Now we have somewhere to get away to. It's quiet here. We can cook, we can walk on the beach, watch TV . . . make love . . ." Char giggled and ran up the steps to the front door. Quickly she unlocked it and stood in the foyer waiting for him to catch up.

Fletcher came slowly up the steps, and looked at her cautiously as though he expected some sort of surprise when he walked through the doorway. He raised his camera, adjusted the focus.

"You look natural there, Char. Surrounded by all that white. Strange how well you look in a mansion." Click. He lowered the camera and looked straight at her. Neither of them was smiling.

"The least you could do would be to say you liked the idea. I did have the best of intentions," Char pouted, peeved that he should put such a damper on her surprise.

Turning away, she walked into the living room. Disappointment raged in her. Even when he put his hands on her shoulders, she couldn't quite forgive him his insensitivity. She shrugged him off, but he came back to hold her and kiss her neck.

"I'm sorry. You did say it was a surprise and you really gave it to me. But, Char, what do we need a place like this for? All this marble and molding? And so far away from Coronado. I thought you loved the island. Not to mention the distance from the factory."

"I do like the island, Fletcher, but I needed a new place. I couldn't stay in that awful little apartment forever. Not now. I can afford something like this."

"Is that any reason to own it? I can afford a yacht, but I sure as heck wouldn't be happy living on it."

"This isn't a yacht," Char drawled.

"Are you telling me this is really you? This is what you've dreamed of all your life as the perfect place to live."

Char looked about, seeing the house through Fletcher's eyes. It was perfect. Too perfect, like the subjects of most of his pictures. She wondered what ugliness that horribly knowledgeable eye of his saw. Scuffing her open toed shoe on the floor, Char shook her head.

"No. If you must know, I always imagined myself in a California house. You know, one of those big clapboard things with a huge porch."

"I didn't think this was your heart's desire," Fletcher murmured into her hair.

"I didn't say that. I said I had imagined myself somewhere else. But then again, I never imagined myself as head of a multimillion-dollar company either. Things change. Now I see myself here quite nicely, thank you. And I see you here with me, too."

Char moved away from him, running her hand over the huge window. When she spoke, she turned to face him, wanting to see the man she loved as he listened to her. His face was an open book. Fletcher hid nothing from her these days. A mere look and she would know if they would move a step forward or two back.

"I think you just say things like that to be contrary," she said. "I think you worry about losing control of your life when I invite you to do something different. You want me to be just the way you are. But I can't be. I can't be molded into something I'm not, or stay exactly as I was when I met you. One of the things you loved about me was the fact that I followed my own agenda."

Char sighed, held out her hands, and let her eyes roam over the beautiful living room before she looked back to Fletcher.

"Well, this house is part of that agenda now. I want it. I want to live here and enjoy what I've worked so hard to make. I want you to enjoy it with me, Fletcher. But you want to fight me every step of the way. It's as though you're afraid to let me have an inch. I'm not asking for a lifetime commitment, although I can't think of anything I'd like more. I only want to love you, Fletcher. Does where I do that make so much difference?"

Though she hadn't intended to, Char began to cry. Tears tumbled silently and she made no move to wipe them away. She wasn't ashamed that she loved him enough to cry for him, and she was too tired to figure out what it was he wanted anymore.

"Why do you fight me? Why is it the more I try to do what I think I'm supposed to, it drives you away? Why is that, Fletcher?"

In the cavernous room there was complete silence. Char's hurt and confusion were so deep that hers were desperate tears, accompanied not by sobs or cries, but by a mute pain that pierced Fletcher's heart. He took a step toward her, then stopped.

Her questions were valid and he had no answers. He only knew he felt unneeded, as though he were superfluous to the grand trappings of her life. Could it be that his jealousy, his envy of her had reached into the very essence of him? Was he truly the one who was causing all this grief and misery? If he was, he prayed he would be released from his envy and be allowed to look at her through clear, accepting eyes. If he wasn't, he hoped he would have the courage to leave and spare her more pain.

Fletcher took another step forward, then another, and he was with her. His hand went round the back of her head as he pulled her into his chest, slipping her silly pink hat off so he could feel the silkiness of her short, curly hair.

"Fletcher," she murmured, her arms winding around his waist, grateful for his warmth and his love. Everything would be all right now. She knew it.

"Char, I . . ."

But before he could speak, someone called from the entry hall. It was a voice unfamiliar to Fletcher but obviously recognizable to Char. Jerking away from him, she swiped at her eyes.

"Oh no, it's Jerry. Fletcher, do I have mascara all over my face?" He shook his head, but Char didn't seem to need an answer. She sniffled, squared her shoulders, and headed out of the room without waiting for him to inspect her makeup.

Curious, Fletcher followed. He was unsure whether he should feel insulted that "Jerry" was familiar enough with Char to walk into this house uninvited, or glad this person had the courtesy to announce himself before barging in further. He found Char deep in conversation with a man of average height dressed in the most unusual combination of muscle pants, tweed blazer, and lycra T. They stood close together, quite obviously acquainted.

"No, don't think a thing of it," Char was saying, her beautiful brow delicately furrowed as she considered something Jerry was holding out. "This is exactly why I left a message where I'd be. I want you to find me if you have questions. Better that than make a mistake that could cost the company thousands of dollars." It was then that Fletcher moved, crossing his arms as he leaned back against the wall to watch. Char caught the movement out of the corner of her eye and raised her head slightly, remembering Fletcher. "Oh Jerry, this is Fletcher Hawkins. Fletcher, Jerry Cordova."

The two men nodded at one another. It was obvious that neither thought much of the other at first glance, but Char's chatter cut through the perusals. Jerry turned his attention to her. Fletcher feeling quite useless, wandered back to his camera, picked it up, and considered the fabulous view of the ocean.

Hearing Char talk, though, he was drawn back to the foyer once more. The sea was no inspiration, Char always was. Standing quietly in the doorway, fading into the background, Fletcher began to shoot as he listened. And as he listened, as he took note of Char's conversation, he realized what he was hearing. He shot faster to cover the anger and sadness that were ripping at his heart.

". . . No, I think you're right. The lace collar would definitely add more to the silhouette. But if we're talking about another five dollars and fifty cents to the wholesale price, I think we ought to can it. You've done a marvelous job on this sketch without the lace. I think we can bill it as a forties' look. Let's maybe do something pretty with the buttons down the front. Something that looks right but only adds, let's say, no more than six cents. When we show it, we'll accessorize it with pearls. The buyers will love it. Never having seen it with the lace collar, they won't know the difference. It's hard to think off the rack after completing the gowns, I know." Char touched Jerry's arm lightly in commiseration as though to say they all had burdens to bear. "But five dollars in this line means a lot, considering our price points are already top of the line."

"Absolutely, I couldn't agree more," Jerry cooed, flipping his short little ponytail for emphasis. Deftly he folded the portfolio, and kissed Char on the cheek in a marvelous show of adoration. But Fletcher had seen his eyes. This man was ambitious. He would adore anyone who could further his career. Jerry grinned, telling Char, "I'll get right on this when I get back. I think I have the perfect button. You're really a genius, you know."

"Don't be ridiculous," Char laughed, though she was obviously delighted with the compliment. "I want to have that fit by Monday. You are cutting it in the brown jersey, aren't you?"

"Of course," Jerry answered, fluttering his eyes in mock reprimand, "and the little leaf pattern in green."

"Fine. Then I guess that takes care of everything. Now, I'm back to my day off. Thanks so much for coming to check this out before you went ahead and did anything."

Char shrugged, patted Jerry's back, and showed him the door. He was gone, zooming down the private road a few minutes later. Satisfied, smiling, exhilarated, Char turned to Fletcher.

279

He took one last picture, then lowered the camera.

"Who was that?" He asked quietly.

"Jerry?" Char looked over her shoulder then informed him offhandedly, "Why, he's my designer."

Chapter Thirteen

"Your designer."

Fletcher's voice was as flat as the afternoon sea, but not as placid. Beneath the words was a tone that strained with intensity, a sadness that was easily observable but hardly understood by Char.

"Yes. My designer," Char repeated with wide-eyed defensiveness. "I hired him about a month ago, but he just started two weeks ago. He's doing a marvelous job."

Char chuckled nervously, not quite knowing why something was terribly wrong, only understanding it was. Smiling, questioning with her eyes, she walked to Fletcher and wound her arms around his waist. He held the camera to the side, looking down at her without returning the affectionate gesture. With his lashes lowered, his hair falling over his broad forehead, Fletcher looked almost foreboding. His eyes were deep pools of pitch that revealed little and hid so much.

"I see" was all he said as he slipped out of her

embrace and tended to his camera, checking this and that as though it were terribly important.

He wandered away from Char, heading out the front door to stand on the veranda. Inside, alone, she watched him with a sense of dread. He had become suddenly alone despite her presence. Legs apart, planted firmly on the veranda, Fletcher looked like a Roman general surveying the field of battle. His slim hipped figure was pulled straight and tall by a rigid spine, his hair lay flat and glossy against his neck. Char could just see a bit of his profile, a bit of his unsmiling face, like a sliver of new moon on a black night.

Char gazed at the huge windows in the house, suddenly aware the interior had darkened as if a cloud engulfed the sun. But outside, the brightness was almost blinding, so she must have been mistaken. Furrowing her brow, she shoved her hands deep in the pockets of her boxer shorts and wandered out to stand next to Fletcher, her heart already hurting because once again he was displeased. She wondered if he had always been this volatile. Had she simply not recognized it in the first blush of love?

"He works for me, Fletcher. There's nothing between us. I swear."

Fletcher laughed, a short, mirthless sound. He didn't even look at her. He couldn't. There was too much in her he loved and too much he had loved that was gone now. He mourned the last and wished the former didn't exist. It would be hard enough to say what he must. Looking at her would make tears come. He felt them already, deep in his throat, filling his chest. This was a pain he had never experienced before and one he hoped never to feel again.

"Char, the thought never crossed my mind," Fletcher sighed wearily.

Just as quietly Char asked, "Then what is it, Fletcher? Why can't I please you any longer? Why is it that just when I think we've gotten over the top, just when we're happy, something I do or say sends you into this impossible mood?"

"It's not a mood, Char. This is just the sound of disappointment. I love you so much, Char, and it's just not going to work."

Fletcher's voice caught, he choked on the unfamiliar fullness of emotion, emotion too great to be completely expressed with words. Every inch of her, every bit of her mind that saw beauty where others saw nothing more than a piece of fabric, was loved by him. But her sight was gone, Char was blinded by what was practical, what was economical. She had given up a part of herself to . . .

"I love you, too, Fletcher. I have never felt about anyone the way I feel about you. Don't you understand that?" Char was close now, her long-nailed fingers digging into his arms as she tried to turn him toward her. But Fletcher rotated away. He didn't want to see the anguish in her eyes, yet Char insisted he look. She scurried around him, forcing him to face her. "Don't, Fletcher. Don't turn away from me if I mean as much to you as you say I do. That's unfair and it's cowardly. I've never known you to be cowardly."

Fletcher stopped suddenly, realizing how right she was. They had loved deeply and would continue to do so. They simply couldn't be together. The only way to begin to ease a pain this great was through honesty. Cupping her beautiful face in his hands, his eyes roaming over every inch of it as though he needed to commit it to memory, Fletcher leaned down and kissed Char, gently, cheerlessly. He kissed her goodbye.

"You're right, Char." He dropped his hands and adjusted the strap of his camera on his shoulder. "I owe you honesty. I owed it to myself months ago. It was Pilar who pointed out that I had been less than straightforward with myself. So I faced my own failings and I confessed them to you. I was jealous of the power, the excitement you were experiencing. I wanted to be part of the force that creates something spectacular like CB Designs. I know envy is a stupid emotion, but it was one I couldn't change then. Luckily that touch of envy has worn off. But then I knew it would. I've already had what you're experiencing. Pilar knew I wouldn't want any more of it, the same way I didn't want it seven years ago. But, Char, there was something she wasn't right about."

"Then we'll figure out how to live with whatever it is," Char assured him, grabbing at any straw. There was such hopelessness in the air she wanted to cry.

Fletcher shook his head, his beautiful lips

tilting in the most melancholy of smiles. "We can't fix this, my love."

"We can do anything, Fletcher," Char whispered desperately.

"No."

Fletcher's voice was louder, stronger now. Char shrank back, not from fear, but from the realization that he already saw the future. And it was one in which he was alone. Frantically she shook her head. Fletcher gathered her to him, shushing her and holding her tight until she stopped.

"You're wrong," Char sobbed against his chest.

"I'm not wrong. Pilar was. She said that all your preoccupation with your business was natural, that you would snap out of it and find a wonderful midpoint where you would still be the woman I fell in love with. She swore to me you hadn't changed. Not really. She said time would prove it."

"She was right, Fletcher. Of course she was. We've been so happy these last few weeks. I hired Jerry and all the others so that I could work less, and I have. It's worked. We've had time for each other . . ."

Fletcher's hand held her head, his skin was warmed by the silkiness of hair. He bent his head and kissed the top of hers.

"Hush. Hush," he commanded gently. "We've been playing at being happy. We've been so worried about one another's feelings we haven't talked about anything important. The only time we're completely relaxed is when we're making love,

Char. And as wonderful as that is, it isn't enough. You've changed and I can't live with it. You've given up that essence that made you what you were. You have deliberately given away your talent. Once you do that, you've given away a very big part of what makes you Char."

"I don't understand." Char leaned back, looking up into his face, trying not to see the pain etched there. Her voice was breathless, her lungs unable to push out sounds of confidence.

"Char, you've hired someone to design for you," Fletcher cried with quiet exasperation. "How can you not see that that won't change you! Designing is what made you whole, and now you let some idiot in a ponytail create for you, and you rubber-stamp his sketches. That's like saying you love your child, then turning it over to a nanny while you sit at the bank and count your money. You put business decisions ahead of creative decisions. You have given everyone in your life a priority number. Ross and your horde of professionals are number one. I'm just not going to stand here and wait my turn anymore. I've got a life to live, too, and commitments to keep and a profession that satisfies me. I want you, but only if I can be a partner in your life. Right now, we're walking parallel roads and I don't see an intersection coming up."

Char's lips parted to protest, but no sounds came. She pushed away from him, anger flaring in every part of her body, her blood running hot and cold with fury. She no longer noticed the ocean or the sky, the house or the beach. Fletcher consumed her consciousness. She didn't hear what he was really telling her. Fletcher wanted the woman who laughed and created and sketched beside him again. He would accept everything else in her life if that part of her could come back. But Char only heard his self-righteousness, his condemnation.

"You bastard," she growled. "How dare you stand there and tell me that I've sold my soul. As I recall, you sold out, too. You're sitting on a pile of money from the sale of your company, and now you're a dilettante who runs around shooting his camera as though you're recording history. Get rid of all those bucks, Fletcher, then maybe you'll have some credibility as a chronicler of world events."

Char stepped forward, then back, hardly finished with him. "Who in the hell gave you the right to judge me? You sound like a simpering idiot, you know that? You sound like you're reading the lines to a bad soap opera. 'Oh, Char, you've given up the best part of you.' " She mimicked him, her eyes blazing as he flinched beneath her fury. "Is that what you're getting at, Fletcher? Well, listen, babe, you haven't exactly been easy to live with either. I don't believe for one instant that you got over that 'little touch of envy.' I think the only thing that's happened is it's grown and taken you over. You can't see anything anymore for what it is. You equate me with my success and yourself with

287

poor judgment. Yes, poor judgment."

Char's eyes flashed, her rigid body quivered in an unexpected response to her anger. Deep, deep inside, she knew she was only proving true what he was trying to point out gently. But Char wouldn't allow herself to consider that he might be right. If she looked at herself, she might lose her tenuous grip on her fledgling company, she might realize that she really is only Char Brody who designs from a storefront on Coronado Island. Pushing her fear into the darkest corner of her heart, she glared at him.

"You didn't have the guts to stand and take control of your own company all those years ago, so you want part of mine. Or do you just want me to walk away like you did, so you won't see me succeed where you failed? Well, Fletcher, it's not going to happen, and I am not going to stand here like a shrinking violet and accept what you're telling me. I don't think you can make a valid judgment about me or anything else. You say you loved me before. Why? Because I was struggling. Is struggle part of your package?"

Fletcher moved, walking toward the flight of steps that led to the driveway. Char erupted, hating the fact that he wouldn't face her.

"Look at me, Fletcher. Look at me!"

Slowly he did as he was told. He looked closely at Char Brody. Her color was high, her eyes bright. She was a stunning creature, thin and healthy, perfect even though she was bathed in the white unforgiving glare of the sun. He loved her.

He hated her and himself. If only this had never happened. If only they had never been tested by the money and the power. But they had been, and both of them had been found lacking. Instinctively Fletcher raised his camera and shot one last picture.

"We're not the people we thought we were, Char," he said when he lowered it. "Neither of us are as good as we wanted to be. Neither of us are as awful. But there are things I needed from you, like the freedom to look at things differently. I wanted to be understood and appreciated by someone who shared my need to create for the sake of creating. I thought you needed the same from me. But what you want is passivity. You want us to exist for one another without really being part of one another's lives and thoughts. When you turned over the design function to that guy, that was the day you turned over a part of yourself. I could no more hand my camera over to someone and tell them what to shoot than I could cut off my arm. I loved all of you, Char, not just the shell of you. Not just your physical beauty, but the energy, the thought process, the soul."

Char picked up her cue, unable to let him get away with the last word.

"And I loved a man who had seen enough of the world to let people be and do whatever it was they wanted," Char retorted. "I loved a man who was fair, who let the world grow and change around him while he documented it. I guess I was the only thing in that world that wasn't allowed to change or grow. Is that it, Fletcher? Behind all the talk of equality, understanding, two souls meeting on the same plane, we really have a guy who likes women to be women and men to be men."

Fletcher shook his head sadly. "You know that's not true. Let's just leave it at this. I've been looking at us too hard, dissecting our relationship because I wanted to find out what it was that was sending it off on the wrong track. You haven't been looking at all. You've simply gone on hoping it would thrive because of what we had at one time. We can't be afraid to let go if it's not working. Face it, Char. It hurts like hell, but it'll hurt a lot worse if we just keep pretending. Let it go, Char. This is no way to live — for either of us."

Char felt her body tremble, a sharp pain coursed down her spine, icy fingers clamped around her rib cage. She wanted to cry out, throw herself at Fletcher, and beg him to reconsider. In the next instant she wanted to throw herself away from him, never look at his face again or remember the feel of his flesh against hers. Indecision, anguish, and anger warred until Char thought she might be torn apart by her raging emotions. Her fists clutched at her sides, tears blinded her. She could see only a dark outline that was Fletcher standing on the steps below her, but she could feel his sadness, his sense of futility. This was not her fault.

Carefully, trying to keep the tremor from her voice she raised her head proudly. She would not be blamed for the dying of this love affair. For certainly that's all it was—an affair. How stupid she had been to think it was the stuff of which a lifetime of dreams were made. Softly she spoke, carefully she chose her words.

"That's it, then. Over and done with, because you've decided that I can't live up to your expectations."

"They weren't my expectations. You aren't going to live up to what you are deep inside yourself."

Char held up her hand. "Spare me the philosophical discourse. I wouldn't want to draw this out. Let me get my purse. I'll drive you back to Coronado. We'll say a fine, civilized goodbye and that will be that. But, Fletcher—" Char checked herself. A tear had spilled over and was coursing down her cheek. She prayed he was far enough away not to see it. Taking a deep breath she continued, "Remember this, Fletcher, when you think of me and what we had. Remember that no one person can change who and what they are. They are changed by circumstances, by their own desires, and by the people around them. They are changed by those they rely on for advice and for support. Perhaps we were simply meant to love one another in a serene world. When we needed to pull together, maybe both of us were just a little too selfish to give what the other needed."

"You're right, Char. I know I did you a disservice by expecting something that maybe wasn't realistic. All I know is where you're going I can't follow. I don't like what's happening to you, and I don't like what's happening to me."

Char nodded. The gesture was so cosmopolitan, so understanding, so worldly. Yet all she wanted to do was scream at him, let her fists fly at him, until she had exhausted her hurt and fury and made him see that she was who she had always been. Instead, she murmured, "I'll get my keys."

"Forget it." Fletcher waved away her offer. "I'll find my own way back."

He was turning from her, leaving her, shocking her. Being alone so far from home was preferable to an hour in the car with her. So be it, Fletcher, she thought as he walked away. In minutes he had rounded the curving drive and was out of sight. Char couldn't see the tears that stained his face, she couldn't hear the undeniable sob that escaped his trembling lips as he walked faster and faster, terrified that he would rush back to her because he was afraid of the loneliness in the world without her.

Char could see none of these things. All she knew was that he left her, quickly and easily. And when she was alone, when only the deserted beach and the endless ocean and the incredible house of marble could hear her, Char Brody collapsed, her knees buckling under her as she cried for him. Hugging the cold, cold marble of the balustrade, she leaned her face against it, sobbing until she had no more tears left, until the only thing left in her was resolve. Without Fletcher, there was nothing except CB Designs and that, she would make sure, would never leave her.

"Carol, get Ross on the phone immediately."

Char stormed past Carol's desk and flung the order at her assistant without so much as looking at her. It was almost quitting time and the office was in the throes of a dying business day.

Char had sat on the veranda of her new home for four hours, weeping, watching, and waiting. How stupid she had been thinking he might come back for her, thinking this was just another one of his little moody, miserable, cantankerous. . . . Adjectives dwindled as they had each time she thought of Fletcher and his virtuous attitude.

At least she wasn't running away from anything, that was Fletcher's specialty. He didn't like the way his company was going, he chucked it all, and hid behind the lens of a camera. He didn't like the way their relationship was going, he walked away, or flew away to Paris. Well, she'd show him. She wouldn't let him escape so easily. She was a living, breathing memory he wouldn't be able to get rid of so easily. She'd show him how a real company was run. Everywhere he turned he would see her face, every store he walked into he would see her work. She would design clothes that were so spectacular even Fletcher would realize that he had been wrong about her. Even he would . . . Suddenly a sob caught in her throat. The fear she thought she had so effectively buried threatened to engulf her again. Without Fletcher she wasn't whole. Without Fletcher she couldn't do this. Without him her mind was a blank, her hand couldn't hold a pencil, she couldn't envision a dress. No, that wasn't the way things would be. She had Ross and she had . . .

"Carol!" The young woman materialized, standing quietly in Char's office doorway.

"You don't have to yell at me," Carol said quietly. Char barely acknowledged her protest, afraid to look at her assistant. She was sure her uncertainty, her struggle to keep her wits about her would show if she raised her face. No one in her position should show weakness to their employees. If that happened, they would lose faith in her, they would leave, too. So Char kept her eyes down as she shuffled papers on her desk.

"Just get me Ross, will you. And do it now. The day's almost gone and I've got to talk to him."

"Char, what's the matter. I'll be happy to do . . ."

"Carol." Char straightened and glared. "Why are you questioning me? I told you what I needed, now I expect you to do it."

Carol looked at her boss with pained amazement. Never had she imagined Char Brody would come to this. She shook her head slowly, sadly and made a decision to solve a problem that had gone unresolved too long.

"I don't know what it is you really need, Char, but it sure isn't me anymore. I think you better get yourself a new girl. I quit. And if the others are smart, they will too. You treat us all like we're your personal slaves and you expect us to be grateful. You gave us a raise that turned out to be more generous than I thought it would be, but even that isn't worth working for you anymore. What happened to the boss who used to tell us what a good job we did? What happened to that fabulous woman who used to say please and thank you? You've sure come a long way, Char. Only problem is the higher CB Designs goes, the lower you do. I'll send for my check since I can't seem to get what I need here."

Carol turned on her heel and disappeared so quickly Char didn't have a minute to think. Instinctively she rushed after the young woman, catching up with her just before she walked out the door.

"Carol, I'm sorry. You can't go now. I really need you. I . . ." Char's mouth was dry, her eyes darted about, she was aware everyone in the front office was watching curiously. Char lowered her voice. "I've had a really rotten day and I guess I just took it out on you. But, come on, I won't let it happen again. You've been with me from the beginning. You don't understand. It won't be the same without you."

"Char, it's not the same with you. I've got to go. It's not good for me anymore, and I have a feeling it's going to get worse before it gets better." Carol took a step toward the door, put her hand on the brass knob then looked back. "Try to remember what it was like before you became so rich and famous, Char. Those times were really good. You used to know how to listen. You used to believe that self-respect was more important than money. I think you were happier then. I know the rest of us were. I'll see you around."

With that, Carol walked out of CB Designs and never looked back. She left Char standing alone in the middle of the beautiful offices she had designed. She left Char standing in a group of employees she hadn't known longer than a few months.

"Ms. Brody?" Char was saved from those embarrassing few seconds by the sweet voice of the receptionist. She was such a young girl, no more than eighteen. Char looked at her without really seeing her. It was a moment before she realized the girl was holding out a stack of pink message slips. Whether they were truly important or it was the receptionist's instinctive nature to save others from discomfort, Char would never know. In fact, she had hardly spoken to the girl since she had come to work; she didn't even know her name.

"Thank you. I'll get on these right away," Char murmured, taking the messages as she looked the young dark haired girl in the eye. The receptionist smiled shyly and nodded. Somehow Char found that reassuring. She walked regally away from the lobby and directly into her office where she dialed Ross herself.

"Ross? Char. I need you. I want you to help me make the name Char Brody a household word. I want it done fast. Can you help? Dinner? Good. We'll talk about it then."

Carefully Char replaced the receiver. With

Ross's aid her name would be everywhere. Fletcher wouldn't be able to hide from her and soon he'd realize just what he had walked away from.

Chapter Fourteen

"I'm so glad you called to ask about it. No, I don't think anyone else has ever rented Disneyland to present a new line. Expensive? Of course, but the drama is going to be well worth it, don't you agree? I do hope you'll be there . . ."

Char swiveled in her chair to look out the window. She continued to mouth the right words. She'd had the same conversation over and over again for the last three weeks — ever since, thanks to Ross's advice, she'd had the public relations agency begin work on the largest gala presentation of a new line the U.S. had ever seen. Buyers and fashion journalists were coming from the four corners of the globe for this one. She was going to be untouchable after this, the greatest star in the fashion galaxy. But when she looked outside, when Char saw that July was boasting glorious summer weather, she felt a touch of something that pricked at her heart.

Just the doldrums, she imagined. It had been a long time since she'd walked on the beach or just sat in the sun enjoying the warmth. But that wasn't unusual, she supposed, with people of her standing. Ross didn't care for the outdoors unless he was controlling a boat or at the wheel of a car. He couldn't see the inherent enjoyment of just sitting on the veranda of Char's beautiful new marble house and watching the sun set. She never realized how much energy Ross had. The problem was, it always had to be directed: toward one of his buyouts, or her, or making more money. Maybe that's why they were getting along so well these days — that's exactly where her energy was directed, too. The problem was, being rich and famous just wasn't as much fun as she thought it would be. Sometimes she felt like a stranger in her own company — sometimes like a stranger in her own body. Tapping her finger against her cheek, Char wondered for the hundredth time if maybe she shouldn't just give in. Ross wanted to marry her. He was committed to CB Designs heart and soul and . . .

Suddenly Char bolted upright in her chair. Voices were raised in the anteroom of her office. Knitting her brow, surprised that anyone would raise their voice in her normally hushed executive suite, Char cut off her caller with a promise to ring back. She was almost out of her chair when the door was flung open and Fletcher Hawkins's tall, broad shouldered frame filled the doorway.

Char resumed her seat slowly, carefully, feeling as though the breath had been knocked out of her. In her shock she hadn't managed to smile, hadn't been able to propel herself out of her chair and run to him, kiss him, tell him how happy she was to see him. That was her first instinct. Instead, a look of wonder lighted her expression, a parting of her lips was her invitation to him.

But Fletcher saw none of this. His anger overrode the electricity that surged through him the minute he laid eyes on her. He had thought, had hoped, he had even convinced himself that his will was stronger than his heart. But how could it be? She was too marvelous to see. Her hair still wisped about her square face, her skin still glowed golden, and her eyes were as misty gray as they were in the moments after they made love. He wanted to put his long fingers around the back of her head. He wanted to feel the silkiness of her hair and her satiny lips on his. All this was thought, felt, and discarded in an instant.

"You can't . . . Mr. . . ." Char's new assistant rushed after Fletcher, took his arm, and immediately released it when his stormy eyes slid toward her. She tried to explain around him, poking her head this way and that to look at Char. "Ms. Brody. I tried to stop him, but he just barged in . . ."

Char held up her hand, "It's all right, Patty. Mr. Hawkins and I are old friends. He's welcome . . . whenever."

Patty looked from her boss to the incredibly good-looking intruder and back again. But Char was in no state of mind to give her any other reassurances. Char was lost in the look of Fletcher, so happy to see him she didn't feel the fury emanating from him.

"Where's Carol?" Fletcher asked, pushing the door shut behind him, and advancing into the office.

"She quit. Better offer." Fletcher raised an eyebrow. Char lowered her lashes. He had seen through her lie.

"Drove her away, did you, Char? Like all the rest of us?" Fletcher asked pointedly, close enough now to splay his hands on her desk. Under his right was an envelope, in his left was a crumpled piece of paper. Char shot to her feet. If that's the way it was going to be, she could play hardball just as well as he.

"Now wait a minute, Fletcher."

"Sit down," he hissed, eyes flashing, jaws clenched. "Sit down."

Char hesitated. But one look at him told her she had best hear him out before she jumped into the fray. Taking her seat, tenting her fingers under her chin, she narrowed her eyes, watching him as he prepared for attack. Yet even now she could say she loved him, even now as he assaulted her. And he loved her back. Char saw, deep in his eyes, that glimmer of desire, the shot of pain, that warred with his rage. She would hear him out. Then . . .

"I'm down, Fletcher. Now that you've burst into my office and terrorized my employees, why don't you say what you've come to say, so I can get back to business."

"This is business, Char. This is the ugliest kind of business I've ever seen. You know, sometimes I'm amazed how easily you gave in to it all. You threw

301

away everything. Your creativity, your love, and now your friends. There's nothing left to sacrifice to the almighty dollar and the god success, is there, Char?"

"Fletcher, I don't have the foggiest idea what you're talking about. I am the same person I always was. If you don't choose to believe that, then that's your problem, not mine. I have no desire to hear your opinion of my business life, or my character." Char raised her pen to her lips, her gaze never wavered as she matched his glare. The pen came down. She dismissed him. "If you came all the way down here to do that, you might as well turn around and head out again. We have nothing to say to one another."

Fletcher straightened and considered her for a moment. The derision in her voice fueled his anger even as it tore at his tortured heart. But angry words had gotten them nowhere. Maybe it was time for something more. Looking down, he considered the envelope and the notepaper he held.

"You're right. After this, we won't have a damn thing to say to each other, ever again. But I couldn't let this go. I had to know why you betrayed Pilar the way you did. I can understand the rest of it, but not her. She made you. You owe her. You owe her so much more than just your success. She's a part of your heart and soul. Or at least she was. But I guess love and honor and respect aren't part of your life anymore. I suppose I just wanted to hear you try and explain this."

Fletcher tossed the crumpled notepaper onto her

desk. Char reached for it and picked it up. She tried to read, but the words blurred, her mind refused to acknowledge what she saw. Confused, she looked to Fletcher for an explanation.

"I don't understand . . ."

Fletcher shook his head in disbelief, the hurt in his eyes as clear as the color of them.

"Char, why do you do this? Why are you playing these silly games? You know darn well what it says. Pilar is begging me to intercede for her. Pilar thinks she offended you somehow. Can you imagine that? How could she have possibly done that? Even if she did, wouldn't you have a moral obligation to keep your promise? You did promise to ship her goods on consignment, didn't you?"

Fletcher waited a heartbeat for her answer, praying that somehow it was Pilar who was wrong, Pilar who had misunderstood. But Char didn't come to her own defense. Defeated, he almost choked on the next words.

"God, Char, the woman's been waiting over a month. If she doesn't get your consignment, she's going under. Can you understand what that means? Pilar is broke. She can't make it. She's hanging on by the skin of her teeth. She turns to you for help and what does she get? False hope because you conveniently forgot to send a dress or two. You know, it's amazing that everything you professed to love is gone, and you don't seem to miss any of it. I'm no longer a part of your life, nor is Pilar, or designing. You've given it all away."

"Okay, Fletcher, stop it this minute. You know

you're being unfair . . ."

"Me?" Fletcher laughed incredulously, but the mirth sounded closer to the choking of a sob. "Char, listen to yourself!"

"No, you listen. Listen to the accusations you're making. Have you even asked me for an explanation? Do you even have a sense of fairness when it comes to me or, just because I'm making money, I'm automatically one of the bad guys? Is that it? I can't be redeemed, no matter what?"

"Okay. Explain this. Tell me why it is you've hung Pilar out to dry without even blinking your eye. You and Vachel both betrayed her. Maybe that's the thing to do once you become a successful designer."

Slowly Char raised the note and looked at it. Now words jumped out at her: *Please, Fletcher. . . . I beg you. . . . Ask Char to help me. . . . Help. . . . Help. . . . Help.* Char felt a knife cut through her heart. She had no idea how to explain this mixup. Now it might be too late.

"I did promise to send her a full shipment, and I can't explain why it hasn't happened. I told Carol to walk it through. I have to check with shipping and inventory. I've . . ."

"Oh, stop it. Just stop," Fletcher shouted in despair, half turning from her. "I can't bear another excuse. I can't stand to hear that it's only business. You know, Char, until this minute I still loved you. I held onto the memories of smiles and talks and touches. But nothing touches you anymore. Nothing except the latest growth figures for this company. What was your net worth last time we talked? In the millions, wasn't it? Well, darling, I hope it makes you happy. I hope all that money and all those reports keep you warm at night. I hope all those consultants listen to your troubles. Because, baby, you aren't the same woman I fell in love with. Not by a long shot. And I don't know where you're going to find someone who loves the new you."

"God, Fletcher," Char broke in, "I'm sick to death of your pronouncements. If it was up to you, I'd sprout snakes from my head and turn people to stone when they looked at me. Am I really so reprehensible? Isn't it amazing that it's only you who sees the monster within? Ross doesn't see it. My employees seem happy enough. The stores actually adore me. Tell me, Fletcher, where is the black hole in my soul? How is it that you've been able to use your X-ray vision to find out how rotten Char Brody is while everyone else just thinks I'm really neat?"

"It's no trick, Char. I think everybody can see it. I just happen to be a little more honest than most. But here. Give it a whirl yourself. Tell me what you see?"

With a flip of his wrist Fletcher tossed the large envelope on her desk, the contents spilling out. Reaching over, he pulled out a batch of photos and fanned them in front of her.

"Look, Char! Look! You tell me where Char Brody went."

With that, he turned on his heel and left her standing ramrod straight behind her elegant white desk. Strewn over the top were photos, all of them of Char Brody. It was a long while before she could sit down and an equally long time before she could bring herself to look at the photos. Finally, slowly, one by one she picked them up and let her eyes roam over them. All the photos Fletcher had shot and never used in that article of his. Carefully she put them in order on the desk, her heart hardening against what she saw. Her throat tightened. Tears seared the back of her eyes. But she would not cry until she had seen every last one.

Here was the first photo Fletcher had ever taken of her. A fluffy-haired, exotic-eyed goddess standing alone in the night, dressed in teal chiffon, her face young and open and fresh. Here was another, snapped to record the first blush of love atop the Eiffel Tower. The night when Paris lay at her feet. Wonderment shone in her eyes, words of astonishment hovering on lips that would never speak them. And here, a picture taken just before they made love in a cloud of black silk, showed the knowing face of a woman ready to give all of herself, body and soul, to a man she adored. That was the picture of true happiness. Success was at her doorstep, love was in her life, friendship was unquestioned, and the world lay before her for the taking.

Char put those photos in a neat pile, taking great care that the stack be tidy before she reluctantly looked at the others still spread over the desk. These she picked up in no particular order because in each one she looked the same. Her expressions had diminished: smiles no longer glittered, caution lurked behind her eyes, there was a sharpness to her lips, small furrows dented the space between her brows, and none of it surprised her.

Hadn't she seen all this herself when she looked in the mirror to do her makeup? Didn't she always look just a bit off kilter? When she dressed, she knew every piece of clothing was technically correct, perfectly suitable. But her body no longer became a part of her fashion, it was merely another way to advertise her wares.

Shoving the photos away, Char turned her head, squared her shoulders, and blinked back the tears that threatened. She had felt this shriveling inside her for so long and she had raced away from acknowledging it. There was always something more to do, something more to worry about, someone who wanted something from her. It had been easy to ignore.

Now, on eight-by-ten prints, Char saw the woman she had become. No longer was she gripped with a verve and energy that came in bursts of creativity. How she was pinched with countless worries about the growth of her business. And the question rolled through her mind like a freight train, the question even Fletcher had forgotten to ask. For all the money, all the fame and accomplishment, for all the things she had acquired in such a short time, was she happy?

As the sun set and her office became dark, while her employees passed her closed door one by one, Char asked herself that question again and again.

The answer was always the same. For a long while Char did nothing but let the understanding of her predicament settle in her mind. Finally she picked up her purse and quietly left her office.

In the corner of the outer offices the cleaning people had already begun their nightly chores. Without a word Char walked past them, pushed open the door that led to the factory, and headed to her car. She hadn't gone far when a light from the small room behind the fabric bins caught her eye. Curious, Char looked in.

There Theresa labored over a lovely persimmon colored gown, its long sleeves beaded with black bugles. *Vogue* had already requested an exclusive shoot with that dress. Char had been thrilled. Now she looked at it and felt nothing, knowing her name would be on the label but that was the only part of it she could claim as her own. Jerry Cordova had designed the dress. Thinking she hadn't been noticed, Char was about to leave quietly when Theresa spoke.

"Is there something you need, Char?" The dark-eyed woman laid the gown on her lap and looked at her employer with frank, sympathetic eyes. Char simply smiled gently.

"You should go home, Theresa. You've always spent too much time here."

"I enjoy what I do. It's no hardship." Theresa shrugged and smiled with affection.

"Thank you, Theresa. I appreciate that. Truly I do. And tomorrow, I'll prove it."

"No need, Char," the woman answered, picking

308

up the dress and resuming her work.

"Yes, there is. There's been a need for a good long while. Goodnight, Theresa. Please, don't work too late."

Threading her needle through the wispy chiffon, Theresa plucked a bugle bead from the plastic dish beside her and hummed a bit as she listened to the sound of Char's high heels echo through the deserted factory. She heard Max the guard say goodnight, then there was silence. Into that silence Theresa whispered.

"The honeymoon is over. Thank goodness."

Char gripped the steering wheel lightly, knowing there was no hurry now. Everything that must be done would be. If fate allowed, she might even reclaim a bit of her soul before the night was over. Heaven knew she had almost lost it forever. She only hoped she could reclaim part of her life in the process.

The drive to her new home in Corona del Mar to change her clothes had seemed endless. Now, though it was late, the drive back to Coronado Island seemed almost relaxing and Char felt surprisingly alert. The exhaustion, the forced exuberance of the last few months had fallen away. Peaceful now, she could pursue what she must with a single-mindedness.

Tilting her chin, she squinted, sighting the proper off-ramp and drove her sexy little Mercedes off the freeway, dropping herself two blocks from the shopping center. Quickly she pulled into the lighted underground garage and locked the car before taking the escalator to the third floor of the huge mall. Her head snapped this way and that, searching for what she wanted. Then she saw it, the little booth amidst the myriad of fast-food stalls.

Determined, Char wended her way through the closely set tables, ignoring the teenagers who watched her with such curiosity. Let them stare, she thought as she entered the booth and pulled the curtain. Obviously they'd never seen a woman in evening dress schlepping through the mall. They'd probably never seen a woman who knew exactly what she wanted, either. Until that night, Char hadn't even known what she wanted. She tendered her money, sat back on the hard little bench, and prayed this would help her get what she needed, and wanted, so badly.

Business finished, Char put her booty in a tiny gold-flecked evening bag and rushed back to her car. Seconds later she was on the road again, flying over the bridge toward Coronado.

It was late and the town was all but closed up when she arrived. As though it would make her passing less obtrusive, Char eased up on the gas and glided through the main part of town, stopping only when she reached her destination. Cutting the engine, she parked and walked up two flights of stairs, anxious to see the only man she knew who could clear up the mess she'd made of her life in such a short time.

Raising her fist, she knocked firmly. There wouldn't be any running away now. Suddenly,

310

though, she was afraid. Scared to face herself and especially frightened to face . . .

"Fletcher?"

He stood in the open door, his expression unreadable, his stance guarded. Char thought she saw a softening behind his eyes as he looked her up and down, recognizing the memory she had purposefully conjured. Gingerly she held up the skirt of her dress, then let the layers of teal chiffon flutter back against her body.

"I know it doesn't look the same without the moonlight, but I thought this dress might be just the thing for . . ."

Just the thing for what? Another scene or a reconciliation? There was no need to find the word she sought. Fletcher held the door open, silently inviting her in. She stepped through.

"I didn't expect to see you." He turned his back on her and settled himself at the drawing board he used for his layouts. Picking up a lovely crystal glass filled to the brim with blood red wine, he tipped it toward her. "Drink?"

Char shook her head. Tentatively she wandered over to the tilted table. She knew Fletcher heard her intake of breath as she looked at his work, but he gave no indication that he realized it touched her.

There, pasted to board, was a collage of her photographs. So many faces of Char Brody. She had no idea that one person could wear the events of their life on an ever-changing face that way. It unnerved her, it shamed her, and it gave her so much to hope for.

"You were so exquisite, Char." Fletcher spoke quietly, looking at his work, not her. Perhaps not even talking to her but to the ghost of a memory. "Look how the moonlight illuminated just part of you here. There was such movement in this shot, even though you were so still. The moon, the wind, your body tensing because you didn't know what it was I was about. We were alone on the beach that night." Fletcher sighed. He looked briefly over his shoulder, as though just remembering she was there before adding sadly, "You're still so beautiful in that dress."

"I wanted to wear it tonight especially, Fletcher. It was our beginning dress. I came to ask for a new one." Gently Char put the tips of her fingers on the back of his chair. She wanted to touch him, thought she might. She stopped, knowing the time wasn't right. "I won't beg, Fletcher, but you have to know that I love you. I can't imagine my life without you. It wasn't until tonight that I realized I would be living it alone forever if I lost you.

"You're a proud man and I'm no less proud. I take pride in what I've created — my designs and my company. I take pride in the fact that I have never intentionally hurt anyone in my life. I take pride, too, in the fact that I am not afraid to admit that I was wrong.

"I'm starting with you, Fletcher. I'm telling you I was wrong. I won't give up everything, but I will not continue as I have been. There are only two things I want from my life now. I want to be content, Fletcher. I don't want to live in fear anymore that I'll lose things that don't really matter in the long run. Security is one thing, excess another. And I want you back, Fletcher. I so desperately want you back."

Char's sigh filled the room as she watched Fletcher's still back. Her fingers shook as she unclasped her evening bag and slipped out her treasure. Looking at it, she swallowed hard, leaned over Fletcher's shoulder, and laid the little strip of paper in front of him. Fletcher's eyes fluttered to it.

Three grainy penny arcade photos stared up at him. Two dollars of hope lay before him. A woman that needed him stood behind, praying he would see her for what she was and always had been.

"You don't have to decide now, Fletcher, but see if you can't find *me* in those photos. If you can, maybe there's a chance. I love you, Fletcher Hawkins. I want to come back."

Gently Char smoothed his black, black hair away from the nape of his neck. He didn't move when she bent down and kissed him lightly just above the collar of his shirt. Char didn't see the tear drop from his eye, nor did she feel him tremble before she turned to leave. She was halfway across the room when his voice stopped her. He didn't want to wait for what he knew was inevitable.

"Char . . ."

Her back to him, she waited for him to go on, steeling herself for pain, hoping for happiness.

Chapter Fifteen

"*Non! Non!* That is not right. Oh, you fools. Higher. Higher."

"Pilar, I can hear you all the way inside. You sound like a fishwife!" Char laughed, skirting beneath the ladder to join her friend on the narrow sidewalk of Saint-Honoré. Like Pilar, she shaded her eyes from the early August sun as she watched the workmen laboring with the sign they were fastening under Pilar's original one. "I think it looks good. Come inside and give those poor men a chance to do their work."

"Oh, but if I don't watch every moment, they will put it on backward."

Char wrapped her arm around Pilar's shoulder as best she could, given the difference in height, and guided her back into the shop.

"You know, even in France it's kind of hard to hang a sign that says CB Designs upside down or

314

backward. Now, come see what I've done." Char pushed open the glass door, propelling Pilar ahead of her. "What do you think?"

"I think that the queen of England herself will be shopping here before too very long. Char, *c'est très élégant*." Pilar twirled into the middle of the shop, looking at it through shining eyes before turning grateful ones to her friend. "I cannot thank you enough, Char."

"You shouldn't be thanking me. You should have strangled me. I'm so sorry about the mixup."

Pilar waved away Char's concern. "It was nothing."

"It was everything, Pilar, and you know it. Because of my stupidity, you could have lost this place. I know how much it means to you. As much as CB Designs means to me. I had no idea that shipping had refused to send the garments because they had found you'd been blacklisted during a routine credit check. Vachel really did a job, didn't he? Then when Carol walked out, nobody picked up the ball."

"Your employees are not to blame. They followed the rules. They only did what they thought was best for the company."

"I knew what was best. You should have had these things six weeks ago."

"But then you would not have delivered them yourself, *ma chère,* and that was worth the wait. Now I am exclusive CB Designs in Europe. Everyone must come to me for them. I shall be your best resource, Char."

"I know you will. Who knows, this might be the start of a retail empire."

Pilar rolled her eyes and groaned, "I think we will pay attention to what we have and nothing more now." She pinched her fingers together. "At least for a little while, *non?*"

"I think you're right." Char chuckled as she reached for her short-sleeved blazer.

She was tired and it was only one in the afternoon. But she and Pilar had been up all night working on the displays. Tomorrow the press would be invited again to Pilar's boutique. This time Vachel would have nothing to say about the success of the boutique. This time Pilar's supplier was also Pilar's friend.

"Listen, I've got to go. I need to look over those reports the office faxed, then conference-call with Jason and Ross in a few hours."

"So. Still working so hard, heh?" Pilar fluffed out the skirt of a day dress.

"Not really. Jason was a wonderful choice for CEO. Now I don't make the everyday decisions, I simply keep track on a quarterly basis. And I have Ross to oversee the whole shebang. I think CB Designs was Ross's allure all along. He loved the business, not so much me. All along we've simply been good friends. We just were too caught up in events to see it. So if anyone has my best interests at heart these days it's him. See, it's just as I told you," Char emphasized. "I'm the designer and the owner. I leave business to the businessmen as much as possible now. I won't let them run the company into

316

the ground, but I won't give my life to it either."

"I am happy, Char. I think you like the fashion the best anyway."

"I think you are right. Now, are you going to be okay taking care of everything else?"

Pilar assured her she would, kissed Char on the cheek, and sent her back to her apartment for some much needed rest. Ten minutes later Char had climbed the three flights of steps to the furnished flat she had rented for an exorbitant fee. Every cent she paid was worth the view she had of the Seine. It had taken her a long time to realize that money was not the be-all and end-all of her life. It was a tool to be used for her pleasure while she pursued what she did best, what she loved. At least that's what he had said that night in his apartment . . .

Char pushed the answering machine button and focused on the messages, all other thoughts flying from her mind. Slowly she slipped out of her blazer and tossed it on the couch. Her chemise was next. A bath, something to eat, perhaps a nap, then . . .

"I wouldn't take another step."

The voice startled her. It was real, talking over the messages on the answering machine. Char froze, her chemise clutched to her breasts, her back bared by the open zipper. It had been warm that day and she had forgone her bra. She heard him move up behind her, his hands slipped about her waist, his long, strong fingers splayed over her bare flesh. She hadn't even heard the front door open. Char trembled at his touch, her chest constricted, the breath inside her struggled to break free. Then

317

she felt his fingers traveling up and up until they covered her breasts and his lips were on her neck and he was whispering, "I wouldn't take another step toward that bedroom without me, Mrs. Hawkins."

"I wouldn't have dreamed of it, Mr. Hawkins."

Turning into him, Char let her chemise drop. Deftly she kicked it away as her lips found his and she was gathered into his arms, swept up and away to the quilt covered bed. Pilar had been right so many months ago when they toasted one another. Held tightly in the arms of her husband, Char truly knew that success and happiness were one and the same.

CATCH A RISING STAR!

ROBIN ST. THOMAS

FORTUNE'S SISTERS   (2616, $3.95)
It was Pia's destiny to be a Hollywood star. She had complete
self-confidence, breathtaking beauty, and the help of her domi-
neering mother. But her younger sister Jeanne began to steal the
spotlight meant for Pia, diverting attention away from the ruth-
lessly ambitious star. When her mother Mathilde started to return
the advances of dashing director Wes Guest, Pia's jealousy sur-
faced. Her passion for Guest and desire to be the brightest star in
Hollywood pitted Pia against her own family—sister against sister, mother against daughter. Pia was determined to be the only
survivor in the arenas of love and fame. But neither Mathilde nor
Jeanne would surrender without a fight. . . .

LOVER'S MASQUERADE   (2886, $4.50)
New Orleans. A city of secrets, shrouded in mystery and magic.
A city where dreams become obsessions and memories once again
become reality. A city where even one trip, like a stop on Claudia
Gage's book promotion tour, can lead to a perilous fall. For New
Orleans is also the home of Armand Dantine, who knows the secrets that Claudia would conceal and the past she cannot remember. And he will stop at nothing to make her love him, and will
not let her go again . . .

SENSATION   (3228, $4.95)
They'd dreamed of stardom, and their dreams came true. Now
they had fame and the power that comes with it. In Hollywood,
in New York, and around the world, the names of Aurora Styles,
Rachel Allenby, and Pia Decameron commanded immediate attention—and lust and envy as well. They were stars, idols on ped-
estals. And there was always someone waiting in the wings to
bring them crashing down . . .